First Printing, 2022

Necromancy, Life After Death

Necromancy, Life After Death

TNK

Lukas Allen

Lukas Allen

Contents

1

The Birds and the Black Knights

Hi, my name is Zach, and I am an orc. My ma calls me "her little Zachary" but my pops calls me Zach. I've always liked Zach in a way, seems shorter, and not so cutsie. I was adopted, and I don't regret it one bit, by humans. A human soldier actually saved me from death, from the other soldiers, and died from his wounds because of it. He was the Sergeant Zachariah, thus I am named Zach. My "real" orcish name was Ren we Gar, which means Maggot of Gar, but I defeated an orc in single combat and chose my name. I chose Zach. I wish ma would stop calling me her "little," but what can I do? She's my ma. Pops said I'll always be her "little" even if I'm a giant, grown old man and she's seventy years old or something. It's a daunting prospect, but I love her all the same.

It's nearly time for my adventure! Pops said I'm old enough to set out on my own, and I can't wait to do so! He said he was nearly half my age when he set out into the world as a squire, and it's time I do the same. I need to talk with Gessa first, my best friend in the whole world, even if she's a girl.

Granted I'm a lot older than her, but I always stuck out for her, keeping her safe from bullies and stupid stuff like that. She seems wise, in a way. Like she's got some sort of eldritch knowledge running through her. Don't tell anyone, but I once saw her bring a dead bird back to life! It flew off, none the wiser that it was actually dead.

Gessa's ma is Aunt Daisy, and her pops is Uncle Marcos, even though my pops and my ma aren't related to them in the least. Marcos taught me a lot about fighting, as he even taught *my* pops about fighting in the past. He teaches peace over violence, and forgiveness and mercy over revenge. It still feels good to beat those bullies of Gessa's to a pulp, but I make sure they're alive after I'm through, so I keep Uncle Marcos's wisdom true.

My pops said that I should always remember his real name, and never forget it. Said we are more than our paternal and maternal names. Said that was some wisdom he learned from my ma's late father, even though ol' Jack said the opposite, that his paternal name is more important. I hated that bastard, ol' Jack. He was a real bastard, and I'm glad he's dead.

Not that I would've minded if he accepted me into his family... but I was a slave in his eyes. A servant. I was nothing but property. Thank God the President Laurel has changed so many things since the great battle ages ago. Orcs are free now, and even get a vote! I'm glad to be a part of her country. The free country of Jericho. It's too bad her term is nearly ending. An eight year term. Seems kinda long, but she sure did make it work. It took a good while for her to even start up the democracy.

My pops's and ma's work bring them all over, and me too, but now I can finally go my own way! I haven't seen Gessa in ages. I bet she's a grown adult woman now. Like I am a man. I hope I don't say anything stupid... Not that I think I'm stupid or anything! It's just... Gessa has always sort of cared for me, as I care for her. I really hope I don't make an idiot of myself...

I've nearly forgotten the orcish language. That shouldn't bother me, but it does somewhat, but some things still ring true. Teck a teck. Blood for blood. Some things you will never forget... like the monstrosity that is my birth father.

He has raped and killed all over the country, burning, looting, and pillaging. One day, I'm going to confront him. I hope, anyway. That's one of the reasons my pops told me to go adventuring, says it changes your perspective, and makes you stronger. I shouldn't have told him about that... but he understood, in a way. Said he always hated his master as a squire, but now that they're older, they get along swell. I doubt that would happen between me and my birth father, my birth father Gar.

But let's talk about Gessa. I'm ashamed to admit it... as I should like more of the orcish girls who come trading... but Gessa has the most beautiful hair! She has the same blonde hair as her mother, and despite that, I think she's gorgeous. I mean... pretty. I mean.... has good hair. Not that I think her mother isn't pretty! She's *very* pretty. I'm always astounded by her grace. Even though some of the stories she tells puts me on edge. Some of the horrible things she has gone through, that have gone through others she knows. She always changes her tone whenever she notices I'm listening, but I can tell she's lived a very difficult life.

But me and Gessa. I always... I mean *sometimes* thought of us together... when we're older. I would be going on an adventure though! I'd have no time for Gessa, so I'd make the most of it in our visit.

I knocked on her door and she said, "Whoooo isss it?" like she always does, even though she knew it was me.

It was a beautiful cottage, I admired it some more, and after I made her wait a little longer, I said, "It's Zach! You know it's me... Come on, Gessa! Open up!"

"Fine, fine... let me put the kettle off the fire." and then she laughed, as she never did like making tea, then opened the door, and I found a stunning, teenage girl of my own age in the doorway. At least she looked my own age. I knew her to be four years younger! Much too young, but still, they say girls grow up faster than boys. This saying didn't seem to prove its worth, as she took me by the arm and talked about clothes and boys. That Gessa! When will she learn. Boys are often after clothes, at least I was as a kid, as I had none, and clothes, like armor, make the boys. Into men, at least. I had worn my most dapperest leather armor, fresh from the armorer! I got it as a present for my birthday. Pops said I should be armored like a tin can, but I preferred a little mobility, for hand to hand fighting. That's why I got these studded gloves! Should be able to do some righteous damage. Gessa was astounded at my mohawk. "Doesn't it hurt?" she said.

"Of course not! It's what all the warrior braves wear. All the great orcs of old. Even Shake Spear had one!" I said.

"But... what about the shaving! You can't tell me you didn't nick your head!" she said.

"Well... only a little bit. Don't tell anyone though." I said. She laughed and said it would be our secret, like it always was.

She took me by the hand and led me to the sofa, seating me down and saying she would get the refreshments. She was a very prim and proper young lass, at least in my own experience. Most girls would seat you on the sofa and talk about their sex life! Most girls *I've* met... and they were all my pops's friends. He'd quickly hush them whenever he heard them, but still, they had some *crazy* stories! Gessa wasn't like them in the least.

We talked about the life, about my soon to be adventure, and how each of us was doing. After we got that out of the way, Gessa said she wanted to show me something... said it scared her. She took me over to the window and showed me... the many, many birds sitting on the trees. "You didn't... bring more back to life? Did you?" I said.

"No. They just all showed up! I *think* they're dead, because most of them don't look too good... That one over there has a broken neck!" Gessa said.

"This isn't good. Kinda spooky, actually. What are they doing? Just watching?" I asked.

"That seems to be *all* they do! They follow me around whenever I go walking, though. I tried running from them, but they chased me! They didn't hurt me or anything, but they're still always there!" she said.

"Do you want me to... y'know... end their suffering?" I said. Gessa, like her mother and father, *hated* death. I think that's why Gessa felt so sad for the bird that was dead, and that's why I think it came back to life. I had seen the dead come back to life... and I knew they were terrifying things. From necromancers. I guess I can tell you... but please, please, *please* don't tell Gessa. Her mother was once a necromancer, too. That's why seeing the dead bird come to life didn't really surprise me. I mean, I was shocked, but it made sense.

"No!! But do you think... you could catch them?" she said.

"Catch them?? Um... erm... fine." I said.

So I left out the backdoor and slowly approached a bird. They were still staring at Gessa through the window. I slowly... carefully... picked one up off a tree branch. Then they looked at me. They *all* looked at me. They began squeaking and chirping, and the one in my hand was trying to escape, but I carefully held it, and tried taking it with me inside, then they swarmed me! They were pecking and scratching me, and the one in my hand escaped! I tried keeping them away from my eyes, and tried swiping them away.

Gessa ran out the door and tried to help get me away from them. They only attacked me, and seemed to ignore her. Then... she said something. I don't know what she said, as it was in a strange language, and the birds stopped and flew away. I thanked Gessa and asked her what she said to them.

"Didn't you hear? I told them to go away!" she said.

"You... You said something different. I think you should talk to your mother about this." I said. Aunt Daisy was very wise, and often knew the best solution to things, besides fighting. Fighting was Uncle Marcos's department.

"I-I can't! I'm terrified of what she'll say to me! Her and my dad... they'd be *furious!*" she said.

"Don't worry. They'll know what to do. I think I have to go..." I said, looking at my pocket watch, "Yep! I'm late for a meeting with my pops's old master! Gotta meet that old fart before he gets too drunk and gets bored and leaves!"

"Alright. Promise you'll come and visit, ok?" she said, then kissed me on the cheek.

"I will, Gessa. You stay safe, ya hear?" I said, running out past the back to the old tavern, the Black Dragon, where I'd meet Barnabus, the grandmaster of the Black Knights.

It was a light, brisk run, and I kept on looking at my pocket watch. My pops said punctuality is the key to any business meeting, and I was four minutes late! But when I got there I didn't see Barnabus, so asked the new owner, Sarah, where he was. She said he never showed up! Nervously I waited at a table and drank a coffee. I never really liked coffee, but as a man going on his first adventure, I thought I should try to like some new things.

I mean, I've been through countless dangers, been almost enslaved and killed, nearly eaten by zombies, and fought an orc for my life, but I don't really count those as adventures. They all happened when I was a small child anyway, and I never had any say in what we were doing. Now, I'd get to make some of my own choices! I laid my axe on the table and continued to drink my coffee, even though it was bitter as all hell, being black coffee, like my pops drinks.

My axe was given to me by my pops, a weapon from a great orcish warrior, one of my pops's friends, who passed away in the great battle. They too, got off on the wrong foot, and fought each other for their lives, but my pops didn't kill him and he became one of his greatest allies. The orcish warrior's name was Athunhel, meaning Brokenskull. I called my axe Skull. I never really needed it, as I preferred taking matters like fighting on with my own two hands, but Pops says it'll come in handy in my adventure, either being intimidating or if I run into danger that can only be solved with an axe, or at least be handy chopping firewood.

I waited for a good hour, always checking on my pocket watch. It was given to me by one of my parents' friends, ol' Dismas the Demon Hunter. Sure, he may be an ex-demon hunter... but isn't that so cool?? He finds and slays monsters! Said he was hunting one, some sort of monster that was destroying villages. He always tried to reason with the monsters in his adventures first, trying to get them to change their ways and become something useful to the world, but if they continued their ways of death and destruction, he would slay them. I think the threat of his sword and shield was enough to convince most monsters to give up their ways, and his ever growing reputation! Most monsters didn't want to tangle with Dismas, no sir.

Finally, an old drunk, armored in black armor, stumbled through the door, asking everyone where the little rodent called Zach was. Ol' Barnabus had a foul mouth on him, but we related on that level. We got into a swear off once, and I nearly beat him! But he pulled out an old racial slur for orcs... with his own added personal touch. It really hurt! But we both laughed it off and then he taught me how to gamble.

"Here I am, you old coot!" I said, walking up to him and holstering my axe on my back.

"Hey! What did you call me? Don't you know to treat your elders with respect? You shit eating little barbarian?" he said.

"Oh! I'm sorry, someone your age probably didn't hear me... *I CALLED YOU A COOT!!"* I yelled.

He laughed an old, drunken laugh, and said I was a mongrel who humps his mother, then bought us some beer from Sarah, saying it's time I get good and drunk before we head off to our destination. "Won't we be late?" I said.

"Little thing you should learn... you're never late when you're fucking the owner." he said.

"What if she gets mad and leaves?" I said.

"Pah. Mary would never do that to me. She's loyal... like a good sword... or in her case, a good sheathe." Barnabus said, as we sat down with the beers, "You're dad ever have the talk with you?"

"What talk? Oh! *That* talk. Yeah... swords and sheaths, birds and bees, all that stuff. And if he didn't, some of his friends told me all sorts of stuff! Do you *really* use butter for the flavor??" I said.

He laughed and said, "I don't know what things your daddy's friends do, but I'm sure butter is probably messy as all hell. You'll have plenty of time to figure things out for yourself. You're looking a little jittery. Are you nervous?"

"No! I've just been drinking a lot of coffee... what the hell is in it?" I said.

"Bah, stimulants and shit. Here, drink your beer... it'll help mellow you out." he said. So I drank it, and eager to impress him and eager to leave, I gulped it all down. "Jeez. You can at least enjoy the flavor. Sarah! Another round for our *little* adventurer..." he said. He knew it annoyed me to be called little, but I stomached it, as I did the beer, and the next one, and the next one.

Finally, I was as stumbly as him, and was slurring a bit. I knew better than to judge Barnabus on his stumble. He *was* always drinking, but was all the more dangerous because of it. In a flash he would lose his stumble, lose his slur, and become as sharp and quick as a brand new sword. He used this many times when gambling, and just when you think you had beaten him, he pulls out the winning hand, and relieves you of everything you have. Or shoots you in the head. He killed ol' Jack, and helped save me and my ma from his clutches. We were going to be shipped off to some dwarven hall, and my ma was drugged out of her mind because of Jack, with some experimental new crap that basically turns you into a zombie. I feared for my life, for her life, in that castle. And it made me very angry seeing Jack... touch my ma like he did. Thankfully Barnabus, Uncle Marcos, and my pops came in when they did and saved us, before Jack could put his sword in my ma's sheathe.

We left the tavern, and Barnabus wanted to see what new moves I had picked up. I put my fists up, and said I was ready. "Damn, son... are those metal studs on your fist? Take those off, I don't want to be killed by my chump ass squire's mongrel boy." he said, so I did, throwing my gloves to the ground outside.

So we fought, and Barnabus was a *very* dirty fighter. Right off the bat he tried kicking me in the nards, laughing as he did. The laugh tipped me off that he was going to do something underhanded, so I swiped my boot at his foot, and he stumbled against me. I pushed him away, because he undoubtedly wanted me to go for a hit, something he could use to his advantage. "Always take the cheap shot first, boy." he said to me, as he took on a real fighter's stance.

I threw a punch at him that he blocked with both arms up. "Come on. Is that the hardest you can swing? Your mommy coddle you too much and now you think you're a woman or something?" he said, so I swung at him again, as hard as I could, and he grabbed my arm and threw me to the dirt. "Never fall for your opponent's taunts. It's all bullshit anyway." he said, as he helped me up, then threw me on the ground again. "Also... never take the enemy's help." he said, and I struggled to a stand, a little too drunk. "You're going to have to learn how to fight drunk, boy. It's probably the time you'll fight the most." he said.

So we fought some more, I blocked his swings as best I could, and he blocked mine. "Lose that grunt, boy. It tips the enemy off to your moves." he said. I punched again and again, and he said, "Square your feet. Don't you know how to fight at all?" Despite myself, I was starting to get a bit annoyed. So I used my jack of all trades move to take him down. As Barnabus punched at me, I dodged and grabbed him by the head, then threw him to the ground, using my hip for the torque, with me landing on top of him. I raised my fist to punch at him in the face, but he said, "Ok. Ok. You've made your point... the Blunt Knight's taught you well. You're going to have to figure out a different way of fighting at some point... in case there's ever a Blunt Knight you have to fight that knows your moves better than you do yourself." so I didn't hit him, got up, and offered a hand to help him up, which he took, and stretched his back. "Argh... I'm not as spry as I once was... Let's go get to Mary." he said.

Uncle Marcos was the grandmaster, the leader of the Blunt Knights, and he taught me all the moves he could in his spare time. I really had only mastered this one... that my pops used as well. But I knew the principles of a lot of the other throws. Barnabus even used some of them on me, and I wondered where he learned them... probably from Marcos. Him and Barnabus were staunch enemies, I think, or maybe they just acted like it. They had saved each other's lives many times.

We got to the station, where my parents' good friend, Mary, was starting up a business of her own, a caravan business, but when we got there, it was empty. "She's just waiting a bit, probably worried where we are." Barnabus said. So we waited, and waited, and waited. He said, "Goddamnit! She must've left... Well, if I was you, I'd hurry to the next town and meet up with her. Good luck, kid." and walked off. I protested, and he said, "Think of it as an adventure! Hooboy... I don't know what your father told you, but adventures are all shit! Have a good one, kid!" and I was left alone at the station. I quickly hurried down the old train tracks, trying to catch up with Mary and the caravan, cursing Barnabus all the way.

2

Learning to Fall

Hi! I'm Gessa! I was named after a friend of my parents' who helped them in their adventures... Gestas the Blunt Knight. He used to be a hateful demon hunter, but he changed his ways, and became a peaceful Blunt Knight. Sadly, he died, as he was trying to offer peace *to* demon and witch hunters... but he will still always be remembered. I go to his grave every day and put flowers on it.

Him and all of my parents' old friends. They knew a lot of people before, and a lot of them died in the great battle ages ago. Something to do with zombies... and vampires? I fear I am becoming one of the necromancers of old.

Zach, my best friend in the whole world, even though he's older than me, just helped me scare away the undead birds that were following me! I brought a bird to life... completely by accident! I just wanted the poor thing to be alive again... and then it was! It was alive! But now... more zombie birds are around! I don't think they're *really* alive... They don't heal! The one with the broken wings always falls to the ground, and I have to help it onto a tree branch!

I've been going out into the forest to meet with the birds, trying to reason with them, like my father says I should with enemies. They just chirp and cheep, and I don't think they're very smart... But maybe they're acting? They're smart enough to follow me.

I've tried to reason with the people who call me names and hurt me... but Zach always beats them up! I think they do it more because of this, even though he means well. It makes him so angry when they pick on me! I have a tough skin though, and I do not want to fight, even though my father says I should learn how. I want peace for all of the gods' creatures.

My dad is going to teach me some judo... I asked my mom if there's any way out of it, but she said to listen to my father. That it will help when words do not suffice, and it is self-defense anyway. So I went to my father's gym, with all the gross old mats of his, and he taught me how to fall.

You'd think that was something everyone would know how to do, you just fall, right? But there's actually a certain way you should fall! I thought it was stupid... but my dad told me over and over again to keep my head up, and slap the ground with all the force I had. The other people in the gym made resounding slaps on the mats, and it sounded like thunder! Mine sounded like a wet fart.

Still, my dad told me that this was the very first thing you should learn in judo, so I *tried* to slap as hard as I could... He said you could tell how experienced someone was in judo depending on how the sound of their fall was. Finally, after he made me do it over and over again, he said the one I just did was good, and to do it again. He was satisfied with the second, and said it was now time to learn some muscle exercises.

He said you should always keep your muscles strengthened, because you never know when you are going to use them. I did some push ups... but could barely get ten! He said that was fine, and that soon enough I'd be able to do a hundred at a time just like him.

We had these weird white gis on when in the gym. They were something Japanese... the founders of judo. I didn't get it, but he said it'll help simulate what real clothes people wear. Long robes... I didn't get it, but he said I would when I learned some throws.

So he taught me the hold of judo. We held each other on the gis, and I was against this girl who was much older than me. One hand on their collar, the other on their wrist. My father said to try swiping at the other girl's foot when she took a step. She did, and I swiped, and she fell over like nothing! I said she was letting me win! So she said fine, have it your way, and fought for real. I never hurt so much as when she threw me over and over again onto the ground, but I learned how to fall. My dad let us fight, and I really wanted to make him proud, but I fear I embarrassed him... a great man like him, master at judo....

After the session, I told him of my fears, that I was a shame to him, but he said I never made him more proud! He said my falls were some of the best he's ever seen, from a beginner, and that I took on real hardship, someone at their best, and that I struggled through to the other side, made him very, very happy.

Even though the people at the gym are very tough, and very strict, I still sort of think of them as my friends. Not like the people at school. They all suck. I get bullied and picked on, but I always turn the other cheek. The boys are crude and distasteful, calling me names, but the girls... they're worse. They're mean and finicky, and very sharp with me. I try to ignore them, but they won't leave me alone! So I tried some of the judo on one of them, and swiped at her foot when she was taking a step towards me, to hit me or something like they do, and she fell to the ground! Embarrassed at the people laughing at her, she said she'd get me for this.

After school, I walked out into the forest, on a shortcut to my way home, and noticed someone following me. She tried to keep silent, but I saw her, all the same. When she noticed me running from her, she came out of hiding and yelled at me, swearing at and insulting me. I wish I was

Zach's age... and could leave school for good. But I ran away from her. Then I noticed the birds following me. I just had had enough! I wanted them all to leave me alone! Then two more girls stepped out from the bushes and cornered me.

"Heya little Gess... how's the love life? Fuck any more dogs? Dogfucker." The girl said to me.

"No! Dogs are good! Leave me alone!" I said.

"I bet you like eating shit. Molly just took a shit. Wanna eat it? We'll feed you..." the bully said.

"No! No! Leave me alone!" and they grabbed me, brought me behind a bush, where there was a steaming pile of poop. The girls tried to force me face first to it. I struggled to get away from them. I didn't know any throws, and couldn't throw them away from me. But then the birds came. They pecked at their faces! They pecked at their eyes! They were everywhere! So, so many birds! The girls ran off, as the birds chased them. One bird sat on my shoulder, and tried speaking, but it lost its voice.

I said, *"Here little guy... have some seeds."* and brought out some seeds from a sandwich, a veggie sandwich with seeds on it from my pocket.

"You shouldn't let bullies stick you in the mud." he said to me, eating the seeds.

"I know... but I don't want to be mean, not like them." I said, not at all surprised I was talking to a bird.

"You should really learn some self defense..." he said to me, *"Or... learn how to control us."*

"Control you? What do you mean?" I said to him.

"You will learn in time. Have a beautiful rest of your day." he said, and flew off. Weirded out, I quickly went home, not daring to tell my dad and my mom about what happened... although, I would eagerly go to every judo meeting, and my dad was proud of me for that.

In randori, or practice fighting, I would get my ass whooped, but would always struggle to fight. I wanted and needed to be able to fight. I didn't want a face full of poop. I was better at pins, and my father saw this and taught me some more of them. Kesa gatame, or the scarf hold, is my favorite. Arm around the head, the other hand on the arm, legs wide as possible, that's how you do it. I bet Zach knows all sorts of pins... I wish I could talk to him about it.

But he had gone, leaving me on my lonesome. He's really a very handsome chap, even if he does like to swear when no one is looking or with that old Black Knight of his. I swore that I would meet with him again, one of these days. "God fucking damnit!" I said, "I'll meet with you again, Zach!" then quickly became quiet, knowing the words that came out of my mouth. You should never take the Lord's name in vain... at least to some of the gods.

My father had a rigorous pantheon of gods, all striving to be his number one. I thought that life is more important than the gods... but there's a god of life too! I didn't know which one to stick with, but my mom said I should at least always try to go to one of my father's masses... at least one. I chose the Buddha guy. He seemed nice enough, and even didn't think of himself as a god. My father taught me mindfulness and patience when we would meditate because of his Buddha god.

We would breathe in, and out. Over and over again. At first I wouldn't know what to think of, and thoughts would roar past in my head, but apparently it's *supposed* to be that way, and you just let them pass by like the breeze, or like a stream. In and out, thinking about whatever, but not being grabbed in by the thoughts. Let them pass, like a cloud that looks like something or other.

My father taught me more throws, and I finally told him about my bully problem... he was furious! He didn't know how someone could pick on a sweet girl like me. I said bullies are like that, and will pick on you no matter what you're like. "Here's something I've learned about bullies. Hit them with the hammer. If they don't like you, that is probably a deeper problem of theirs... but if they cause you harm, then hit them. I know you and your mother strive for peace... but sometimes the bullies will respect you more if you put up a fight. And if they don't? Whack them to hell." he said.

I said that wouldn't I get in trouble?? Wouldn't the teacher be mad at me??

He said, "Well... erm... I suppose... Maybe you should go to my *friend*... the Black Knight, Barnabus. He has dealt with bullies his whole life."

"Really? *Him??* He seems more like a bully himself." I said.

He laughed, and said that no one knows about bullies more than the Black Knights. So I went to Barnabus Dread, scared for my life in the tavern, just being a girl... but no one paid me any mind. They just thought I was a dumb kid. I found Barnabus betting with a friend of my parent's... Jacob. Jacob was really a scoundrel, out of all the friends of my parents.

"You fucker! How do you have four aces and a joker?? You're supposed to take those out!" Jacob said to Barnabus.

"All part of the god of luck. She's converted me. Oooohhh god of luck! WE THANK YOU FOR THIS VICTORY!! Now hand over your cash." Barnabus said to Jacob, and Jacob grumbled and gave him a check. "Nuh uh. *Cash.*" Barnabus said.

"Listen, we at the Wheel have gone through great efforts to achieve mobile banking! We've gotten good at it!" Jacob said.

"And I bet your friends at the Tower are eager to stick a knife in my throat, before I cash this check. *Cash.*" Barnabus said, "Oh, lookie here! It's my *friend* the Blunt Knight's kid! The rest of you scram. I gotta talk to little Gess." and the rest of them left the table, but not before Barnabus could grab Jacob's arm and get him to fork up his winnings. "Here. Sit here, little girl." he said to me, patting a seat beside him.

I sat next to him, and said, "Hi, Mister Dread. I'm having a problem..."

"What's that, girl? No sex life now that your boyfriend, Zach, has left?" he said to me.

"Um... no... He's not my boyfriend!" I said.

"Ha ha... and I'm not your elder. What is it you want?" he said.

"Well, I'm having a problem with bullies... They keep on picking on me! My dad says I should just beat them up... but I don't know how.... and I don't want to!" I said.

"That's your first mistake. If everyone thought of sticking a dagger in everyone else who thought of sticking them with a dagger, they'd be perfectly happy. Now, some, like your mother and father, think it prudent to be wise and merciful to those who would end you. I say you stab them, and shoot them for good measure. Just in case." he said, taking a sip from his beer.

"But I can't kill my bullies! If not for the *birds...* I'd be eating a pile of shit!" I said.

"What's that? What about birds?" he said to me.

"Well... um... don't tell anyone, please! But the birds have aided me... attacking my bullies... one said I shouldn't let bullies stick me in the mud..." I said.

"You've been talking to birds? Not taking on the sickness of your mother's, have you?" he said, taking another sip.

"No! I know she has schizophrenia, but I don't have anything like that! She said I'm *very, very* lucky... But the birds have helped me! The one said I should be able to control them!" I said. He spilled his beer at that.

"These birds of yours... they're not dead, are they?"

"Um... they *might* be..."

"Gessa. You need to fight these bullies tooth and nail! Don't let them push you around, but always be the better man, er, woman. Be the better woman. And don't tell anyone about this, ok? I need to do some research... learn some things. Keep it silent, *ok?* And have peace. Something your Blunt Knight has taught me. Keep the peace." he said, then got up, saying he had a prior engagement, and excused himself, very politely.

I wandered back home, very confused. What did Barnabus have to learn? What was he so upset about? I didn't have a clue.

3

Coyote Daddy

I wandered down the road, and it was nighttime already... I thought I'd make it to the next town before nightfall, but I guess I'd have to hope I'd get there before daybreak... It made me so angry! If I had just left *without* Barnabus... but whatever. I still thought of the moves of his, and wondered how I would integrate them into my own fighting style. We're always learning, every step of the way, and if I can learn from some old coot like Barnabus who made me late, then the more the merrier.

My anger seemed to be waning, as I took on the quick march to the next town. Barnabus, like the others, *had* taught me invaluable skills, so I was thankful for him, despite my fury. Figaro, Fadaro, Pigaro, Padaro, I said, hoping Mary hadn't forgotten about me.

That's a little saying my pops thought of. Means good luck and love. Said it came to him in a dream, and I wondered what dreams were capable of.

I had dreamt of me and Gessa, in my sleep, and as we were having tea, there was *something* else there, always asking for more biscuits. I can't quite remember it... but I was annoyed at it, as I was fearful of it. But no matter. Dreams are dreams, even the greatest of them can have no meaning at all. The thing looked like a giant skeleton, whatever it was.

I hurried down the road, but I was starting to get tired. My pack was starting to feel heavier... but if I kept walking, I believed I would make it in time. It was just a little after four o'clock in the morning, anyway. I had to get there before they left again... So I started jogging, then started running, then sprinted for a little bit, then jogged some more.

I was soooo tired... all the drinking really made me feel sleepy... but running helped sober me up. Finally, I got to the next town, seeing the outskirts in the distance, the little houses and an end to the forested terrain. I walked off the old train tracks and hurried to the next inn where the caravan was supposed to stop.

They were closed and locked up, so I waited outside. Not able to do anything, I smoked a cigarette. I was keeping them for a special occasion, and usually *never* smoked, but I wanted a treat so I bought some, finally being old enough to do so. My pops hided me verbally when he caught me smoking as a kid... but let me finish the cigarette, as he smoked it with me. It was a very difficult time, when I smoked as a kid, and it helped my nerves. It made me feel calmer in a way, and as I inhaled deeply and coughed, coughed a bunch, sitting on a bench, I could feel the stress passing, and got up. Suddenly I felt very woozie, like heavy in my legs. It actually felt pretty nice, if a bit tiring, so I sat back down and waited until sun up when the inn would open.

Finally, it was six o'clock and someone changed the little sign that said "closed" to "open" and I hurried over to go inside. The little bell tinkled as I opened and closed the door. "Hello." the thin little man said, sweeping up, "Welcome to Helveta Velour."

"This is an inn, right?" I asked him.

"Why, no! This is a clothing shop. Can't you tell?" he said. I then noticed clothes stacked and ordered, hanging from racks. I had thought the manakin in the window was a little odd...

"Didn't Mary and her caravan stop here?" I said.

"Mary... Oh! Yes, brown haired woman with the braid crown? She's staying at the Broken Cow. You should probably go there... or buy something... now, you look terribly out of fashion, would you care to see our assortment?" he said.

"No, I'm sorry! Thank you for your help!" I said, running out the door. I could hear him swearing at me underneath his breath as I left.

I ran to the other side of town, and saw the caravan leaving the inn. They had a mule and horses, and lots of baggage. I shouted out, "Hey! Wait up! It's Zach! Mary, it's Zach!"

A brunette turned to me, and laughed, saying as I got up to her, "Finally got here, eh? Good thing, too! We were just about to change stops on our route. I told you that we would leave with or without you... What took you?"

"Barnabus... He said you'd wait up!" I said.

"Little tip. Never trust a man on his drunken word. And every word that man utters is drunken... Well, I'm glad you made it. We have to make trails! This is so exciting! My business is really booming! I never knew it was so fun, trading. Since the Chariot is taking a break, as your parents are on holiday, I get to do my own thing! Marvelous, I really needed the break, too. Even though being a mercenary is a thrill like none other... I always wanted to try a side business." Mary said.

My pops was the leader of a whole mercenary company called the Chariot. They had grown a lot since the small band of members that they had in the past, the seven of them. Mary was one of the original members, and is my pops's right hand woman, besides my ma. Mary took care of all the little things in the company, which all turned out to be big things in the end. A cough a soldier got had to be treated quickly and have him quarantined, before it spread to the rest of the troop. A loss of supplies could mean hunger for the Chariot down the road, so always had to be resupplied. A thief in the ranks had to be sussed out and caught, before they decided to work their way up from stealing grain to stealing all of their paychecks. Mary was a master at handling all sorts of things like this, which is why she wanted to start up a caravan. Mary had an innumerable assortment of skills, from managing, to healing, to fighting.

She was a very pretty woman, although war had not been kind to her features. What was once a pristine shapely body, covered in armor, was now a wreck of scars. She had one long gash down the side of her face, she had another big scratch on the back of her hand. She said every scar is a story, however, and she had a *lot* of stories.

She would regale us of stories of her adventuring days, as kids. She used to be married to a biker, and she was a rogue knight, and they had traveled the world and saw its many sights, and got into many fights. They decided to settle down, after a long spell of hardship, and made the Black Dragon what it is today, even though Mary's former employee, Sarah, now owned it.

As we walked down the road to the next stop, I told her about all the drinking and fighting Barnabus and I did. "Do you drink a lot?" she asked.

"Never! I don't mind the taste... it's just that I always say stupid things when I do. I made Gessa cry once when I was drunk, and I never drink anymore. Barnabus said it was a good thing to do at the start of my adventure... but if I hadn't, I wouldn't have been late!" I said.

"How many drinks did you have?" she asked.

"A good six or seven of that new beer Sarah is making." I said.

"And you still managed to fight off Barnabus? That beer is the most alcoholic we've ever created. Bless Sarah for figuring it out. I never could get the concoction right... Well, that just goes to show orcs for you. They can hold their own no matter how deep they are! Deep in their cups, that is!" she said, and laughed.

As we kept on walking she told me the history of alcohol, and how each place has its own unique brew, and if they didn't, it probably was a shit place to visit... So, on the road, she made sure to stop at each new tavern, the best in town, and would sample their booze. Said it was all part of the fun of being an independent business owner, you can get drunk whenever you want.

The other workers, as there were two besides me, were a dwarf named Lasso and a woman named Shekinah. Lasso would always drink with Mary, but Shekinah was very quiet, and did not. When I finally did talk to Shekinah, after trying to for a good while, she said she used to be a slave, and that like orcs, a lot of people held her in disdain. At least in this country. Her ebony skin was dark as night, and a lot of people ignored her or tried to insult her, but if Mary caught them, they soon wished they hadn't. Don't pick on women and you won't find out what she did to them.

Lasso was a bit of a ruffian, saying he used to be a bandit in the past, being banished to the surface by his dwarven clan. He had to quickly do anything he could to survive, after the great stone doors were closed to him, and was thankful for Mary for offering him a job and putting him straight. Those two would always stumble out of each new tavern... and then brawl, like good friends. They made sure to never hurt each other too much when they did, but still, they threw some wicked punches! I asked them if I could join in, but they said they didn't trust my studded gloves, and my sobriety. When I got good and drunk with them, then I could brawl. I didn't feel like making any more stupid mistakes though, so remained sober, and just sat with Shekinah in the night when the work was done.

It was lonesome sitting in the dark on the ground, but at least Shekinah was there so I wasn't lonesome alone. I didn't want to be tempted by going into the tavern. I made Gessa cry when I was drunk by saying that people die all the time, and that they should because they were so horrible... I really regretted it, when I sobered up. I had never taken a life, and I don't plan on doing so... but I was angry at all the people that hurt others, who hurt Gessa. I would say those people should be dead, but I shouldn't. Gessa says everyone, no matter how horrible, deserves life. Said that's something my pops said to her, when she asked him how many people he's killed.

My pops had killed a lot of people in the past, and regrets most of them. But he strives to make Uncle Marcos proud of him and not kill, but they still get into arguments whenever they talk about war. My pops defends a lot of killing he's done, saying if he didn't then innocents would perish. I fear that Marcos doesn't understand. My pops has saved innocents around the country, around the world, and always strives for good, even though he's a mercenary. Uncle Marcos always reminds him that goodness cannot be snuffed out, even through the most horrible conditions. My pops quickly relents after they argue, and they talk about fighting again, like brothers.

I don't... *ever*... want to accidentally kill someone, like Uncle Marcos had said he's done. He said it was the worst feeling imaginable, and haunts him to this day. He always tries to disarm or dissuade people from battle, but sometimes he hits a little too forcefully, trying to break an appendage, or knock them out, which turns into a death swing accidentally. The Blunt Knights use only blunt weapons, and always try to convert people to peace, and even though they must sometimes fight to do so, they wish to never take a life.

The Blunt Knights... well, most of them... are even vegetarians! This seems impossible to me. Meat tastes so good! Especially if you've hunted the animals. I've hunted all sorts of things, usually with my bare hands. A squirrel is easy to catch if you don't alert them, and boars are difficult as all hell, but just stay away from their tusks. Still, there's never such a rewarding meal as when you've hunted an animal before.

I used to eat animals raw, as a kid, but I quickly learned the wonders of cooking. My pops likes things a little undercooked, but I like to get them at least medium well. I asked Shekinah if she wanted to hunt with me, but I think she was a little afraid of me, so said no.

I stalked through the undergrowth, alert to any sounds in the night. I quickly heard a rustling in the bushes to my left, so stalked it, and chased it when it ran. It then turned and growled at me, being a coyote. Coyotes taste fine if you cook them right, so I growled back.

It then lunged at me, and I had a sort of wrestling match with it, keeping it away from my neck. But I got it around the shoulders, underneath its armpits and broke its neck. I then heard yipping beside me... and found two coyote pups. I've never felt so bad. I took the coyote and the pups back to Mary with me.

She said we could cook the coyote, and may as well throw the others into the stew. I couldn't do it... I couldn't kill the pups, and I gave them to Lasso, asking if he could do anything for them. He said they were far too young to care for themselves, and I begged Mary to take them with us, saying I would care for them. She said, "Fine. But if we get into any trouble because of them, it's all on you. If you harm this caravan in any way, I *will* send you packing. So sharpen up, and don't look so glum. I'm sure you'll make a fine coyote daddy." I thanked her endlessly, and bought some cow milk from the store to feed the coyotes.

We still ate the coyotes' mother... but it was a little too salty, and shame filled, for me.

4

Waffles and Pancakes

Little Gess... I didn't mind being called little, but I wish people had time for my full name. It's Gessa, with an a at the end. Now, I didn't mind when Dismas called me Gess, said it reminded him of both of his brothers, but I wish people would call me by my real name. Dismas had come to visit, a friend of my parents, and he had his great shield and sword with him. I looked up and wondered at the Christian cross tattoo on his forehead.

He had traveled the land, fighting monsters, and I was always so surprised at the monsters he had come into contact with! Plague witches, trolls and ogres, even a fatso wurm! I never knew half the things he told us of existed, but he said life will always strive to be out of the norm, to get a jump on us, and that we should never let our guard down.

I sat on Dismas's lap, like I always did, even though I was getting too old for that sort of thing, and he showed me the book of monsters he was making, and how they came into life. Their origins, their upbringings, and most importantly, how to slay them. He said there was a page at the end he was saving for the monster he was hunting... a monster of evil and darkness, that could not be reasoned with, and was one Zach's dad and him fought before.

The two had been to so many places! After Gestas, Dismas's twin brother, died, Dismas was looking for a friend, for a family, and Zach's father and the Chariot provided him with that. Said it gave him another reason to live... said the first one was that he had to remember his brothers, and fight the monstrosities that they died fighting. Gestas was a Blunt Knight, and didn't fight monsters, I thought, and I asked him about this.

"Well... some monsters are human. Don't ever forget that." he said to me.

I suddenly thought of the birds... was *I* a monster too? I whispered in Dismas's ear, when my parents weren't looking, and told him about the birds. He turned pale. It was supposed to be a secret, between me and Barnabus, but it's hard to keep a secret! Only when it worries you so.

"Little Gess has something to tell you two." Dismas said to my father and mother.

I buried my face into his coat, and said that I couldn't... that I wouldn't! That they would be mad at me...

"Now, now, Gessa... we could never be mad at you. Please tell us." my mom said.

"Come on, Gess. It's alright. We all love and care for you." Dismas said, with me at his shoulder on his lap.

Cryingly, I said I brought a bird back to life... that more birds came about. They didn't understand me at first, crying as I was, so I wiped off the tears and tried saying, "The birds... they came back to life! I'm *so sorry!!*" then resumed crying onto Dismas's shoulder.

My mom asked me what I meant... asked if what she thought I was saying was true. I said, "Yes... the bird was d-d-dead! It came back to life!" and resumed crying.

My father and mother looked to each other meaningfully, and my father said he would get the tea, and that my mother had something to tell me.

She said, "Gessa. There was a time in my life when I could do the same thing you could... bring the dead back to life. It is a horrible skill, and has brought much suffering into the world. But do not worry. It is nothing to be ashamed of. When I brought the dead back to life, it was only to save the living. The ones who fight death. I wish you to remember the same thing... that the living are worth fighting for. I will help you in this matter, and make sure *nothing* happens to you... I will be there for you, my love."

She always called me her love, even though it was kind of annoying at times. But I still thanked her, glad to be loved by my parents.

So after Dismas left, and gave me a big ol' hug, saying everything would be alright, my mom took me out into the forest, so that I could show her these birds of mine.

They squawked and chirped at her, and she told them to be quiet, but they wouldn't listen. I said, *"Please, please be quiet!"* and they did.

My mother looked at me, astounded, and asked me what I said. I said, "I told them to be quiet."

"Ah, yes. The language of necromancy. It brings a chill to my spine." she said.

"I'm sorry... Mom..." I said.

"Don't be! Without me, the forces of the living would've surely perished! And if not for Zach's parents... we would all be dead... and undead." she said.

"What do you mean? You *saved* Zach's dad??" I asked.

"In a sense." she said, "We saved each other."

"I thought he didn't need help from anyone... him and Zach's mom... they seem like very well off for themselves." I said.

"We all need the touch of the living, every once in awhile. And their saving grace." my mom said, "Zach's dad... saved me from zombies before. Saved me from the unholy. And his mom made me feel loved and cared for. There is so much the living can offer... do not be sucked in by these... birds..." she said, looking at the birds.

"But... they saved me! They saved me from the bullies! They *seem* good..." I said.

"Then it is probably an extension of your will. The birds do not think, do not know. They are the dead. Come, let us let your birds rest. Let's go back to the cottage." she said, putting her arm over my shoulder and leading me away. I still looked back at the birds looking at me.

So I continued the next few days... always telling the birds to leave if I saw them following, which they did. Although still, the bullies left me alone for a while, afraid of the "bird girl" and let me play by myself. I was kicking a woodchip on my lonesome and a boy stopped the woodchip. I looked up at him, and he said, "Heya, bird girl... so how do you do it? Are you a bird yourself?"

I ignored him and walked away, but he said, "Heyyy... I didn't mean no offense! I think it's cool you took on Molly and her gang."

"Leave me alone please..." I said.

"No, seriously! I think it's badass! Molly's a real cunt... never even shaved yet, and she's got a goatee!" he said.

I looked up at him and laughed. Molly did have a little thing growing on her chin. I said the birds help those who help the birds.

He said, "Well... that's really cool! Wanna be my girlfriend? You're... very pretty, even if you are a bird girl."

Blushingly, I said that was fine, and he said that he had to go tell some of his friends. Little Gess had finally picked up a love life! That's what he said.

I was just glad to not be called "dogfucker" anymore, really.

I've never fucked a dog! Nor do I wish to, or even now how to! Sex is a mystery to me... I wish I could explore it, but I was just so embarrassed! I just wanted to kiss some of the boys... Kiss! That's all... but some of the boys thought differently than me.

The boy I went with showed me eagerly to his friends, and they were astounded by me. Saying how ever did a beauty like me ever end up in his hands! I've heard the same thing from some of the friends of my father, although they just thought of me as a baby kid. Zach's dad was always nice to me, he was a nice sort of person, and he told me to not ever trust in boys and their compliments... like I was doing now.

I foolishly believed them, thinking I really was pretty, but then the boys turned mean. They asked me to show them my cunt, asking if it was as tight as Molly said it was. I walked away, and the boy I went with said to not be intimidated by them... and asked if I really did have a tight cunt. He said that would be hot.

I ran off, crying, and found a bird of mine. The one with the broken wings. It struggled to get to me, and I helped it onto my lap. The poor little guy... he had no wings, just like me. I wish I could just fly away from all of them.

"You shouldn't let boys mess you around." he said to me.

"I know... I hate them all! They all suck." I said to him.

"I'm sure you'll find them differently... when they get what's coming to them." he said.

"What do you mean? Get what's coming to them?" I asked.

"You'll find out. Everyone goes through it eventually. Your bullies will probably go through it sooner than others. Let them pass." he said, and I thought of my Buddha god.

"Yes... let them pass. Like a cloud!" I said.

"Exactly. Let them meet the ethereal. There will be time for mourning later. First... I need you to help me." he said.

"Is it about your wings?? I know a veterinarian, if you'd like. Zach's mom trained to be one actually, and knows a lot about animals." I said.

"I'm sorry. No. It is about the cycle of life and death, and how it must be overthrown. I will speak to you about this later. Good day. Have a beautiful rest of your day, and remember to stick the bullies with anything you can muster." he said, then waddled off through a hole in the fence.

I suddenly became very angry, thinking of the bullies. I wanted to beat them up so bad! I did, actually, throwing the boy I met onto the ground, and pummeling the girl, Molly, to bits, and I was expelled from school later that day. My dad taught me well... a little too well, it seemed.

He didn't know what to do with me, as I sat on the couch. On one hand, I had done what he told me to do, and on the other, I had threatened society. I told him of the day, except for the bird, and he sympathized with me every step of the way, but could not condone me getting kicked out of school. It was hard put on him, him saying he would've done the exact same thing.

When my mom got home, she was furious! She had just had a meeting with Absinthe, the owner of the courier service, the Wheel, and also a distributor of medication for people like my mother.

She said maybe we should just send me out into the woods like Zach's parents did with him! I said that would be fine by me. That I hated school, and that it was all bullshit anyway. "*Young lady! What* did you say?" my mom said.

"I said it was bullshit! *It's shit, shit, shit!*" I yelled.

My mom turned white and furious. I'd never seen her so mad. She said to get to my room, *now.* So I did, quickly. I could hear her and my dad argue throughout the night...

When I woke up I found pancakes sizzling on the stove. My mom was cooking for a change, and said that if school isn't what's best for me, then I didn't have to go. I nervously looked at the pancakes, wondering if there was some sort of catch. She told me to eat up, that it was good maple syrup we had, and to not waste it.

So I drizzled the syrup on the pancakes, and took a bite, only *then* did I regret it. She said, "Oh! And by the way, we've found you an apprenticeship! If school's no good for you, you should get an education somehow! Venny the goblin has agreed to take you on as his apprentice."

"A goblin??" I said, astounded.

"Short little blighters, green, with pointed ears? That's them! You'll be working for pay from now on! You're a working girl! I'm so proud of you!" she said, then went up and hugged me. I thought of what insidious secrets pancakes foretold, and went to my goblin mentor after breakfast.

We had a goblin in school, but they always called him nerd boy. He was always stealing from everyone, but I made sure to punch one of his bullies on my rampage.

Venny was nothing like him. He was shy and antisocial, with a horrible hobble and a bit stunted, and made me clean out his boots first, of all things. He said he didn't know what to do with an apprentice, as I couldn't grasp what the hell he was talking about when he showed me some of his schematics. Some sort of engineering thing for the future. So I just cleaned his boots, and washed his knickers later. I regretted punching those bullies, because of this.

But it wasn't so bad. He was a very nice goblin, even though he got distracted at the littlest things. He calculated the trajectory of a falling leaf and explained to me how gravity works, when we were walking through the forest.

"So... so you see! There is always a maximum velocity of falling things, and *everything* will fall at the same speed, eventually, but some things, like that leaf, have air resistance and fall slower! I had been thinking of something to reduce falling speed... something for when you need to drop from far up! It perhaps may save many a mountaineers life, one day. I just need to find the right fabric and geometry of the thing..." he said.

"When we were kids we'd drop those little twirly leaves and watch them fall... something like that?" I said.

"Perhaps... but that would make the faller so dizzy! Twirling, and twirling... like a gyroscope! Like the world! Spinning, twirling... forever, throughout time... I wish I could see it, in all its glory, one day... the *whole* thing, all at once! That would make my heart fly." he said.

"With a camera? I looked through the one you gave me and it was all black! Couldn't see a thing." I said.

"Well... my dear, remember to take the lens cap off!" he said.

Embarrassed, I said I would, and our day ended. I didn't really do all too much work, besides trivial things like sweep up his little cabin and wash clothes. I couldn't really cook, but that was alright. Venny made me some of his famous waffles for lunch. So it was all in all a good day, of waffles and pancakes.

5

Presidents and Whores

We were getting farther and farther from the homestead, and Mary said she was starting to make a profit! When we got to the city of Jericho however, she gave away the clothes she bought to an orphanage, and she said it never made her more happy. "When you're finally settled up with life, it's good to give back every now and then." she said to me.

The city of Jericho used to be called the City of Thieves, as the thieves guild, the Hermit, was its ruling factor. I mean, they still are, as a lot of the members of the thieves guild became politicians, saying it was even easier, and more legal, than thieving. They're some damn good politicians, I'd say! Always seem to be able to get things done, under the new democracy that President Laurel started. I wondered who would take Laurel's place when her stay in office had ended... I hope they don't muck everything up. Jericho brought peace and order to the land, and even though it has very icy relations with the dictatorship of Gregory's, they still do trading and have open borders.

Gregory started his dictatorship after the King, ol' Jack, bit Barnabus's bullet and the land was thrown into chaos. A few heirs to the throne stepped forward, but were assassinated as soon as they made their claims. One of the heirs to the throne is my ma. She is an illegitimate bastard brought about from the union of Gregory's wife and King Jack. My pops and my ma *have* tried to become king and queen, once, long ago, but they said that ruling was always a hassle, so never pursued it further after the resistance put up by Gregory and those who remained loyal to him. The country was split between Jericho and Gregory, right down the middle, after the great war from my childhood.

My pops and ma had just had a terrible time in the northeast, some place called Russia. They fought to help a teeny tiny country regain its independence, and were paid moderately well, but lost many of their troops. The country became free again, after the help from the Chariot and other mercenary groups, but my ma and pops were frustrated that everything that could go wrong did, and needed a vacation, before they were to rebuild the Chariot back to its former glory.

I had wanted to go traveling with them for ages now, but they usually kept me at home near the Black Dragon so I could be with Aunt Daisy, Uncle Marcos and Gessa, if things were inordinately dangerous. They always hugged and kissed me goodbye whenever they would go on a very dangerous excursion, wanting their last words to me to be something positive. I made the case that I could be a soldier in the Chariot, and try to recruit others, but they said I'd need a tad bit more experience before I strove to fight with them, and even though it was nice going on family vacations, my ma and pops wanted "some alone time" so put me on an adventure instead. I am happy with the decision, as I wanted to go adventuring forever now.

School was always kind of boring to me, except for the fighting, but that was too easy. No one wanted to fight me, because I'd beat them up so bad, and made sure it didn't show, so they couldn't try to tattle on me. I only beat up the bastards who picked on little kids, like Gessa, or who tried stealing from and intimidating others. Always fight for good, as Uncle Marcos says. I had a few friends because of this, but mostly only if they wanted something from me, like protection. Some even tried to pay me! I told them to keep the gold, and that I'd help them if anything bad happened.

A gang tried recruiting me once. They all dropped out of school, skipping every class, but would extort and threaten everyone, even some of the teachers. I had to use my axe, Skull, on them, for nothing but a silent threat, and told them all to leave, forever. They threatened they'd get me one day, but I've never seen them since. Everyone just thought they moved on, and disappeared. It felt good being a silent hero, and I only told Gessa what I did. It was nice having that cloud of fear over the school pass, as the gang left.

I could go on learning, but I think my talents lie in fighting. This world will always need fighters, people to keep the peace and protect the innocent. My ma and pops gave me all sorts of books to read, and I struggled to get through them as a kid, not knowing English very well, but I've found out that books can be some of your best friends. History is kind of boring, as is poetry like my pops likes, so I always stuck with the adventure stories, as I wanted to go adventuring so bad. I love the history of Shake Spear though, the great orcish warlord. His history always reads like an adventure story, anyway. Samay somon samay, to be or not to be, he said, deliberating if it was wise to start wars or not. He was a very noble orc, always trying to better his people's lot in life, and fighting against innumerable odds for his freedom. Nothing like the cannibalizing, murdering rapist that is Gar. Gar ate the orc I beat in single combat for my name, his very own son, like I was his.

I never knew Gar growing up, until our paths crossed in the great war of my childhood. He laid with my birth mother, I don't know if it was willingly or not, and I was her brood. She died from the soldiers, and I'm sad to say I don't really remember her.

But my pops and ma have been the best parents anyone could ask for, and all their friends are like the family I've always wanted as a kid. My ma said to look to the family that passes all bonds of heritage. Said that was something that kept our little family together. There's Barnabus, like the old drunken great uncle, there's Mary, like an aunt, there's Dismas the monster slayer, like an uncle, there's Uncle Marcos and Aunt Daisy, and Gessa too, there's Jacob the courier, a bit of a scoundrel, but always helping out in his own way, and then there's Aunt Melissa the Empress, and Uncle Simon the Emperor.

They're really an emperor and an empress! Melissa is the half sister of my ma, and Simon is the son of the old Emperor, which allowed him to regain his standings and claim a lot of the old lands under his father's domain. I don't get to see them much, as their duties keep them very busy, but they've invited us a couple of times to see them. Melissa has so many dogs! Melissa and Simon are working on making their own child, I heard them say, but are having difficulties. I bet they'll get one eventually if they keep trying. I heard them say to my ma and pops that they're quite enjoying themselves.

Melissa was one of the soldiers who fought my people, the orcs, but she's changed her ways. She was in the grasp of a horrible evil throughout her entire life, and it warped her to all hell. As soon as her curses were lifted, she immediately seemed more buoyant and cheerful, and always tries to spoil me a bit. I'll still remember her throwing that dagger at me, killing Sergeant Zachariah, but I really can hardly picture her like that anymore. Her and Simon are one of the best fighters I've ever seen, and my pops had to fight each Simon and Melissa for his life once, and said he nearly perished both times. It's strange, but the people my pops fights all seem to end up being his friends. Even him and my ma have fought each other, and now they're happily married!

So I wandered down through the City of Thieves, and my pops said if I could I should visit the red light district, which my ma snapped at him for, and said to stay away from it. Said I'd find a nice girl all on my own, and didn't need to pay for sex. I think I'll trust my ma on this... but I still wanted to see what it was all about.

Mary told me to meet her at the gates in an hour and a half, and that I had some free time to use however I wished. She was about to tell me to not get into any trouble, but she looked at me with my studded gloves, my axe, Skull, and my bulging muscles, and she said to not cause any trouble instead.

I left the coyote pups with Shekinah and Lasso, and Shekinah was playing with one as I left, and Lasso tried to ignore the other, but then broke down and picked the other one up and said, "Aren't you the cutest little mongrel! Yes you are! Yes you are!" so I knew they would be safe.

I stayed away from the Broken Compass inn, the one that Mary and Lasso frequented while we were there. It seemed like a gathering place for all manner of devious people, thieves, assassins, gamblers, drunks, and prostitutes, but Mary said they had some good whiskey, so they always went there.

So, after walking around, noticing the sights, I circled around the red light district, then finally, cautiously, approached it. There were really red lights! I thought that was some sort of sexual innuendo. I saw gorgeous maidens in their glass booths, dancing, enticing me to join them. One of them gasped at me, and said however did such a handsome man walk into her neck of the woods. I chatted with her for a bit, and she said, "You wanna blowjob? I'll give you a discount... handsome man..."

Feeling very aroused at this mysterious maiden winking and flirting with me, I said I better not, and walked away, she said next time to look her up, said her name was Chastity. What a strange name.

And then I walked straight into the President of Jericho, Laurel, as my attention was focused on more of the prostitutes.

Her and her vice president, Horatio, were checking up on some of the ol' girls, as prostitution had been legalized and pimping abolished.

The prostitutes were now independent business owners, and anyone who started a *hint* of pimping was quickly thrown out. Laurel had known many prostitutes in her time, being the head of the thieves guild and the president of Jericho, and hated pimps. She wanted the power to mercilessly end them, but needed them as the thieves guild. Now she did have the power, and saved a lot of women and even some men from practical slavery.

Horatio was a huge man, and not what you'd expect from a vice president at all. He was very good with people, and I think his excessive muscles helped in that matter. He used to handle all sorts of things for Laurel in the thieves' guild, and was now handling all sorts of things as vice president.

Laurel was a sandy haired woman, dressed kind of manly, and you could tell she was powerful just by her demeanor. She didn't flaunt it, she didn't lord it over you, but she was, anyways. I think it was the *not* saying how powerful she in fact was which showed how powerful she really was. She was the person you least wanted to cross in her country, and the one you wanted to most aim to please. So I bowed.

"Is that... Zachary? It's been ages! So nice to meet you again." Laurel said, grabbing my hand and giving me a firm handshake.

"This can't be Zachary... Zachary is tiny! Wasn't he just a kid?" Horatio said.

"That's the problem with children... they always grow up. Just ask Absinthe about ours." Laurel said, "I'd know Zachary anywhere." Absinthe was owner of the Wheel, and the country's first husband.

"Yes, it's me, mam! Honored to have your acquaintance." I said, grinning.

Horatio laughed and said *now* he recognized me. It was my smile, said the first time he saw that he was amazed at how sharp orcs' teeth are, and it stuck with him to this day. "So... just looking for a good time, eh? What brings you to Jericho, lad?" Horatio asked me.

"Oh! I was just curious. I'm on an adventure! Currently I'm working for Mary with her caravan business." I said.

"Well, you should come and visit with us. How much time do you have?" Laurel asked me.

I looked at my pocket watch, and said, "Almost 58 minutes left before I have to go back to the caravan..."

"Punctual, to a point. I like that in a man. Come, let's go to my friend Trinity's place. I've been dying to ask her about her biannual profits... I was wondering because of the legalization of her trade if it hasn't been dipping yet." Laurel said.

"She's a... a courtesan? A lady of the night?" That was what you're supposed to call prostitutes, my pops said.

"She's a damned dirty whore, is what she is! But she's one of my best friends in the world. Let's go." Laurel said, and I followed her and Horatio down an alley.

You're probably wondering why the president was walking so freely down shady alleys in a shady city, but if Horatio wasn't enough protection, then her many loyal followers were. She had people *everywhere* who thought of her in the highest regard, the most of them situated in the city of Jericho. She nodded to a cutthroat balancing a knife on his finger, and we walked down a couple of steps and she knocked on the great metal door. The peep latch opened and shut, and the door opened and a bunch of loud music came out, as well as a thin, but shapely, smiling prostitute, with a lot of makeup on. "Laur! My dear ol' bud! I mean, *Missus President!* Please! Come in! That Absinthe didn't up and ditch you yet, did he? But I mean, how could he? You're the biggest ball and chain in the country!" she said, as we followed her inside.

It was a strip club.

Laurel said, taking Trinity by the arm, "No, we're doing well off. Our children are still annoying little babies, but they're growing up *so* fast. Little Firenze is taking his first steps already! And Tobias almost said his first word!"

"I'm *so* glad you didn't name them all after alcohol, like Absinthe is named!" Trinity said.

"Oh, believe me, if he had his way there would be a little Lager and Ale in our cribs... That man... I swear I don't know what to do with him sometimes." Laurel said.

They walked past the strippers to a back room. One of the strippers winked at me. Horatio was talking to a few of his old buddies as well, old thieves guild bouncers and muscle men, and "his darling señorita," so I followed Laurel and Trinity into the back room.

We got to a spacious office space, with a lounge. There was a huge aquarium with all sorts of tropical fish, and a big TV. We sat on the red sofas and Laurel asked Trinity how her business was doing. Trinity said, "Well, ever since I've opened up this joint I don't have to work on my back anymore! I still 'open the gates' to a few of my loyal, well paying customers, but it's fantastic! The girls only strip, or sleep with whoever they want, and I make sure they get checked for STDs and illnesses every month. Who is this *darling* young lad? I don't believe we've been introduced... I'm Trinity, an entrepreneurial working girl!" and offered a hand to me, in that way ladies do. I never had someone offer their hand to me like that, so I lightly took it, and gave it a little peck, looking up at her eyes wondering if I did the right thing. She giggled.

"This is Zach, the King's kid." Laurel said.

"*The* King? The one who fought the undead hordes??" she said.

"That's him. Leader of the Chariot." Laurel said.

"My, oh my! The King's kid! I suppose that makes you the Prince, eh sweetheart?" she said to me.

Clearing my throat, as I was a bit nervous, I said, "I don't know about that. I'm just working for a caravan right now... Pops said I'm not experienced enough to join the Chariot, not yet, anyway."

"Oh, it really does all come down to experience... Passion can only get you so far! I'm sure you'll get there in time, sweetheart." Trinity said.

Laurel and her talked about business, and the decrees and laws she had enforced. They talked a whole bunch, and Trinity was a very worldly prostitute. She eagerly followed everything in the news, and knew what happened to her friends and many, many lovers seemingly before they knew it themselves. I politely sat and nodded, unless they asked me what my opinion on something was. Some things I didn't have a clue what they were talking about, like city ordinances and public council, but others, like when they said they threw a drunk out who kept on groping the girls, I could relate on. The headlock they told me about was a bit common, but it worked well in almost any scenario. "Well! If you're ever tired of caravaneering, you should come back and I'll give you a steady job. We can always use more bouncers, some get too old or too bored, and we lose some of the quality compared to a fresh bouncer." Trinity said. I thanked her for her offer.

Laurel seemed to be able to keep the time without a pocket watch, and said it was time I got going, or else I'd be late... I didn't know how she did it, but when she said I had 15 minutes left to catch up with my caravan, I actually did only have 15 minutes, so thanked Trinity and Laurel, and said I must be on my way. "Don't be a stranger to Jericho, Zach. You're always welcome in my city." Laurel said, waving me out the door. Trinity blew me some kisses as I left.

I got to the caravan just in time. Mary thought I might lose track of time again, so she gave me a little shorter time than what I really had. She said we were all set, so could leave, and we left the City of Thieves behind, with its strange, worldly pleasures.

6

What's a Barcough?

I would continue going to Venny's every day... and today he really needed someone to do some physical labor. My dad told him, when he came over for tea once to talk about how I was doing, that I was a strong lass, and needed to put my muscles to real tests.

So I dragged his house.

It wasn't a very large cabin, in fact it was a very little one, perfect for a tiny little guy like him he said, but I didn't know how the hell to do it! He told me to use physics! I didn't know the first thing of physics, so I tried pushing, then pulling it, but it wouldn't budge. He said he wanted to move it to the next hill over, so he could get a better reading on the stars and more sunlight, but that seemed like a long, long way away, even though really it wasn't very far.

We tried jamming a plank underneath it, and that kind of worked, but I had to pull the whole house up the plank, as the ropes were wrapped around the house. He said that it was just firm in its base, and that once I got it moving it would be easier. So I struggled to pull it up the plank, and got it an inch up the thing. "Very good!" he said, "Now, get the logs and put them where you want the house to be!" so I picked up some logs and put them next to the plank, and we sort of rolled the house down the hill to the next one.

It went too fast though! I had to keep removing the logs and putting in the next one, and still, it moved too fast! It fell off the last log, and was in the dirt again. "Now get the plank, and try again!" Venny said to me.

Uphill was a struggle, going downhill was easy, if a bit hectic. Venny was very crippled, which is why he used his brain instead of his brawn to get things done. Which is why he needed *me* to use my brawn to get things done. I was thankful for all the muscle exercises my dad taught me, as I struggled to pull the house up the hill. I was making progress though, and every time the house fell off a log, I'd just try again. When we finally got the house on the hill, he went inside to check the lighting. He said, "Yes! Yes. It's perfect! Thank you, Gessa! You may have the rest of the day off! I would like to let the sunlight go in through my window and think about things..." so I left him, saying goodbye.

I was just so tired... and sat on a log in the forest for a good bit, breathing in and out heavily. Then my little birdie, the broken wing guy, showed up. *"Tough day?"* he said to me.

"I just moved a house!" I said to him.

"Very commendable work. I congratulate you. Do you have time to speak? I wish to notify you that not everything is prim and proper in your kingdom." he said to me.

I picked him up and put him on my lap, and he looked at me, even though one of his eyes was a bit buggy. A lot of his feathers were ruffled now, and he felt cold. *"My kingdom? What does that mean?"* I asked him.

"Well... how do I put this... You are the Queen. The Lady of Life and Death." he said to me.

"The Queen?? But... Laurel is the president! I'm not a queen!" I said.

He seemed to be smiling to me, and said, *"You are greater than the greatest living ruler. The Queen of All."*

But then there was a rustling in the bushes behind me, and I put the bird on my shoulder, and stood up. "*What* did you call me?" Molly said, coming out of the bushes, with a bowie knife.

I stumbled back, terrified, as she approached me. "N-Nothing, Molly! I didn't call you anything!" I said.

"I heard you! Talking to your *bird.* You said I was something or other! Did you call me fat? I'm going to kill you, little Gess... for everything you've done." she said.

"P-Please! Molly! We can talk this out!" I said.

"Nuh uh. You made me bleed. I think you deserve to bleed a little yourself..." Molly said.

"Please help." I said to my bird.

"Stop talking about me!!" Molly said, then rushed me, wielding the knife and screaming.

The bird fell to the ground, dead.

She tackled me, and tried stabbing me with the knife. On the ground I struggled to keep the knife away from my face, as she was pushing with so much force. She was drooling, frothing at the mouth. A big bunch of spittle fell on my face, as I lay under her terrified.

But I twisted her arm, quickly, and surprised by my strength, the knife accidentally impaled Molly in the neck. She struggled to say something, but coughed up blood. I didn't know what to do. I wanted to scream, but nothing came out of my mouth. She fell limp on top of me, and I struggled to get out from under her.

She wasn't breathing. She was still bleeding. I was silently terrified. I had just taken a life.

"Please!! Please don't die... Don't die! Please!! BE ALIVE!!" I said to Molly's unmoving corpse.

And then she got up.

"Wha- Why is everything so dark? Where am I?" Molly said.

"Are you ok?? Please, let's take you to a hospital!!" I said.

"Nuh uh. I'm going to- I'm gonna- but, why can't I?? Who am I?" she said, rubbing her neck, getting her hand all bloody. I thought I was going to be sick. I *was* sick. I threw up on the ground, as she felt the inside of her neck.

"What should I do?" Molly said, her voice changing, becoming sort of lifeless.

"Please! Go to a hospital!" I said.

"It will be done." she said, running away from me into the forest. I ran for my life, leaving the bloody knife on the ground. I didn't know where I was running to, what I was running from, but I ran all the same.

I ended up at the graveyard of my parents' friends. Gestas's Cross. They had all been cremated, so I hoped none of them would come back to life and talk to me. I had realized that I was a horrible, evil necromancer at this point. That I deserved to die, so wanted to be with the dead. I sat in front of Gestas's grave, and didn't move, didn't make a sound. I just thought, the image of Molly's corpse stuck in my head, like someone jammed it in there with a sledge. I stayed there through the night, shivering from the cold.

Eventually, my father found me, knowing that I brought flowers to all his friends' graves, and said, "Gessa! We've been looking all over for you! We were so worried!" and he got down on one knee and gave me a hug. I didn't hug him back. I felt like I didn't deserve it. "Come on... let's take you home." he said, and picked me up. I was still in shock, and didn't make a sound, but eventually, after I tried shutting my eyes *so* hard, trying to close them from the image of the body, I began crying, and crying, and crying. "There, there... It's alright, Gessa. It's alright." my father said, trying to console me.

When we got home my mother rushed to me, asking if anyone hurt me. I just cried and cried, saying I felt sick. My mother turned white, as my father took me upstairs and tucked me in bed. My mother stayed with me all through the night, trying to comfort me, singing to me and issuing reassurances that it was alright. It was hard, impossible, to believe her, but I was glad she was there. I kept on seeing Molly's corpse in the shadows, and when I shut my eyes. I just stared at my mother, as she held me, whispering that I was her love.

Eventually, I fell asleep. I didn't dream of anything that night, and I'm thankful for that. But before I fell asleep, I saw a huge skeleton in the shadows, completely decayed.

When I woke up, my mother was talking to me about flowers. She loved flowers, and told me about all sorts of them. It was soothing hearing her talk. "Can you tell me about what happened?" she asked me comfortingly.

I shook my head, and she said, "There, there, that's alright." and held me some more. She was crying, ever so slightly, and looked very sad, "They found Molly dead in front of a hospital... They think there is a killer around. Did anyone try to hurt you?"

I thought, *a killer...* I was a killer. I buried my face into my mother's breast, and simply sat with her, as she rocked me back and forth.

"Everyone is in a panic. Right now a mob is mercilessly rounding up some wanderers, and your father is trying to calm them down, trying to issue some of his Blunt Knights to catch the killer." my mother said, "If you can tell us *anything* about what happened... then it would really help. The killer will be imprisoned, but will be shown mercy by the Blunt Knights... if only your father can get to them first."

Mercy?? What mercy could *anyone* show me?? I was scum. I was the worst person alive.

My mother sighed, and said, "There is something I want to tell you, that I fear for all of my life has happened to you. I wanted to tell you when you were older... but I wish you to know the truth. In my younger days I was an adventurer, trying to find a cure and answer to my illness with your father and Gestas. We went through many hardships... and we found a man who was like me. Who had schizophrenia. He was in much worse a hell than I ever was in, and caused much harm because of it. He... kidnapped me, and raped me. I believed he didn't understand what he was doing, and because of his later actions of change, I know so. I wanted mercy for him, despite my awful hatred and fear of him. I saw a part of myself in that man, some evil part, that is schizophrenia. Your father, Gestas, and I eventually found the answers... and also realized I was pregnant. With you. Did anyone... touch you? Did anyone... hold you in a way that you didn't like?"

I looked at my mom awestruck. What was she saying? My father wasn't my father? "N-No. I-I-I wasn't raped..." I said.

We then heard howling outside, from what must've been the biggest dog alive. It was scary. Was it the mob coming to get me? To bring me to justice? I cowered next to my mom, and she said she would see what is outside.

I could hear her slowly open the door, and then open it up completely, and the howling stopped. I heard her sounding almost happy... if not for the concern and worry that she continuously had for me. "Gessa!" she called up the stairs, "I have someone I want you to meet."

So slowly... very cautiously... I crept down the stairs... Then I saw the dog at the bottom of the stairs. I froze in my tracks. It was a big German shepherd mutt, that was only looking at me curiously so far, with his head cocked to one side. I could hear my parents chatting with someone in the living room. The dog whined at me a little bit, then wagged his tail. He looked nice enough, I guess.

"They thought *I* was the person stalking around! How could I be, if I stalked Barcough would bark and howl! He always catches dinner before anyone is the wiser, and maybe he can catch the killer." I heard someone say.

"How are you feeling, Edgar? Not low on medication?" My mother said to the man.

"I am very well, thank you. Thanks to both of you. I have found Barcough's lost love, a mountain lion, and they hit it off very well, but they are taking a break. Whenever they cuddled he would end up being scratched to ribbons!" the man said.

My father said, as I was at the bottom of the stairs petting the dog who seemed very happy with it, "Yes. Now that Barcough's unfinished business is taken care of... you have some that you need to take care of as well." and then he looked at me. They *all* looked at me. The dog barked a little bark then curled up at my feet.

"Yes..." the man said, "I've been dreading this day forever... But the King found me again after a while, in the strangest park next to a carnival, and convinced me, after we had a little fight, that I 'shouldn't leave quests unfinished...' So here I am. With Barcough, too."

Perking up the courage to speak, I said, "What's a Barcough?"

The man waved to the dog at my feet.

"Before we... erm... continue with this, maybe we should make sure everyone is safe..." the man said, "Barcough! Do you know who the killer is? Where he went?"

The dog looked at the man. Then looked up at me. Then my parents and the man looked at me again.

"I see... This is not good..." the man said.

"What? You can't mean... There must be some sort of mistake!" my mother said.

I looked down at the dog, then crouched next to him and pet him, and pet him, and pet him. Then I started crying. The dog was just looking up at me smiling, then put his nose underneath my arms that were held to my face, and put his head next to my head. My parents and the man were silent.

Finally, I stood up, and said, "I... *I killed her!!* She was going to kill me! She attacked me with a knife... and the knife sort of... went into her neck. I didn't mean for it to happen! I was so scared! I am scared... Please! Please don't let them get me!!"

"But... they found the body at the hospital..." my father said.

"I... It happened in the woods, next to Venny's house. I told her... to be alive! And then she was! I told her to go to a hospital! The knife is probably still there..." I said.

My mother let out a long worn out sigh, and my father quickly went up to me and hugged me. I finally did hug him back... afraid, alone, and a murderer.

The man said, "I will tell them it was me. You do not need to worry..." and the dog howled at that, and went over to him, raising a paw to shake, which the man shook. "It was good traveling with you, my friend... but I must meet my end." he said to the dog, and the dog howled again.

"No. *No, Edgar."* my father said to him, "We do not need more injustices. I will look for the knife. Molly's father said that one of his was missing, so he suspected a break in and kidnapper... but I will look for the knife." and charged out the door, but not before my mom gave him a kiss, and she told him to come back soon.

So we waited, nervously on the couch. The man, Edgar, seemed to be the source of all nervousness. Barcough sat on my lap on the couch. My mom busied herself in the kitchen, making tea and biscuits for us. I heard her crying, mumbling that no one was going to take her baby away from her.

Finally, my father came back, holding the knife wrapped in cloth. He went next to me, and said, "Is this the knife, Gessa?" and unfurled the cloth, showing me the knife. I nodded, and he quickly wrapped it up again and put it on the table.

My mother came in, and put the tea and biscuits on the table. The teacups and teapot were rattling on the tray in her hands. She finally sat down, and did something she never *ever* did, smoked a cigarette. My father was very surprised at her, and said, "Daisy! Where did you get those?? This is not like you at all!"

She said, "From Jacob. Apparently nicotine helps with schizophrenia. I learned that from one of Brittany's books. I never wanted to start, but I kept a pack, just in case. I just need everything to be quiet for a while... I *don't* know what to do..."

"I will give them the knife... and tell them the truth." my father said. My heart sank to my stomach at that.

"We can't! You know the people of this village! Most don't even trust me! If you weren't a Blunt Knight I'd be rounded up with the rest of those people they're butchering!" my mother said.

"The Blunt Knights have stopped them before they could wreak any-more harm. If we have to... we will leave. With Gessa. No one will take her, I promise." my father said.

"But after all the work we've put in... We've built this home! We have friends, family here!" my mother said.

"Well..." the man, Edgar, said, "It is not my place to offer this... but what if Gessa just... disappeared, for a while? After you two calm the hive. Necromancy is hated, everywhere, and you will always be hunted if you tell them. I, and Barcough, can give Gessa a safe place, or places, to hide out for a while. At least until the anger and fear has passed."

"Yes." my father said, "I know a detective who can verify your tale, Gessa. I have not touched the knife. Did you?" I quickly shook my head. "Then the truth will be revealed, but it will take a long while..."

"Let her go?? With him? But... but..." and my mother puffed again and coughed, and said, "Please. Do not tell them it was necromancy. Tell them you don't know how the body got there... and that someone must've dragged her there. Please, do this for me. Do this for Gessa."

"If... she went there on her own, there should be no marks, there were no drag marks... I... suppose... but we will have to tell them, one day." my father said.

"Then she will go with Edgar, for a while. Keep her safe, please, Edgar, and if *any* harm comes to her, I will rethink, rethink hard, on all the mercy we have given you." my mother said.

The man smiled a sort of sad smile, and said, "It will be done. Do not worry. Barcough will keep her safe, if I cannot. He seems to like her already!"

So my mother told me to pack quickly and take only what I needed. Frantically I put everything in a pack in my room, then took some things out, and put more back in. I was just so terrified, but I took what I normally take when going on vacations, and said it was just like a vacation. Just a vacation.

So we stood by the door, and Edgar and my father shook hands, my father saying again to keep me safe, and they went out the door. My mother hugged me with all her might, and said, "Edgar... is your genetic father. Despite this, I want you to remember your father and all the love and goodness he has shown you, shown all of us." I cried a single tear, and said that Marcos was my father. My only father, and that I loved him and her with all my heart, and will miss them. My mother cried back, and didn't seem to want to let me go, but finally, she did, and waved goodbye, saying, "Be safe, Gessa, my love."

I took one last look at her, then walked out the door, into my new life.

7

Aphrodite and Nickels

We got ambushed, one morning, on our way down to the next town.

Shekinah was the first to spot them. She took out twin blades of hers, Lasso wielded his axe and shield, Mary took out her sword, and I put my fists up. "You should probably use that... Skull, of yours, Zach." Mary whispered to me. I shook my head, which she shrugged at.

A bunch of spitting and grinning bandits walked out from the forest, as we were stopped in front of a fallen tree. The leader, a very thin man who was very tall with a hood over his head said, "No sudden moves. Hand over your goods and you may just walk out of this alive." and brandished his own sword, "We've got rifles pointed at you in all directions... So be smart, kay?"

These bandits seemed very poor, just by looking at their clothes and rusty weaponry. I didn't think, or feel, anything was pointed at me. My instincts usually kick in when someone is stalking me, but I was worried about Gessa, thinking about those bullies of hers, so I was distracted... but still, I didn't think anything was pointed at us.

There were only six of them, and by the looks of them, they looked like they hadn't eaten a decent meal in days. One kept on coughing. I took out my pouch of gold, all I had, and offered it to him. His eyes glinted, and he said, "Now. Throw it to my feet." so I threw it at his face, the hard gold coins exploding from the pouch and blinding him momentarily. I then tackled him to the ground and began beating him up. He was shit at defending himself, and began getting bloody and bruised under my studded fists.

The others stepped into action, and chased the bandits away, as the lot of them ran. I was still beating the man up, but Mary yelled, "That's *enough*, Zach." so I stopped, and got up off of him. He was cowering and crying, afraid of me. "What's your name, man?" Mary said, helping him up.

"Please don't call the law on me! Please!" he said, "I just need enough money to feed my daughter! She's all I have!"

"That was stupid of you, claiming you had rifles... Anyone could see you're a dirty, homeless, bum. Your name, please." Mary said to the man as he whimpered.

"My name's... Keith. My daughter's Charlene." he said.

"Well, here's some coins, Keith, and if I were you, I'd take on a different trade, before someone a little more ruthless than our orc comes and ends you." Mary said, giving the bandit some money. I was about to protest, but she stared daggers at me, and I shut up.

"Th-Thank you! Bless you, bless you!" he said, then ran off with the others.

"I thought you learned something from Marcos, Zach... it was good of you for being so quick, but we do not want to cause more suffering than what's already in the world. If I were you I'd search for those coins of yours... because we're moving this tree and leaving as soon as we do." Mary said to me. I nodded, ashamed, and looked for the coins. I found seven of them. I also found a tooth from the bandit... which I kept, to remember that day.

When we stopped later to camp, I asked Mary how she knew the bandit was telling the truth. "He could've been a ruthless scoundrel! He could've been a murderer!" I said.

"I know, it's difficult for you, being so young... but most people simply want to live a good life. Most aren't out to get you, whoever they are. Most are just like you and me." Mary said.

"But haven't you gone against some of the worst people imaginable? Haven't you gone against ruthless tyrants, and malicious evildoers?" I said.

"Yes. And I showed less mercy to them than our bandit friend, Keith... But I know they're very rare, and if they are out there, they are usually in some secluded lair somewhere, fearing for their life from all the people they've wronged."

"But... What about *true* evil? Like... Gar." I said.

She sighed, and said that she didn't know about Gar and his followers... but that her and my father would have to end them, one day, when they get enough troops again. "They may have been like the Black Knights were, once. Like our friend, Keith. Like Lasso was." and Lasso nodded and took another sip from his brew, "Simply trying to survive in a cold world. Perhaps they started enjoying it... the cruelties that they had to do. Perhaps they became, like the ones Dismas fights, monsters amongst men. Fear not, balance will always prevail. People like that can't do what they do forever, before they eventually get what's coming to them. That's why it's so important to do as much good as you can in the world, so people realize that they don't have to be monsters."

I didn't know what to say, but I took her words to heart. Dismas said that monsters are people, and that people are monsters, and that the saying worked each way, and you should remember both sides of the coin... Barnabus said that anyone who pissed him off was probably worth slitting open, if they couldn't drink their weight with him first. I thought that I should figure out my own principles, my own technique in fighting evil, and stick with it. I should have a code of honor, like all the great warriors had. So I thought of this:

1. Always fight with your bare hands first. It isn't as lethal, even though it can be just as dangerous, as fighting someone with a weapon.
2. Protect the innocent. Some people may not seem innocent, but there are both sides of the coin, and you should always find the truth of things and protect those who do no harm.
3. Subdue and discourage. Do not aim to kill, whatever you do, and give the living peace, as the dead cannot enjoy the same peace.
4. Always learn from every fight.
5. (One I learned from Mary) Make love, not war.

I wondered how Mary and Barnabus got along so well. Like, how Barnabus always mentions fucking her, and that Mary quickly told me to shush when I told her about that... They seemed like opposites. They were both great warriors, but while Barnabus seemed to think of himself first, and then the ones he cared for, and then for the general peace of things, Mary seemed like she cared for everyone, no matter what their origins. I knew to not take this as a show of weakness, because if you messed with those she cared for, you would quickly lose an eye. She had always wanted to be a mother, so I suppose she thought of herself as sort of the mother for all of our little family, and we could go to her for anything. She was a bit older than my pops... but still, didn't have a problem shacking up with Barnabus, who was about the age of my pops's pops age, if my pops's pops wasn't dead. I wondered about relationships, because of this. I day-dreamed of Gessa, imagining her doing that little twirl of hers when she was happy.

When the others were sleeping, Shekinah told me she wanted to show me something in the forest, after I put my coyotes to bed in my pack. She brought me to a moonlit pool, and began disrobing. I asked her what she was doing, and she said, "You are great warrior, no? You like?"

Looking at her ebony body, naked to the moonlight, seemingly a part of the woods, I quickly nodded. She dove into the pool, and asked me to join her. I undressed, amazed at her beautiful body, at her white teeth smiling in the moonlight. I went into the water, even though it was very cold, and swam with her. She was circling me, as I was circling her, then she went to me and kissed me. She did an astounding thing with her tongue, and I kissed her back.

When we got out of the pool... she did something with her mouth on me, that was really very enjoyable, but something I've never had before. When she finished we dried ourselves off and clothed, and got to the campfire to warm up. She fell asleep in my arms, with her hand on the inside of my thigh. I fell asleep, strangely, very happy.

When I woke up, the others were all ready to go, and Shekinah didn't seem to be acting any differently towards me... but I did always catch her smiling at me, and I smiled back, which she quickly turned her head at and giggled.

Later on the next night, she took me out again into the forest, after a relatively uneventful day where I caught a couple hares, Shekinah laid on top of me. She said I was the first man she would take for pleasure, over duties to her old master.

So we had sex.

I was very bad, I fear, but she took control most of the time and helped me through it, on top of me, gently telling me to put my hands here, to thrust there... I felt very good after that night.

But we never saw Shekinah again, after I fell asleep, and all of our gold was missing the next day.

Blood filling in my face, I kept silent as Mary was furious, biting my and Lasso's heads off. I had sex with a thief, for my first time. She even stole my few bits of gold, and Keith's lucky tooth. "That's it. Never trust a bitch who doesn't drink. From now on, you're drinking with us every night, Zach, or I'm kicking you out." Mary said. I stammered protests, but she simply smiled... and I knew I had no choice.

So the first night after that, I drank very heavily with Lasso and Mary. I woozily wandered away to take a piss, and missed the tree I was aiming at, even though that doesn't matter.

Mary went up to me and grabbed me over the shoulder, and looked down as I was taking a piss. Shocked, I quickly stopped the stream, and pulled up my pants. "*Not*... like... I haven't seen it..." then she hiccuped, and said, "before..." and then squat down, and took a piss right next to me. Drunkenly I laughed my ass off, which she did too, laughing at me. We laughed at each other, and then walked back to the camp. "You'reeee... a gooood *kid*... Zachary... Don't ever fall in love with a thieffff... They'll take your hearttt... and sell it..." she said.

Embarrassed, I said, "You... knew? How come?"

"I thought itttt... was harmlesss..." and she hiccuped again, and said, "Your little giggligllinggg game..."

We got back to the camp, and Lasso was playing with and naming the coyote pups, "You'reee Aphrodite the Fair... and you're Nickelssssss!" he drunkenly said.

"Are you... ready? Lasssso?" Mary said to him, arm over my shoulder.

"Oh yeh! I'd love to see this new blood take us on..." then he grinned, and I wondered what he meant, but not after Mary walloped me in the face with her other free hand.

I lay on the ground, shocked from the blow, as Mary almost fell over laughing, and Lasso laughed too, getting up and putting his fists up.

I quickly got up, and then Lasso charged at my legs, actually picking me up as I flailed around, then threw me down with a takedown. "We said we'd let you fight, when you were ready..." Lasso said to me on the ground again, "Don't let us down." and he offered a hand to help me up, but remembering Barnabus's words, I didn't take it, and got up myself. Lasso shrugged at this and threw a swing.

So I blocked, and swung back, but that was one *tough* dwarf! He could take anything, and I punched him over and over again, him not even blocking. He just laughed at me, and said, "Is there a mosquitooo around here? I hear one buzzing..." then gave Mary a tag in, and she swung, swung *hard* at me, right in the stomach. I threw up from the force and from being drunk.

I kept on throwing up, hunched over, and Mary helped me up, saying, "Comeee on... don't you have a thicker couple of livers than that? Get angry. You were robbed and taken advantage of by a thief and a whore."

So I thought back on the encounter with Shekinah... and I *was* starting to get angry, every nice kiss, every fond caress... It was really pissing me off! So I fought Mary and Lasso, taking every punch, the anger making me stronger, in a way.

I threw Mary with an ippon seoi nage over my shoulder, which took her completely off guard, and the fighting ceased, as each of them wanted to know how I did that. So I told them how, actually being able to pull it off in drunken determination.

"Welll... you grab their arm, turn, take one step back with your left, one fooooot forward with your right, lean over, and pow! Onto the ground." I said, stumbling a bit, "Remember to kick a bit with your lefttt foooot..."

"Woooahhh... that's like... *Blunt* Knight knowledge..." Mary said, and the two did a little jig, saying, "Blunt Knight! Blunt Knight! Doesn't even put up a fight! Until they hit you just, just right!"

"Hey!" I said, "The Blunt Knights are a very noble order!"

"Yeahhh... they're just a bunch of pussyfests..." Mary said, "Marcos is one of my best friends... but he needs to fight for real one of these days! I saw him at the great battle, and he could take on the entire garrison of Stockholm all on his own! If he wasn't burdened by his *morality...*"

"What... What do you mean?" I asked.

"When the hammer comes down, you either get out of the way... or you fight back. Marcos needs to use that hammer... and then maybe he could join us! But instead, he fockin' *hates* mercenaries... damned fool... I wish I was like him, and could be a noble knight again... but I forsook my vows, and became a rogue... I am the epitome of shame! I fell in love with a worthless biker that got killed by his own pets!" and she began crying. Lasso went over to the fire, and got her some more beer, which she thanked him for and drank. We then all went to the fire and sat down, and watched the coyote pups, Aphrodite and Nickels, play in the glow.

After sniffling some more, Mary said, "You don't need to fight, if you don't want to, Zach... You don't have to try to find the goodness in people, no matter how far deep it is buried... You can go home, if you want to."

Shocked, I said that there was nothing I enjoyed more than fighting, and that if I can try to find goodness in people, then I will. Mary was like a second mother to me, and when she and Lasso finally accepted me, it felt really, really good. I said there was nowhere I'd rather be than with this caravan.

"That's good of you, Zachary. I'm feeling sleepy... Good night..." and she fell over. Lasso laughed, and we played dice, Barnabus taught me how, even though we had nothing to gamble with, we just played for fun.

I never felt more happy, and more drunk, than when Mary had accepted me into her pack.

8

Like Cats and Dogs

My father, Edgar, and Barcough took me out past the woods, where Barcough and Edgar were leading us. Edgar said there was nowhere safer than in the wilderness... so after we got over the next hill, my father, not wanting to leave, went down on one knee and hugged me, even harder than my mother. I squeaked at the hug, and then he gave me a gentle one. "I love you, Gessa. You are the world to me... please come back safe." he said. I said I loved him too, and kissed him on the cheek, which he cried and smiled at. "Well... it's time I get this all sorted out. Please, either meet with a courier of the Wheel or come back, in a few months." he said to me, "The Wheel owed our family a great favor, and will deliver your letters at no cost, no matter what the distance."

"Really? I will always keep in touch with you!" I said.

"Lay off on contacting us, for just a while. But you can message Zach if you want to." my father said. I thought of the mohawked warrior I met with before everything turned sour, and I felt happy. I said I will, and my father gave me one last hug, then walked off, looking back at us and waving.

Edgar was nervous, saying he didn't know how to do this, and I said, "Just take me to wherever you want to go... I don't want to talk to you. You hurt my mother." he said he would, and became very quiet, even though Barcough barked a lot and led us down some path.

Then, Barcough suddenly ran off, and Edgar too, very silently. I waited for them wondering if I should follow? They just ran off! But they came back in a bit, as Edgar dragged a dead moose through the wilderness. "I have dinner for you! Just you wait! It will be delicious!" he said.

Looking disgusted at the moose, I said I was a vegetarian.

"Oh? How does that work? Do you know of veggies to eat?" he said, looking at me.

Embarrassed, I said I didn't... that it always didn't seem very interesting to me, and I couldn't tell which ones were poisonous, like my father could...

"Then... I am sorry, Gessa, but you *must* eat! Otherwise you will starve, or catch a sickness, or something horrible!" Edgar said.

I said I'd starve.

He dragged the moose for a while, and we stopped on top of a hill in the forest, and he started a fire. He skinned and cooked the moose, saying that knives were handier for that than with bare hands... even though he said he hunted and killed with his bare hands. I thought I was going to be sick, as he cooked and ate the moose, and gave a big portion to Barcough.

Ashamedly, looking at the two eating the moose, I did feel hungry... but I couldn't eat one of the gods' animals! That would be evil! My stomach growled, and Edgar offered me a bite. I shook my head quickly.

I didn't know what I'd eat... I tried eating a leaf when Edgar wasn't looking, but I don't think those are right to eat... I ate some wildflowers, but they had a weird taste, and I don't think they were right to eat either... Edgar had stored a lot of the moose in his pack, saying we didn't need to hunt for a while. It made me sick the whole while, as he portioned it up and wrapped each piece of moose in cloth. He must be some sort of monster, I thought.

Not like Barcough. He was the cutest dog imaginable, always whining at me wanting to be pet... I didn't know how the two could be a pair. Barcough was a good boy... Edgar was a rapist. I didn't trust him, but Barcough did, so I tried to, anyway.

When we stopped for the night, Edgar told me that every part of everything was special, was important, was all. He wasn't drinking, saying that that screws up his medication... but it sounded like something a drunk person would say. He said that the most important thing in life is to not waste food, and if you must take a life, then you should eat it.

Edgar always took medication for the night and the morning. Said it helped stop the voices of his. I always wondered about schizophrenia, as my mom had it, but she never talked about it with me. Said it was very frightening, and wanted desperately for me not to have it. I never heard, or saw, anything which made me question my sanity. Besides the birds, but it turned out the birds had been real! Thank Buddha they weren't following me anymore.

I asked Edgar about schizophrenia, asking why it was so terrible. He said, "It... is like someone else is in your head, commenting on your thoughts, tormenting you and hating you, for no other reason than that you are there... I thought they were real, once, and was terrified, and caused much harm because I was so scared... I thought everyone was out to get me, was going to get me, but people like your mother and father, they make me feel like I've let in a draft, thinking that way... like it was the stupidest thing imaginable, thinking of. The voices were not real, were never real, and are just my mind playing tricks on me. I don't listen to them anymore."

"Who is 'them?'" I asked.

"Well... I don't really know. They used to have names, but they really aren't the people they claim to be, so I don't call them anything. They said they were these terrible people, terrible at least to me, but I'm sure they aren't really so terrible. I'm sure they're normal. Like you. I'm glad that you're normal." he said.

"How can you be sure? What if they really are terrible people? Like... Molly was." I said.

"...I don't know. We will see one day. But I'm sure that it is my mind playing tricks on me. Please, do not make me fear and... doubt. It is only hallucinations. Even the worst people aren't as terrible as you think them as..." he said.

I thought about him, and I became quiet. Barcough snuggled up to me, and we fell asleep in these sleeping bags that Edgar brought, close to the fire. He always put a new log on when he noticed me shivering...

He was always awake before me! Scouting out the land... but I did catch him sleeping once, when we camped in the middle of the day. Barcough guarded his side, and kept vigil. I decided I'd sneak away for a while, but Barcough barked at me once, and I said, "I won't be long! Just gotta take care of lady business!" and he wagged his tail at me. Barcough seemed like a smart dog, too smart, and smart people can always be deceived.

I ran into the forest, running away from Edgar and Barcough, but Barcough caught up with me... he may be smart, but he wasn't stupid. He had all the animal instincts of an animal, and the intelligence of a human, at least that's what Edgar said. He whined at me, and I said, "I'm leaving! I've had enough! I want to go home..." but he came up to me, standing so alert and vigilant in front of me. I just held his fur coat and cried into it... wishing that none of this ever happened... telling the dog that I was starving, and sad, and lonely, and missed Zach... He licked the tears off of my face, and brought me back to Edgar.

Edgar yawned and woke up, saying why was I so glum? I just said I wanted to keep walking.

We did, and as we settled down for the night, under the rising full moon, I noticed a big pair of eyes staring at me in the darkness. Barcough seemed to be wagging his tail more, but I was terrified. Edgar said, "That'd be Jillian. Don't worry... Barcough converted her on not killing humans anymore."

And Barcough ran to those eyes, yipping happily.

I cried out, saying that shouldn't we help him?? That was some sort of big cat!

"No... I'm sure we'd just get in the way. They have a very 'complicated' mating arrangement..." he said, taking out some moose and cooking it.

Then we heard growling, and howling, and barking and hissing. I was scared as all hell... but then, to my complete astonishment, a man and a woman came out from where Barcough was, holding each other in their arms. I quickly asked who they were.

"I'm the Barcough that you know! The one and only..." the man said.

"Yes! I'm Jillian. Who might you be, dear lady?" the woman said, offering a hand for me to shake which I did. This was something Edgar just said! I was flabbergasted.

"I-I-I'm Gessa." I said.

"Nice to meet you, Gessa! We're just going to take a sleeping bag... and be on our way." Jillian said.

"Now, now, Jillian, like you always said, company before fun stuff. Let's talk to little Gess and my friend Edgar for a while..." the man called Barcough said.

So Edgar talked with Jillian, saying that they shouldn't be so loud! That that only attracts others. Jillian said, "It's no fun if you're *quiet!* Arguing and having fun is always so much more fun when you are as loud as possible!"

The man, Barcough, laughed, and said, "Yes... My Jillian was always a squeaker. I suppose that's why they turned her into a giant cat!" she hit him at this gently.

"Wh-Wh-Who are you??" I asked.

Barcough looked to me gently, like so many times as the big dog, and said, "I'm a weredog, little Gess. And Jillian is a werecat. We were 'changed' when we were human, and turned into animals. It was a very long time ago... and you shouldn't worry yourself about it. We've made our peace."

"You mean she doesn't know?? It makes me *so* angry... but I suppose we should let the old Shazians pass into dust... I'm sure we'll become the source of many a good ol' folktale eventually!" Jillian said.

"Yes. We're getting old though. I don't know how many more times we can do this." Barcough said.

"Fuck that! We're going to live forever... or at least, until we've fucked enough to feel like we've lived forever. Come on! Company can wait." Jillian said, so she took Barcough and a sleeping bag and went into the forest. Then... the loudest sounds of lovemaking imaginable assaulted our ears.

Edgar was simply smiling, saying he was happy for his friend.

I tried covering my ears... but they were so loud! They'd wake the entire forest! I tried going to sleep... but they'd argue, and fight, and then start up again! It was a never ending cacophony of groans and moans!

Edgar said sleeping is easier on a full stomach.

So I took a bit of the moose, and slowly... carefully... put it to my mouth, and took a bite. I was disgusted at first, I felt like some sort of cannibal... but it tasted good, after a while. I asked for seconds, and he cooked a slab up for me, which I ate carefully... and I asked for thirds, and he cooked up another which I ate ravenously... for the fourths, I finished half of it, and struggled to finish the rest... but I did. Then I really did feel sleepy, despite the endless noise, and fell asleep in my sleeping bag.

Barcough and Jillian were using Edgar's, so he stayed up for them, and talked with them when they thought I was sleeping, after I woke up again, used to the noise that ended.

"So this is the girl of the girl you hurt?" Barcough asked Edgar.

"Yes. I wish her to understand that I was not sane, that I was a terrible human being..." Edgar said.

"Come now. You helped everyone, with me, in the past. Don't think of yourself so bad." Barcough said.

"Yeah, and you found me! Noticed there was a cat out there who wasn't totally a cat!" Jillian said.

"...I know... I just feel so awful... like I should die, whenever I think of her... It was the worst thing I ever did, and I hope her and her child can forgive me..." Edgar said.

"Worse than when you ate people? Come on, people don't taste that bad! Kind of good, if you hate them." Barcough said.

"But! But! That's not who I want to be! You have the liberty to do anything you want, but I must answer to the human race! I must repent for my actions!" Edgar said.

"There's always a place for you, with the dogs, if you want." Barcough said.

"And some of the cats! I really don't know what my owner thought of... when he turned me into a giant cat. Was the easiest thing imaginable, to maul him to bits. Ha ha!" Jillian said.

They laughed, and they talked about strange things of the past. I was never so frightened.

When I woke up again, Barcough was a big German shepherd mutt, like he'd always been, and I wondered if it was a dream.

But it wasn't a dream. Not like the dreams I had sleeping... I had a really good dream. It was a lucid dream, and I figured out it was a dream when Zach's dad was behind me then in front of me again. The dream didn't really know who to be at first, but became him, as I thought it may as well be someone I love and care about. I had thought all the flying and floating around in the dream was weird, if very fun, so had my suspicions up unto that point. I thought Zach's dad could give me more insight into some things, as he was always a source of wisdom in my dreams, and when I said I had to grow up quick, he said, "Well, would you rather grow up quick or go quickly to your grave?" and I thought that was some fine wisdom.

I then tried escaping the boundaries put up by the dream, the weird hotel setting around me I was put in, opening doors and windows, and even trying to smash through the closed shutters of one. I debated reality with Zach, like we did when we were kids, and even though I knew it was a dream I said this was real. That the apartments, that the soft grass, that everything in it was real, still. He shrugged and said I would know. Eventually, as my family kept on blocking me, preventing me from leaving the setting, I said screw it, my family and friends were here, and that made me happy. I thought if this was a coma, and would never wake up, that I may as well make the most of it. I was sitting on a soft couch chair, and all my family and friends were around me, and even though the army was there to keep me in, I wasn't scared of them, as they were all dancing and handing around refreshments. Then I heard this great song... something about a story and lives, and I woke up. But I was still in the dream, even though everything looked real enough, and I said this was real, and that was real. I heard a cluttering from a closet, and then I did wake up. It was much different than the reality before me, of Edgar throwing a piece of meat over me into the forest, and some loud purring coming out of the bushes right next to me.

Having to pee, I didn't want to disturb Jillian while I did so... so crept away from her to the other side and did my business. I went back to the camp, and Edgar was all ready to go. I asked him, "Where the *hell* are we going??"

He shrugged at me, and said that life always finds a way. I think he misinterpreted the saying... but maybe he was alluding to himself as life? To our little pack of humans and animal humans? I think he was just lost and didn't want to admit it... but he kind of did. I think he just made up the direction and path as we went along... but while I always stumbled in the undergrowth, he and Barcough seemed to walk down a path only they could see.

Jillian always stayed away from us, and was a bit wild. I did catch her drinking from a stream once, as an enormous mountain lion. She was a beautiful animal, if a bit scary to be around.

I hadn't washed in days... and was beginning to stink. I was embarrassed to ask the question if I could be alone and bathe when we got to a lake, but Edgar took off his clothes and dove into the water, not even giving me a second thought! I looked at him and Barcough playing in the water... and I said I was going to find a quiet spot to bathe. "Stay out of the shallows, Gessa!" Edgar said. I ignored him and found a part of the lake under some shady trees, and took off my clothes and bathed. There were a lot of mosquitos in the shade... so I tried staying in the water as much as possible, and washed myself. When I got out... I was covered in leeches! I screamed, and tried pulling them off of me, but that hurt a lot, and they were stuck to me.

Edgar quickly went over to me, naked as he and I was, and removed the leeches. He said to me, calmly, carefully removing the leeches and flicking them away, "Find its mouth... which is on the thin end... slide your fingernail underneath it, and push it away... remove the sucker... and flick it!" I was crying as he removed the things... It was like something filthy attached to me, draining me of life! Only after Edgar removed all the leeches did I thank him, and become embarrassed that I was naked. I quickly clothed myself, and Edgar averted his gaze. "Don't... Don't get any ideas!" I yelled at him.

"There is no worry... I would never hurt myself, anymore, and you came from me... in a way... I would never hurt you, Gessa." he said, with his back turned to me.

"I'm not you! Leave me alone!" I said, and walked away. I heard him gently crying, as Barcough sat next to him and Edgar pet him... and I felt bad about it... later... He *was* nice, if a bit bare to the bones... but the things him and Barcough said! I wondered who was the real monster here... was it them? Or was it me? No. He was a rapist... But he was nice! I decided I wouldn't think about it anymore, after the thoughts went around my head in a circle... and we continued walking.

9

The Necromancy Book

I trudged up the hill, I trudged down the hill, following the caravan. This was the longest walk we've ever done. Mary had been commissioned by a halfling to go to the great library in another country, on the edge of Jericho, to get some rare books for him. The walking was good for cardio, but I'd never been so tired. We left early in the morning, and rarely stopped for rest. Mary said walking was the best way to fight a hangover... but I felt like acid was in my stomach, rumbling around and going into my throat. The pack animals, unlike me, were unphased.

We had two horses carted with supplies and goods, and a stubborn old jackass who made a lot of noise if anyone approached him besides Mary. That jackass, Ferdinand, bit, too.

I asked Mary why we couldn't just ride the animals, and she said, "The animals have enough burdens already. We would be making the same time with or without riding, and if we rode, we'd lose a lot of our cargo, as the animals couldn't carry both it and us. Do you even know how to ride a horse?"

I said no, I didn't, but it couldn't be that hard.

"Well, I'll teach you, one day. But keep up, you're lagging." she said.

So I hurried up next to Lasso and Mary, and tried distracting myself from my aching muscles by admiring the scenery around us. It was a lot more wild at the edge of the border. There were large trees, blue and yellow wildflowers, and some strange vines growing up a lot of trees. I asked Mary what they were, and she said, "They're kudzu. They're a bit of an invasive species... They would be everywhere around the world by now, if a religious group hadn't burned them down and discouraged their growth. They had a religious text where the writer mentions 'the trees being drowned from sunlight' so they interpreted that as the kudzu being a sign of the apocalypse, so they tried to prevent the world's end. They're no good for a lot of plants, and they do get tiring to look at after a while... but still, here they are."

We kept walking, and stopped to rest at the edge of a palm oil plantation. Mary said these were special palm oil plants, being native to colder, temperate regions. The owner had cut down anything around the plantation to discourage the kudzu growth. Mary said the palm oil trees were just as bad as the kudzu, as nothing would grow underneath them, besides grass and a few stubborn plants, and animals wouldn't even travel underneath them. Workers were harvesting the palm trees, as palm trees can be harvested many times during the year, if a little less for these types of palm trees. Elves were climbing up the trees and picking the plants.

A few stopped working to look at us, and one raced away. Soon, a fat elf came out of the palm forest to meet with us. "Howdy. What brings you to our lands?" the fat elf said.

Mary said, "We're looking for the great library of Alexander. I think we may be a little lost... Would you be able to help us?" I didn't expect that she was lost! She seemed like she knew exactly where she was going, wherever she was going.

So Mary showed the owner her maps, and the owner said her map was out of date... as the Emperor lost some holdings in his lands to a rebel group to the southeast. But, if we kept walking down this road, the library of Alexander should show up on the horizon. Mary thanked him and we continued on our way.

I asked Mary if maybe we should get new maps. She said, "I knew exactly where we were going... Don't you worry. People look kindly on lost travelers, and not on foreigners who disrupt work."

"Aren't we the same thing? Foreigners and travelers?" I said.

"Yes. But there's a difference. Think of it like the kudzu. Some foreigners invade and inhabit the land, making it difficult for the natives to continue their way of life. Everyone *should* be able to inhabit wherever they want, but you'll find most people don't like having something strange and maybe invasive in their homes. Some people may not even like foreign caravans. We'll be more like the migratory swallow, and inhabit the land for a short while, for a season, and then be going on our way." I nodded, understanding. *I* was something foreign and invasive, to most people, being an orc.

So we walked for a while, muscles aching, Lasso's joints popping whenever he would walk too vigorously. He sounded like popcorn popping, when he strode with vigor. And then we saw it. A great building arising over the next hill, green and grey, old masonry covered with vines. "That'd be it." Mary said, and we hurried to it, Lasso actually breaking out into a run holding the pack animals' reins.

"H-Hey! What's up?" I said, running after him and Mary, running away from me.

"Always take the final stride as strong as possible! Come on, yeh orc! Let's see how yeh sprint!" Lasso said.

The horses and jackass didn't seem to slow Lasso down, and I hurried to catch up with Mary and him, Lasso's joints sounding like a xylophone as he ran.

I was very tired, but I did what I usually did when I had to sprint for something, I imagined hunting my prey. I saw Lasso and Mary as my game, and I would take them down. They heard me growling and roaring, and Mary said, "Oh shit! The orc's gone bloodlust! Fuck, let's run!" and they ran even faster.

I was catching up with them, I was gaining on them. When Mary turned her head to look at me, something you should never do when someone is chasing you, caught up in the moment, I tackled her to the ground. "Ach! Fuck, my back!" she said, so I quickly got up off her, then she sprinted away from me, laughing. "Last one there has to clean the sweaty clothes!" she said.

Lasso had already made it to the great doors of the library of Alexander, and it was between me and Mary now. I was at her pace eventually, striving to hunt Lasso now, putting his hands on his knees and making grunting, out of breath noises. I was nearly ahead of Mary, but she turned her head to one side, and said, "Shekinah!" so I turned my head to look, which then she quickly tripped me and I fell to the dirt, flat on my face. She laughed and got to the doors.

I walked up to them, trying to dust myself off, as Mary was sitting on the ground breathing heavily. "That was a dirty trick, Mary." I said.

"Come now, you'll get over her eventually. The Library of Alexander keeps a washing pool, let's see if we can acquire permission." Mary said.

A monk of the library, one of the librarians, as the Library of Alexander was deeply sewed in with religion, books being a holy thing to them, came out to greet us, and Mary asked for permission to wash in their pools. The monk, gasping from our stink, quickly said yes. I left the coyotes, who were still sleeping after I fed them, in my pack with the horses.

We went to the bathhouse and disrobed. Mary popping off her armor, and Lasso taking off his rough clothing, struggling to get one of his boots off. "Go on. Let's see what your girlyfriend found so attractive." Mary said to me, so I took off my clothes.

I am not embarrassed about being naked, usually. I was proud of my body. But I was getting naked in front of a naked Mary and Lasso! They submerged themselves in the pool, breathing out a sigh of comfort. I quickly went into the waters with them. I didn't stare at Mary, and she wasn't at all interested in my naked body, but I did admire her many scars, and she told me a bit about a few of them. "This one... I got from picking a fight with an orcish chieftain, when I was their guest of honor. The orcs all love making hooch, and I loved drinking it, and when I drank a few of them basically to their deaths, I said a faux paus to the chief. We had to brawl our way to peace, and that orc... sure did like to bite. This one... I got from wrestling a lion in an arena, when your father and I had to fight as gladiators to win a mercenary contract. This one... I got from a c-section, after I miscarried."

She seemed sad, after that last one, so I didn't pry further. We washed and bathed, and I had to wash up all of our stinky clothes... It sure did reek. That's what happens when you walk all day, I guess...

We left the clothing to dry, and were given spare clothes by the monks. We had these long robes on, and I felt we looked a little silly. It was what all the others wore though, so I suppose we were taking on the native custom. We were going to the head librarian, looking for the books, and I heard a familiar voice, saying, "Come on! You don't have a *single* thing on necromancy?? What kind of bloody fuckin' piss poor place is this!"

"Barnabus?" Mary said, as we turned a corner and looked into an aisle of bookshelves.

And sure enough, the old Black Knight was antagonizing one of the librarians, a short girl of my own age. He turned to look at us, and said, "Mary! My sweet! Whatever are you doing in this shithole?"

"Barney! You drunken old fool. This is a library, with books, something you've never heard of..." and the two went to each other and gave each other a kiss.

It was a very long kiss... and Barnabus had his arm around Mary's waist, and Mary had her hand on his cheek. I coughed, unsure of what to do, as they kept kissing. Barnabus stopped kissing, and looked over Mary's shoulder, and said, "What's that? I hear a fuckin' bird chirping, disrupting the mood..."

"Zachary finally made it to us, and this is Lasso." Mary said. Barnabus was glaring at Lasso as Lasso was glaring at him, but they shook hands and grinned. My pops said you can tell a lot about a person by their handshake. "We're just getting some books for a contact. What are *you* doing here?" Mary asked Barnabus.

"Erm... Well, it's top secret. A secret mission for the Black Knights, yeah..." Barnabus said.

"Well, let's go talk about it. Outside, as these monks sure do love their quiet." Mary said.

"Fuck their quiet. If they knew what I was doing, they'd be in an uproar, eager to help me. That's right you fuckin' monks! You'd be *begging* to help me!" Barnabus yelled. Mary hushed him and took him outside.

Lasso went to get the books, as even though he was a bit of a ruffian, he loved his books, and knew how to approach a library for information. I was left on my own, and Lasso said to check some books out and thicken that thick skull of mine.

I went to the librarian Barnabus was yelling at, who was nervously trying to continue categorizing books, and asked if she had any books about Shake Spear. She said, "No! I don't have any more books for you people! Wait, what did you say?"

"I'm looking for books on Shake Spear. Don't worry about us or Barnabus." I said.

She was a pretty maiden, if a bit mousy, and said, "Well, a lot of orcish history was 'requisitioned' by some orcs who wanted their history back and out of human hands, so I'm afraid we have no more books about Shake Spear. Are you one of those orcs?"

"Not at all!" I said, "I think it's neat if as many people as possible know about Shake Spear. He's one of my heroes!"

"I always did find it interesting how he met with those witches who offered to give him unlimited power if he would kill his generals and those he cared for, and denies them, and eventually has to fight the witches with their magic and necromancy. And how it turned out the witches were trying to subdue and destroy Shake Spear and his people. 'Orc! Thou time will come! You will be forsaken and forgotten! You will be shrouded in shadow! You will be risen again, and none will know your true name...' was the last words of the witch."

"That's one of my favorite stories! I also like the one where as a young orc he tries to win the heart of a maiden of a neighboring clan, and an ensuing feud takes place between the families, but as Shake Spear is gravely wounded, and his love is about to kill herself, he stops the dagger she is about to thrust into her heart, and saves her life, saying, 'With a kiss from my love, I live.' and she kisses him, and he is immediately rejuvenated, and brings peace to the clans. Almost the same thing happened to my ma and pops." I said.

"What do you mean? Are they great orcs too?" she asked.

"Nah... I was adopted by humans. My pops lay dead, and my ma tried bringing him back to life with CPR, but eventually realized there was no hope, and kissed him. Then he got up, and lived!" I said.

"Well, sometimes a jolt to the heart can fix near death, but I think you must be misleading me..." she said.

"Not at all! I was as astounded as you are!" I said.

"I always wanted to be kissed like that... but I'm a monk of the library, so I don't really have a chance to go out much." she said.

"They don't even let you kiss some of the other monks?? That doesn't seem fair." I said.

Blushing, she said, "Well, they're all old, anyway... I was left here, abandoned by my parents, as a small babe, and the monks took me on and raised me. My name's Cheri. Who are you?"

"I'm Zach. It's nice to meet you." I said, and shook her hand. She smiled at that.

"Why... did that old Black Knight... want books on such *evil?*" she asked me.

I said, "What did he want? Barnabus has his ways, but he's changed the Black Knights and himself over the years, and is a mentor of mine."

"He wanted to know the origins, the foundings, even the principles of necromancy! Said it was important, or something. That stuff all needs to be locked away..." she said.

"Do you have something that he's looking for? Don't tell anyone... but I actually know a necromancer. Maybe something on necromancy could help her." I said.

"You *know* a necromancer? But... But... I thought it was abolished after the great war! Where our Emperor fought against the hordes of the dead, and saved many lives!" she said.

"Oh, you must be talking about Uncle Simon. Yeah, he was there and him and his people saved us many times." I said.

"What?? *Uncle?* You were *there??*" she said.

"Yeah! I even fought a couple of zombies! I was never so frightened, but if I hadn't, they would've made horrible violence in the camp. Someone had to do it, and it may as well have been me." I said.

"Now I know you must be misleading me..." she said.

"No! I swear! My pops is the leader of the Chariot." I said.

"The *famed* Chariot?? We have a few books on them and the great battle, and it did mention them saving an orc... You're really *the* Zachary!" she said.

"Well... I've never been a *the*... Just call me Zach. Can you help me and Barnabus?" I asked.

"Um... sure. But don't ever let them know. And be silent! Let's go... this way, to the forbidden section... *the* Zach!" she said, walking away as I followed her through the maze of bookshelves.

She told me to wait for a while, and that she had to get the key. She snuck off, and came back a few minutes later with a lamp and the key to the gates in front of us. "The master always sleeps at this time of day, so we're lucky. Let's see if this works..." and she inserted the key into the padlock, and it clicked open. She carefully opened the gates, and we crept inside to the dark, unused part of the library, the forbidden section.

We snuck through the bookshelves, and Cheri said the books are all very unordered in this section, but are put together by topic, so we looked through the many names and titles of the books. "How to Sell Human Flesh," was one, another was, "Speaking to the Dark Gods," and another was, "How to Create Angels," there was even a book on the Shazians, the sinister race of old, and their many misdeeds.

We eventually found a corridor of bookshelves with all black books, all titleless and dark. At the end of the corridor was a book on a pedestal, with strange leather... and Cheri was fearful of it as I picked it up. "That book is made of real people." she whispered, and I nearly dropped it in shock. I opened it very carefully, and the title was *"Necromancy, Life After Death,"* and the words denoting the author were, *"The Lich."*

A gust of wind went through the corridor. A few of the open books laying around fluttered their pages, and Cheri's lamp went out. She said we had to leave. So quickly, we left with the book and Cheri locked up the gates behind us. She said she didn't want to get in trouble, and must return to her duties. I thanked her, and on a second thought, gave her a kiss. She blushed, and said thank you.

I went to get my clothes, hiding the book underneath my robe, and dressed up in my clothing and armor. I quickly put the book in my pack, next to the coyote pups who were getting hungry, so I fed them some milk while I waited for the others.

10

Something for Someone You Like

"We should be near the town of Burlington... We should go around it..." Edgar said.

"No." I said, "I want to send a letter. We're going to Burlington."

"But... But... there's all the people!" Edgar said.

"Too bad. I want to talk to my friend, Zach." I said.

"Gessa, we need to stay secluded! Hide out for a while... I cannot do this." he said.

Barcough barked.

"Do this, or I *swear*... I'll do... something! Something you'll regret!" I said.

He seemed to ponder at this, and said, "Why do you want to talk to this Zach?"

"I... He's one of my best friends... He's one of my *only* friends... We've always cared for each other, and we get each other, even though we're different... Please?" I said.

"I suppose... We all need friends... Very well. We shall go to Burlington." he said.

Barcough wagged his tail, then showed us the way to the nearest town. I took a picture of him, as he looked back at us, with the camera Venny gave me. The picture came out of the camera, and that dog... is a very photogenic dog.

I asked Edgar to take a picture of me to give to Zach. I didn't want Zach to forget about me... I felt like I looked dirty, and rugged, and nothing like I did before, but I still wanted him to see me. I told Edgar which button to press, and how to put it into focus. He said, "Oh... this is some of that new magic they made... I always stayed away from it, not that it isn't nice to have for people. Ok... one, two, three..." and then he clicked the camera. I looked at the photo, and I looked... like... a wild woman! A meat eater! Thankfully, I didn't shut my eyes, but there was a twig in my hair! I didn't want to waste the film though, so didn't take another... so this will have to do.

We got to the edge of the town, and Edgar was starting to get nervous, and Barcough stayed at his side more often. When we got to the town, a few people were astonished at us, and I could feel like they could tell we were outcasts. Edgar told me, "Even though I... am not your father, please tell people I am if you get into any trouble." I said that was fine, and then proceeded to ignore him.

We were looking for the Wheel, and I asked a few people, a man and a woman, where the Wheel was situated, but Barcough barked at the couple, and they walked off quickly. "Please be quiet, Barcough! You'll scare everyone half to death with that bark!" I said to the dog. He whined a bit.

We asked a no good looking man smoking a pipe filled with something strange where we could find the Wheel. He red eyed looked at us, and said, "Damnnnn... that's a huge dog! Shouldn't you, like, put it on a leash?"

Edgar remained quiet in the town, but I said, "No, he's very well behaved... to people who like us."

"Well... I like you! That's a good dog..." he said, as Barcough wagged his tail, "To people I like, I've got something special... for just a few coins! For people I like... And if you like it, then I can show you where the Wheel is located..." He then waved his dreads around and proffered his hand for the money.

I nervously gave him some money, and he offered the pipe to me. Edgar was starting to say this wasn't a very good idea, but I shushed him and I inhaled on the pipe. I then coughed a bunch, which the man laughed his ass off at. It was so harsh! He then put something behind my ear, and said, "Toking is always nicer with people you like... Have a joint. The Wheel is the big building, used to be an inn, on the southeast side of town. Can't miss it! It's got a huge wheel on the door!" I thanked him and we went on our way.

We wandered down the streets, but everything was starting to look so strange! I feared I would get lost, but everything was just so new and exciting! The people on their day to day business... I wondered if they were really part of Gregory's army, and why they looked so normal then. Shouldn't he be taking the town by force? Probably had to use dragons. Yup, dragons would do it. Too bad dragons all went extinct... I felt bad for the dragons then. I stopped to look at some huge flashing lights, awed by the electricity coursing through them, for a diner of all things. Why did a diner need such big flashing lights?

Edgar always had to stop to hurry me along, and I heard some music coming out of a building. It was astounding music! It was breathtaking! Some players were playing some jazz, practicing, and even if they missed a note, it still sounded fantastic. Even better when they missed a note!

I looked at a goose ambling through the streets, and started wondering if it was like Barcough. Would people turn people into *geese??* That wouldn't be a very good lifestyle. Most people eat geese! I wanted to give the goose a hug because of this, saying it was alright, and would only eat it if I was very, very hungry, but it ran off.

But I was starting to worry. Maybe going into town wasn't a very good idea... Did that man looking at us know of my crimes? Was he part of the mob that wanted to bring me to justice? I felt like they were *all* looking at me, knowing that I was a killer. I started to get very, very frightened, and I clung to Barcough as Edgar led the way. His fur was the softest thing imaginable, and I couldn't stop petting him.

We eventually got to the Wheel, and entered the building. They sure did have a big wheel. I was glad to be safe from all the *people* outside. If people were really what they were. Maybe they were people who turned into animals, instead of the other way around!

I went up to the clerk and very nervously said, "I... I think I want, to, um, I want to, um... write a letter?"

He looked at me for a long time, then offered me a piece of paper and a pen. "Please give that back, when you're finished." he said, talking about the pen.

So I wrote a letter on a chair next to me while I was sitting on one. I told Zach about everything that happened, and that I wish he was back home, and that I missed him, and asked him about how he was doing, and all sorts of things. I was rambling a bit though, so ended it after talking about how dragons and geese were the same thing, in a sense. Dragons ate geese... but geese ate the grass that the dragon's dead body decomposed on. It was the circle of life, and we're all predators and prey, in a sense. I wondered how to sign my name, but feeling for this orcish warrior, my friend, I said, "Love, Gessa" and ended the letter.

I gave the letter to the clerk, and said who it was for, and he asked for payment, and I wanted to say my father was Marcos the Blunt Knight... but what if they knew who I was? They were supposed to know who I was, but what if they knew I *killed* somebody?? Edgar was tapping his foot, waiting for me to finish up, and Barcough wanted to go back outside again, and was chasing his tail.

But I was saved by none other than Jacob. He walked out of a back room, saying he was going on a cigarette break, saying managing was a real pain in the ass, all the time, and then he noticed me, with an unlit cigarette in his mouth. "Gessa! The little one! Right? You're the little one? How's it going, darlin'?" and then went over to me and patted me on the head.

"I-I need to send... a letter..." I started saying.

"Well don't worry about that. My outpost is swamped, and I have to manage the shitty thing, but I've got a courier, one of my fastest, who can get yours delivered. Who's it for?" Jacob said, out of the corner of his mouth not filled with a cigarette.

"Zach." I said.

"Alrighty... give it to me. I'll make sure it's delivered. Last I heard him and Mary are out by that great ass library in the next country over... I'll make sure it gets there, darlin'! Run along. I've got a business to run. Edgar, you take care of her, kay? Marcos told me everythin'." Jacob said. Edgar nodded and smiled.

Jacob got into an argument with his clerk, saying how things should be categorized, and put his cigarette break on hold. He didn't seem to notice us, so we left. I was astounded by his niceness. He never seemed like a very nice person, just thinking of me as a kid, but he actually *was* nice! Maybe he was always nice, but didn't want to have to deal with children.

I told Edgar I wanted to go back to the woods, and he quickly took me back through the town, away from all the staring people, and then I realized I had stolen the pen, hidden in my left pocket. I felt so bad about it! I thought maybe I should go back and return the stolen property, and I told Edgar this, but he laughed and asked if I noticed the tens of them on the desk, saying it was alright, and that he wouldn't miss just one. I breathed out a sigh of relief.

We quickly went to the safe, hidden forest, and I felt good again, listening to the birds. Jillian was watching us as we got further into the forest, but prowled off into the trees. I said I was very thirsty, and asked Edgar for some of the water we had. He gave me the canteen, and I drank greedily, and it was the tastiest liquid ever. Water, really is, the nectar of the gods.

Edgar said that was kind of fun, and that next time we go into the city we had to get me some more gear... I said I never wanted to go into the city again. He stared at me for a second, then laughed and laughed. He said, "Be careful what you put into your system. My drugs help me, the drugs you took are for other things."

Drugs? What was he talking about? I asked him this, and he said, "Well... it smelled like you smoked marijuana, but it could be anything! If I was you, I'd learn to grow it, so you know exactly what you're getting."

I sat down, feeling calm again, listening to the birds. There were so many of them, and I even heard a woodpecker. I then remembered the joint behind my ear, and took it out and looked at it. I thought I should just throw it out... but it was kind of fun, in a way. I decided to keep it for later maybe. It'd probably be nicer in the forest.

So it was uneventful, the rest of the day, and I could feel the drug leaving my system, even though I felt a little hazy throughout the day. I really hoped Zach liked the pictures I sent him. I had brought a mirror, on a second thought, and I stared into it and combed my hair. I looked pretty skinny now. My legs felt strong from all the walking. At first I would gasp and be out of breath, but now I could go for miles without stopping. I still did my push ups, and could get a good thirty of them now. I kind of wanted to fight someone in randori, like the old days. I'd probably whoop them now.

Edgar never fought with me, and never talked about fighting with me. He said fighting is for killing. This made me *sure* that I didn't want to fight him. He sharpened his knife, and said it was a tool, that fighting is a tool as well, and it all depends on how you use it... but if you use a dangerous thing, it should only be used for a dangerous objective. I said that sometimes you need to fight for people to understand they don't need to fight, like my father told me. He said, "Sometimes... but some people cannot, will not, ever, be swayed. Thankfully I am not one of those people, and your father and mother fought me, and showed me mercy... but if I was them, I would've just killed me."

"What... What do you mean??" I said.

He sighed, and said, "I know that everything is special, that everything is all, but some people... and *things*, like the zombies, want to end it. Want everyone to die, for some foolish whim, or simply because death is in them. Is it not wise to end them before they end you? End everything that you care about?"

"You... You sound like a villain, who wants to die, and be done being a villain..." I said.

He laughed, and said, "I am a villain. I will never be a hero. I fought the necromancers with Barcough and the dogs, but perhaps simply because I felt like living, perhaps because I just liked dogs, and didn't want to see them die. Maybe I just wanted to fight."

"You should be wary of playing the Devil's advocate." I said, "Because sometimes... you might actually be the Devil."

"Those are some wise words. I will not speak of death and killing with you, unless you ask me and wish to know how." he said.

I thought of Molly. She would've killed me, if I hadn't fought her. Maybe I wasn't a horrible murderer... Maybe I was just acting in self defense, and it was an accident. I said I didn't want to know how to kill, and would remain true to my father's wisdom. Enough death happens accidentally, people didn't need to do it on purpose.

Barcough snuggled up to bed with me, and we slept until morning.

11

Name in Blood

After we stayed a night camping outside the library, a courier, a thin, tall woman approached us as we were about to leave. She said she had a message for me! I took the letter, and began reading it. The first thing I noticed was a picture of Gessa, and the big dog she said she made friends with. It made me happy seeing her. She looked very fit! I noticed the muscles under her jeans, the biceps under her shirt, and she looked much stronger these days. She never was very tough in body, but it seemed that was changing. I wondered if we could fight one day, and she could show me all the moves she's learned like she told me about in the letter. The letter... was a different tone than what I normally associated from Gessa. She seemed a lot more philosophical of late! Maybe all the struggles she went through had changed her somehow. I hoped she hadn't changed too much. I felt sad, reading the letter telling me about the hardships she went through... but happy to hear from her. I felt my heart skip a beat as I read the words, "Love, Gessa." She never said she loved me! I shook it off, I did love her too, in a way, and thought maybe she was just being polite.

Barnabus and Mary were arguing again, and they decided to stick together for a while, at least until they talked to me. I wondered why they wanted to do that. No matter, they're probably worried about Gessa too, and I told them about what she'd been through with the letter. They looked at me wide eyed, as I told her about the girl she accidentally killed and brought back to life. Barnabus said, "Tell your girlyfriend to hush up. Sure, the Wheel may be a little more 'sophisticated' than it was in the old days, but we don't know who is listening. I don't even trust your courier over there, watering her horse..."

"Oh, she'll be fine. Quit worrying! I'm going to write a return later." I said.

"Yeah... and if you do, you're giving it to *me.* No one else. I have to tell the little lady how my search turned up dead ends, anyway..." Barnabus said, and we walked down the road, and I bid the courier goodbye. She waved back and started off on her horse, going as fast as a bullet.

I said, "Well... I um... found something. Just so you know. And I'm worried about Gessa! Can I go with you? Sorry, Mary, but she sounds like she's in real trouble!"

Mary said, "That's fine, Zach. You do what's best for the family. I'll always be around, and as soon as your father and mother get back into the country, we're going to get back to *real* work. Lasso joined up with the Chariot, and I've been secretly recruiting more soldiers on the side. I bet you were wondering what we were doing in all those taverns. Well, now you know. Soldiers love to talk about work after a few drinks, or a few brawls."

"I thought you just loved booze??" I said.

"That doesn't matter. We all love a good drink, every now and then." Barnabus said, "Now, *what* did you find?"

I nervously showed him the book, when we were far away from the Library of Alexander. I thought perhaps they could somehow sense there was a missing book, like libraries do, if we weren't careful. We were sitting down for a rest, and Barnabus was sitting down and drinking his morning brew, and he opened the book up to a random page, dropped it in shock, and hurled all over on the ground beside him.

"Th-The fuckin' people! All those poor fuckin' people! What... *what the fuck!* I'm going to be sick..." and he threw up again, and said, "I'm... I'm going to quit drinkin'... for a lil bit... Those fuckin' people!"

"What? What are you jabbering at, Barney? It can't be that bad..." Mary said, then picked up the book and looked at the page, then turned white, slammed it shut, and put it on the log beside her. Rubbing her eyes, she said, "That... That can't be real..."

Lasso laughed at them, saying books are harmless, then looked at the book, opened a page, and cried out, "My darling Reah! *Reah! No... no...*" and was staring, ghastly awestruck, transfixed at the page. Mary whacked at the book, out of his grip, and Lasso sat down on the dirt, still in shock.

Mary grabbed up Lasso, and said they needed to go on a walk, Lasso mumbling something about Reah. I picked up the book... carefully... slowly... opened it... and saw... nothing. The pages were blank.

"Huh??" I said, and turned the book at different angles, wondering if it was some sort of trick image. But still, it was just blank pieces of paper.

I turned back to the front page, saw the title and author, turned a page, and the only words were, *"You will die."*

Well, everyone dies eventually, I thought. I put the book away, as Barnabus was cradling himself back and forth, and Mary was walking around with Lasso, seemingly in a daze.

"That... That fucking thing needs to go." Barnabus said.

"We can't! It's about necromancy! We need it to help Gessa!" I said.

"But... but... it's fucking evil! IT'S FUCKING EVIL!!" he said.

"So is necromancy, which is why we need to help Gessa control it." I said.

"...Fine. But don't ever let me catch you reading the thing. I don't want you to get any horrible, horrible ideas from it." Barnabus said.

"The pages are blank. I really don't know what all the fuss is about." I said.

"What? Can't you fucking read? Didn't you even see... the pictures?" Barnabus said.

"No. I can read fine, and I don't know what is going on, but I'm going to find out." I said.

Mary and Lasso came back, and while Barnabus wasn't drinking anymore, Lasso took Barnabus's brew and slurped it all down, splashing a little bit of it on his face. Mary said, "You... You should think hard about what you want to be, when you get older, Zach. I... would rethink a lot of my past choices if I could... like looking at that book..."

Getting a bit annoyed at all of them acting so strangely, I said we should keep walking, and they followed me, all seeming to be lost in thought.

Gessa said that she was last in Burlington, and would be traveling in the forests for a while. I vowed to find her and help her in any way I could. Burlington was quite a long way away, but we could make more time if we sold the rest of the things we were carrying. We were honorbound to deliver the books we got from the library... so that would be our first stop.

It took all day to get there, but we got to the halfling's home in the night. The rest were extremely quiet the entire day, and while I tried to make conversation with them, they said one word responses, or trailed off as they were trying to start up a sentence. Maybe the book was some sort of hidden evil that only some people could see. Maybe you had to learn a special language, to see the words? Nah, I thought, I read a sentence from the book, so maybe it was just hiding from me... like something to be hunted. I thought maybe I should hunt whatever was lurking in the pages, but how could I hunt a book?

I knocked on the door, and a halfling woman opened up, with a child at her breast. I asked for Percy, and she said her husband would be there in a minute, and was just finishing translating the elven saga of Tirago. A thin halfling with spectacles came to meet us, and bid us to come in. The others were starting up a campfire, and declined, so I brought the books and went into the halfling's home. I gave him the books, and he paid me the second half of our payment, and thanked me relentlessly, saying that his work was translating and deciphering. I thought of an idea at this point, and wondered if he could translate the necromancy book.

We went into his study, and he sat at the desk, and asked me to show me the book I wanted deciphered. I took it out of my pack and showed it to him. He opened it and immediately his eyes went wide with shock. "The... The knowledge... The power! This... This needs to stay..." he said. I tried to grab the book back from him, but he snarled at me! He then wielded a penknife, and with the fiercest eyes imaginable, said the book was his! This wasn't at all like the gentle halfling he was just a second ago! I punched him hard in the face, knocking him out, and took the book and quickly left, as his wife asked what was the problem.

I told the others we needed to leave, *now.* So they nervously followed me out of the town. Mary asked, "Was... Was it the book?"

"Yeah! The guy turned into some sort of monster! He paid us at least... Here it is." I said, trying to hand her the coins. She sighed, and told me to keep it. "Think of it as an investment into your adventures. You tell me all about them, one day. And keep that Gessa safe, ok?" she said.

"You're... You're not leaving? Are you?" I said.

"I need to gather the rest of the Chariot. Keep strong, little Zach, and strive for good." She then hugged me, out of the blue, and kissed me on the cheek. She told Barnabus, "Be kind, my love. And keep the children safe. " and she shook Barnabus's hand... which quickly turned into a hug... which turned into a kiss... which turned into a makeout session... and then they said they needed to say goodbye to each other properly, so went out into the forest.

Lasso shook my hand and said that he wished all orcs were like me, and not butchering each other in war. He said, "Find yer home. Find yer family. I lost mine ages ago, fer fallin' in love with the wrong woman... Keep them safe."

Barnabus and Mary made love, saying goodbye in their own way, and I didn't hear it, which I'm thankful for, besides one loud moan coming from each of them... which carried through the air like a sonic boom. They came back, and hugged, saying goodbye one last time, and she and Lasso walked off down the other direction, waving.

I waved back, and Barnabus said, "Well... let's find your gal. Hopefully she didn't kill the entire town she was staying at and raise them back to life already."

"Gessa would never do that!" I said, as we walked down the road.

"You'd be surprised how well you really know people. I hope she's still the sweet innocent kid she was... I guess she took my advice on her bully problem... Fuckin' hell. I should keep my big mouth shut." Barnabus said.

Thinking that whatever he told her must've not been very good advice, we kept walking and eventually went into the forest to camp away from the road. It was getting very dark, as there was no moon. Barnabus quickly set up his tent, and I brought out my sleeping bag and slept underneath the trees.

I heard him snoring after a while, and started up a fire, as I couldn't sleep. I was too worried, and it had been such a strange day. The flint sparked in my hands, and a little fire went up. I sighed a sigh of relief, thankful to be in the nice comfort of a good fire.

I thought I'd give another try at the book, even though Barnabus told me not to. I took it out in the light of the campfire, as my coyote pups slept soundly. They had been sleeping a lot, but I made sure to let them run around during the day. They were getting a bit bigger, and Lasso said I could feed them meat soon.

I opened up past the title page, looked at the words, and there was a new sentence. It said, *"You will die. Now live again."*

And then miraculously, after I blinked, the page was filled with words. I read it, eager to figure out this new dilema. It read, *"The first of the four is Gerich. He will guide you on your journey. You will hate, and he will always be there. I have bound him, in this work, and he will never leave. Be thankful that you are not he. I pity you, for now you must be his vessel. You will never know love again. The words to summon him is thus, 'Asta Terro.' Use them well, for even if you do not summon him, he will still be there.*

The second of the four is Biona Callus. She will bring you hardship and struggle, but you will grow stronger because of it. She will tempt you and taunt you, and you will never know peace. Fear her, for she is every splinter, every scorn, she is hardship and woe. She is malicious and vengeful. I have bound her, in this work, and she will never leave. Be glad that you will have a love again, for your love is now the struggle of life and death. The words to summon her is thus, 'Shel Bion.' Use them well, for if you do use them, you will regret meeting her all the more.

The third of the four is Teckus. He is the living essence in all, the reason that our work is so disdainful. You will feed and feast on the living and dead, drink of their blood and gain their strength in his name. I have bound him, in this work, and he will never leave. Praise him in all his glory, seek out suffering and drink in its pleasures. He is the reason you are not dead yet. The words to summon him is thus, 'Sinful Sake.' What can I say? He's always been sort of a jokester. Use them well, and drink of death and woe.

The fourth of them all has no name. It is the power and will of death. It is the stranger, the vagabond, the cold and dark. It will bring you to me, as you can never escape it. I have bound it, in this work, and it will never leave. When you finally meet me, you can thank this entity. There are words to summon it... but you will never know them, for the words are silent.

Now, bleed for Gerich, Biona Callus, Teckus, and the nameless, and you will never have peace again, and true power will be yours."

And awestruck, moving my hand down the page, I got a papercut, and accidentally smudged the page. My blood seemed to reveal a word, and it said, *"Zach."*

I quickly shut the book.

12

Wild Woods

The next day, I was out in the woods, just wandering around. I wasn't trying to escape anymore. I had become accustomed to the forest, and I didn't have anywhere to go, anyway. I hoped my father was getting everything sorted out though, and I could come home eventually. I was staring at a tree, wondering how it ever got so big, and Jillian surprised me by rubbing up against my legs.

I didn't know what to do, as she kept on rubbing against me with so much force, making loud purring sounds. I tried petting her, but she quickly made a grumbling sound in her throat, so I remained still. She licked my hand, gave a little nibble, then left me, long tail trailing behind her. It was actually pretty frightening, but cool. I suppose not many people at all would be rubbed against by a mountain lion.

I went back to Edgar and Barcough, and Edgar said, "There are people roaming around... hunters. Should we hunt them? They may be after us."

"No. Let's just try to get as far away as possible." I said.

So we kept on walking, very briskly, and I followed Edgar through his twisty paths and through harsh undergrowth. We got to a river and crossed, and my whole bottom half got wet. I just kept walking though, and ignored the discomfort.

We stopped for the night, and there was no sign of Jillian, and Barcough kept going out into the forest to look for her I think. He disappeared for a good while, but came back, barking and howling. "Barcough? What is it? Is there trouble?" Edgar said. Barcough turned around in a circle and scratched the ground with his paw. "He wants us to follow him." Edgar said.

We did, and he would always come back, after he went too far ahead, wanting us to go faster. So we ran with him, and what I saw made me very angry.

There were hunters jabbing at Jillian with spears and swords, and she was wounded with a few arrows. She growled at any who came too close, and swiped with her claws at the hunters. Barcough quickly jumped in after her, biting a hunter on the ass. Edgar rose up and howled! This froze all the hunters, before they could stick Barcough with a sword, and Barcough ran up to Jillian and growled at the hunters, defending her.

"I-Its a bloody werewolf! Fuck, let's get 'im!" a hunter said.

Jillian and Barcough ran off quickly, and Jillian was limping as she ran. Edgar had his hands out in a strange fighting style, ready to grab at anything. It was actually a bit like judo, but he tensed up his hands, and sort of crouched. Edgar ran at them and brought one of them down, as I hid behind a tree. He quickly dodged the others' spears and swords, and when he got up off the hunter, the hunter was dead. One tried stabbing at him, but he caught his wrist, and snapped his arm.

This didn't stop the one with a bow from shooting him though.

An arrow went into Edgar's side, and he grunted in pain. He made sounds like a beast! Like an animal! Another hit his side, and he was getting weaker, and was stumbling a bit. I had to do something! I quickly went up beside him and told them to stop! "Stop! Or I'll kill you all!" I said, threatening them.

They laughed and told me to go home, that this was no place for a girl. They said either I'd leave, or they'll rape and kill me. I didn't know if it was just a threat or not, but I didn't want to find out. Angry, I told the dead hunter to kill them. They were shocked at the strange, unholy words coming out of my mouth, but even more shocked when their dead comrade got up and stabbed one of the hunters in the back.

"Sh-She's a witch! Run!!" one said, and the dead hunter chased them, and killed two more of them, who got up and chased the others.

Edgar collapsed beside me, and I struggled to remove the arrows. He said, "Pull hard. Pull quick. I'm... sorry. For everything."

I told him to shut up, and I did what he told me. He grunted in pain after each one was removed.

"I... will probably die of the sickness... the sickness after getting hit, which is why I try never to get hit..." he said.

"I'm taking you to a hospital. Or... someone! I don't know how to fix you!" I said, "Can you stand? Put your arm around me, and let's go! Now!"

I helped him up, and he put his arm over my shoulder, and struggled to walk with me. We kept on walking, and I didn't know where to go! I cried... but kept silent. I knew there had to be *some* way to save his life! There had to be!

He was bleeding a lot, and he put his other hand over the wound, and when he tripped and stumbled against me, his bloody hand got my arm all bloody. That didn't matter though, because my shirt was already all bloody from having his side against me.

And miraculously, there was a small cabin in the woods. It looked occupied, so all the better. Maybe there was someone who could help. We got to the door, and I knocked three times on it.

A woman, an old crone, answered the door. She was terrified of us, all bloody and everything, and shut it quickly. I begged her to help us. "Please! My father is wounded! He needs help!" I said, remembering to call Edgar my father in case we got into trouble. I guess people look more kindly on a homeless father and daughter than two outcasts with nowhere to go, because she answered again, and nervously told us to come inside.

She said, "I will help your father. Put him on the bed, please."

She got to work, and disinfected the wound and patched Edgar up. I didn't know what to do, so went outside to find Barcough and Jillian. She protested, but I said I would be back.

I was looking around the forest, looking in the direction Barcough and Jillian went, and I heard a rustling behind me. What came out of the forest were the hunters, all dead. *"What do you want us to do... witch."* one of them said.

"I'm not a witch! You can't talk to me like that! You people tried to kill my friends!" I said.

The hunter seemed to laugh, a horrible gurgling sound, and said, *"Yet you killed us. You killed us. You killed us."*

They began saying this over and over again, and I said, *"Stop! Stop talking! Go to sleep!"*

They were quiet then, but were still standing, staring at me with that mindless, accusing stare. Finally, I said, *"I... I killed you. Now go to rest."* and they fell over, finally dead.

I crouched down and cried. It didn't matter what weapon I used, *I* had killed them.

I heard whimpering and growling coming from afar, so followed the noise. I found Jillian snarling at Barcough, and Barcough trying to gently approach her, but she swiped at him whenever he got too close.

I said, "Jillian! I need to help you! Please, calm down."

She grumbled at me as I approached her, but didn't swipe at me, even though it was terrifying, her looking at me so menacingly. I went to an arrow, and she growled even more, but I pulled it out quickly and sharply.

I went to the second, and did the same. I went to the third, and did it again. I went to the fourth, which was close to the jugular by her head, but missed thankfully, and pulled out that one. She made a sort of whimpery sound, and began licking at her wounds. Barcough stayed with her to the side, and I told them I would be back later, which Barcough barked at.

I went back to the cabin... and found Edgar covered in leeches! The crone was putting them on him! I yelled at her, and told her to get away from him! She said, "This will take out the rest of the infected blood. He needs this..."

But I ignored her and pulled off the leeches, just like Edgar told me how to. I flicked them at the crone. I wanted her to leave... but I couldn't kick her out of her own home. So I defended Edgar from her, as she sat on a chair in the corner, fuming. Edgar was passed out on the bed, but was still breathing thankfully.

I stayed up with him throughout the night, but I dozed off accidentally, over Edgar. The crone somehow slept on the chair, and was making breakfast... and told us to leave. I quickly went to her and apologized, saying, "I'm sorry... My friends and Edgar were being attacked... *I'm so sorry!*" I broke down, remembering the night.

The crone seemed to change her attitude, pitying me crying and trying to hide my tears in my arm, so said, "There, there... My husband is coming home soon. He'll know what to do with you."

She offered me breakfast, eggs and mushrooms. I suppose eggs are less than meat, but still it's *sort of* like eating meat. I ate it anyway, and said thank you. I had eaten eggs in the past... but still, I wondered if it wasn't like animal slavery, to make animals give you eggs and milk.

An old lumberjack came to the cabin, and he was surprised by all the people in his home. He asked his wife who his guests were. She said, "A girl and her father, who is gravely wounded."

"Will he live?" the lumberjack asked.

"We will see. If not, I suppose we always did want another daughter..." the crone said, looking at me sadly.

"I-I have a family..." I said.

"Is this not your father? Or isn't he?" the crone asked.

"He... is sort of my father... in a way... but I have a real family to go back to..." I said.

"Are you an outlaw? And so young, too..." the crone asked.

"No! I just... This man is my genetic father... and my parents thought it would be good for me to travel with him! We were going camping!" I said.

"It sounds as if you're lying, dear." the crone said.

I didn't know what to say to this, but I begged them to please not kick us out! I said I'd work for them! Would clean the place up!

The crone looked a little huffy, and said, "It would be wise not to insult those who take you in. Our home is as clean as it can be." It *was* pretty clean, even though there were pine needles everywhere... "Well, you can begin at once." the crone said, "As payment for healing your father. Please, gather the eggs from the hens out back."

I didn't want to insult them again by asking if Edgar would be safe... I suppose I'd hear something if they started butchering him, but what if they were silent killers? What if they were cannibals, like the old witches in the stories? I guess I wasn't one to talk, being a necromancer... And if they did kill Edgar, I'd raise him back to life and kill them both.

I was thinking more violent of late... I suppose I just didn't want to see my friends and family suffer. Maybe once you get a taste of it it's a never ending stream of bloodlust. I think it was just the power of it. I could kill anyone! All I needed was a corpse. I began to get a little fearful of this feeling, this anger that was festering in my heart... so I tried thinking of positive things instead. I thought of Zach.

I daydreamed of him holding me... like he did when I made him play marriage with me. He'd always make jokes when we did, and I wanted him to take it seriously. I wanted the perfect wedding, and he just wanted to wrestle and fight. We both loved nature though, so always held our weddings out in the woods. When we kissed, we never thought much of it, just being kids, but now when I thought about kissing him I felt all hot and woozy. I decided to think of something else, while I picked up the eggs and put them in a basket.

I thought of my mom and dad. So peaceful, so hard working... My mom strove to help all sorts of sick people, with all sorts of maladies, and my dad worked hard to keep the peace, and even if you did think about harming someone, having a Blunt Knight around was enough of a threat to make you think better of it. This made me feel kind of sad, though... thinking of them holding me, too. Of our family picnics. Of the never ending love they gave me.

So I thought about Edgar, and wondered about him. But this would make me worry. He was a good person, even though he thought of himself as a villain. He seemed to be a part of nature itself, and I suppose if you must judge someone like him, you should try judging nature too. It's impossible. Nature will kill you without a second thought, but will also nourish and care for you. I hoped he would live, and I could bring him back to my parents. No matter what their history was, I wanted him to live.

I brought the eggs back into the cabin, and the two were arguing about us. I caught the word "authorities" being thrown around, so I worked harder for them, doing anything they asked. I cleaned boots, swept up the pine needles, did the laundry, cleaned the stove, and the lumberjack said I was doing good work, and asked me to chop up some wood for the night. We never had lunch. They only ate two meals a day, they said.

I struggled to chop firewood with the sort of blunt axe. I wish I had that axe of Zach's, Skull. That thing was always sharp, as Zach made sure to keep it in pristine condition, even though he never used it. I chopped one, kinda going halfway through. I hit it again, feeling angry at the wood, at life, at those hunters, at everyone, and the axe went through the wood.

I attacked another piece of wood with the axe, and it went easier the next time, and the next, and the next. It was very therapeutic, in a way. I then picked up some sticks around the cabin, and brought them back inside for the fire. The old crone was looking content, ruthless taskmaster she was, and fed me a light meal of porridge with partridge bits in it, which I ate ravenously. She said it was ok if I used a spare mattress they had. They also slept on mats, and I put mine by Edgar's side, then said I had to go outside for a bit. "Don't be long, dear. There are wild animals about. I will give you thirty minutes before we lock the cabin."

I went to where Barcough and Jillian were, and the two were snuggled up together, strange as it was seeing a German shepherd and a mountain lion in peace. Barcough wagged his tail at me, and Jillian stretched and shook her head at me. I pet them both, then went back before the crone locked me out.

I was really actually worried she would, and would get some sort of sheriff to catch us both, but she didn't, and bid me goodnight, and the two fell asleep. I sat next to Edgar awhile, listening to his ragged, soft breathing, then laid down on the mat, and fell asleep instantly.

When I woke up there was a knight at the door. The lumberjack answered the knocking, and the knight asked if they knew of the hunters around the area who went missing, that showed up all dead. "It seems they had some sort of infighting... which is strange, because their bodies don't look as if they had a recent battle, just their wounds." I then noticed the heavily armored knight was a woman! You couldn't tell by her armored body, but it was her voice! She was a woman knight!

"No, we've just been nursing our son in law back to health after he had an accident. And this is his daughter. I'm afraid I've been busy of late, where did you say the bodies were?" the lumberjack said.

"You're a local, right? Maybe you can help me with this conundrum. Please, follow me." the knight said, and the lumberjack went with her.

"Was it you and your father who killed them?" the crone asked, sitting on the chair.

"No! I don't know how they died." I said, quickly noticing that I talked louder when I was lying. "But they did attack us, and our dog... who I've been going to see. He's a bit wild, and I think they thought he was a wolf..." I said.

"And the mountain lion?" she said.

"I..." I didn't know what to say, so I said, "She's nice! She's a good cat! She would never harm anyone! Edgar and our dog tried to save her... They ran from them, because they were so frightening... but I didn't see how they died." I quickly learned the best lies have a bit of truth in them.

She sighed, and said, "You should know better than to keep wild animals as pets. But, I suppose she was in the forest, where she belonged... Your father is getting better, and I fed him while you were sleeping, so you should be able to leave soon."

"Thank you, for everything you've done. My name is Gessa." I said.

"I am Anne, and my husband is Hance. Do come by to visit sometime, when you've found that family of yours." she said, very nicely. I was just so overwhelmed by everything, so I quickly went to her and gave her a hug, and she gave me a nice hug back. The old woman, Anne, was smiling at me.

We left the next day, and the knight didn't ask any more questions, but still, I think she was following us... and I hurried Edgar along, even though he was very tired, and couldn't walk so fast because of the pain in his side. Barcough and Jillian would catch up with us when they were ready, or maybe they'd go their own way, being wild like the woods.

13

A Love Lost

I woke up the next morning after a dream where Skull was trying to say something to me, but was all muffled and I couldn't hear the words. A talking axe, I thought, as I woke up. Seemed like it would probably be helpful. Could probably watch your back as you fight.

I looked back at the book in my pack. It just seemed like a weird leather book. It wasn't shouting and screaming, it wasn't trying to devour my soul... but still, I was terrified of picking it up, to open it and see what new horrors would be on the pages. Barnabus asked me why I was acting so strangely, and I just gave an excuse that I was worried about Gessa, only Gessa, and wanted to get moving.

So we walked down the road in the plains, keeping silent for the most bit. Barnabus was in a much better mood, and kept his word that he wouldn't drink for a while. He was swearing less, and seemed like he had a bounce in his step. "That Mary... She sure does know how to say goodbye! I wish I could get together with her again just so I can leave her!" he said.

I thought of Barnabus and Mary, then of Gessa, and how she said she loved me... she was a bit younger than me, but I wondered if it was alright if maybe... we would be a couple one day? I felt a little silly asking this, because I thought the answer would surely be no, but I asked, "Barnabus... you and Mary seem to get along so well... could the same thing happen with me and Gessa?"

"What? You mean like last night? I doubt you would have the skill to pull off what I pulled off! A triple lay, all in one night!" he said.

"No... I just mean, like, I care for her... and she cares for me. Are we too different? Is there too much of an age gap?" I said.

"Listen, son. You're almost a grown man, and Gessa is almost a grown woman. I'd think about it before you tie yourself in with someone, but follow what makes you happy. As long as you ain't diddling kids, that's alright with me. And based on what I know of Gessa so far... she ain't no kid anymore." he said.

I thought that would be swell, one day. Even though I didn't want to do the things like I did with Shekinah with Gessa, I did want to protect her, to stroke her hair and tell her it would be alright. Embarrassed, I told him about my time with Shekinah. He laughed, and said, "Well, that's women for you. Be thankful she was so up front about it. She at least took your gold and still gave you what you wanted! It's a lot easier with a forward transaction, when each party knows what they want from each other, and gives willingly. Like a good, professional whore."

"My ma says I don't need to pay for sex." I said.

"Trust me, you'll be paying for it either way, with gold or something else. Women always get something out of sex, whether it be simple pleasure, children, or a lifetime of servitude from the man." Barnabus said.

"But shouldn't you only really have sex with people you love??" I said.

"I thought you had this talk. Remind me to hide your father. I know he probably told you you *should* only fuck someone you're married to and love with all your heart and blablabla... But really, it's not so simple. Some people fuck for love, some because they're just bored, and others fuck eachother because they hate eachother. And some people... well, we won't talk about some people."

"Fuck eachother for hate?? How... How can that be a thing?" I asked.

"You'd be surprised at how much a good argument can heat up the sack. Relationships... People have all sorts of them, and you'll never find one that's exactly like the other, no matter what some 'players' say. Relationships are as complicated and unique as each person alive." Barnabus said.

"Do you love Mary?" I asked.

"Uh. Erm... yes. Don't fucking spill it to anyone though. She's mine, you hear? But we both have a little fun on the side... so, we're both complicated. We never did feel like tying each other down. We prefer being professional lovers, free to the wind."

"How the heck can you be professional at love?" I said.

"Well... we've both been around in our time. Mary tried having a go at married life, but it turned sour quick, and then your father came in and put an end to that romance... I always did hate that bastard of hers. I was homeless, broke, mute, and fucking cursed. Mary saved me from death, saved me from myself. And if I hadn't by chance met with your father again... I'd probably have ended up killing myself." Barnabus said.

This was heavy to hear, but I thanked Barnabus for telling me, and we continued walking in silence.

I had a fleeting imagination of Gessa... but it quickly passed, like it was snatched up from me. I tried thinking of her again, but it was gone in a flash. I tried hard to imagine her hair, her body, her face... but someone seemed to grab her away from me. I couldn't make heads or tails of it. I thought hard, trying to picture her face, and I couldn't picture her! She was blank to me! I frantically took out the picture, and looked at her. I looked hard at her, and sighed. Then I seemed to notice someone in the distance behind her, but when I blinked, he was gone. I put the picture back in my pocket, and just kept her in my head for a long time. That's all I thought about, and if I forgot her face, I'd look at the picture again... but every time, it seemed like the figure behind her was getting closer. This was beginning to terrify me, and I was about to ask Barnabus for help, but he was just humming ahead of me, and I didn't want to worry him. I thought perhaps I was losing my mind. But if I was... why couldn't I picture Gessa?

I asked Barnabus, "Does... Does drinking make you forget things?"

"Sometimes, but only if you drink a lot. Usually I can remember pretty well, if a bit fuzzy, if I only drink a little bit. Sometimes you black out, and can't really remember anything, and when you wake up, you're next to a ladyboy covered in chocolate. I was pretty sure it was a prank... but it does make you forget some things." he said.

"Like... does it make you forget the face of those you love? Does it make you see things?" I asked.

"Uh... You've been drinking a lot with Mary, haven't you? I've never seen anything except on this weird green alcohol... absinthe. Like the owner of the Wheel. Don't know how I could forget a word like that, but I more associate the word absinthe with Absinthe instead of the drink... strange, how time flies. He sure made a name for himself." Barnabus said, and continued humming.

I forgot Gessa again, and looked at the picture... and there was a man shrouded in shadow directly behind her. This brought me goosebumps. I asked Barnabus to look at the picture and tell me what he saw. He said, "...Just Gessa. She's a cutie, isn't she... Don't look at her too much, or you may fall in love!" and laughed.

I looked back at the picture, and it was only Gessa now. I decided to leave the picture in my pocket before the man got her. I figured out a way around losing her image. I remembered her voice, and if not her voice, then her words.

I reread the letter over and over again, and I could practically hear Gessa talking behind those words. I thought of all the times we've shared, of all the jokes we've made, and her laughter. She has the prettiest, nicest laugh in the world. It is never directed at something mean, and is only when we make silly jokes and laugh about the most uproarious things. I read the letter again, but the first words, *"Dear Zach,"* seemed to change... seemed to come from another voice, a low, manly voice in my head. I didn't read the letter anymore, but when I tried to remember the letter, the voice would still be there. I told Barnabus that I needed to rest.

As I sat on the ground next to the road in the plains, Barnabus said, "You feeling alright, kid?"

"I... I think I'm losing my mind." I said.

"Oh boy... Then you really must be in love. Listen, chap, love can be a beauteous and wonderful thing, if you do it right. Love of all kinds. I loved your father's father, and his wife, who went by some stupid nickname that I can't really remember... They were my best friends in the whole world, even though he and I argued to all hell. It was a shame he bit it before his son could really know him, and I had to fill in the gap... I never strove to be a father, but I did try to be a mentor. You've got a father, kid. Just try to remember your parents, remember they love you." Barnabus said. I thanked him, feeling a bit better, and kept walking.

But when I tried to remember my pops's and ma's face, it was snatched away from me.

I could remember Barnabus's face, hell, he was right in front of me, but when he said, *"Follow."* I could've sworn he was someone else. We quickly went off the road, and hid behind a hillside. We peaked out over it, and there were cavalry going past, a whole regiment of them.

"That looks like it'd be Gregory's forces... They should know better than to traverse this far inland with such heavy cavalry..." Barnabus said.

"Should we tell Laurel?" I asked.

"No." the voice said, and then Barnabus said, "She probably already knows, anyway."

I was staring at Barnabus, and he looked at me and then looked again, and said, "Why the hell are you staring at me like that?"

"Y-You sounded like somebody else." I said.

Then it was as if the voice was taking pieces of Barnabus's words, twisting his speech, and said, "Listen, *Zach*, I don't know *what* you're *do*ing, but *you* need to cut it out! *Want* to eat some lunch?"

"I want Gessa." I said.

Barnabus laughed, and it seemed like the voice was laughing instead, and said, "*No,* Zach, lunch! Aren't you hungry?"

"I'm going to save Gessa!! And you can't stop me!" I said, then walked away from Barnabus.

Barnabus was getting worried for me, and him and the voice said, "Listen, maybe you need to *take* a rest... Let's *just* wait for a while... *What* is going on with *you*? *Need* a proper rest?"

I turned to Barnabus, and I was fearful of him saying anything else. I asked him if we could just take a nap somewhere... in quiet, as I wasn't feeling very well.

"*Sure*, kid, *let's just rest.*" they both said.

We settled down for a good nap on the hillside, and I felt myself getting sleepier, and not listening to that horrible voice anymore. I took out the picture of Gessa, carefully looked at it, and saw a man staring at me, with horrible, hate filled eyes. Gessa wasn't in the picture. I stared at him for a long time, thinking this was my new foe, then put it away and didn't think of anything for awhile, and tried to keep my mind blank.

I dozed off, listening to the quiet, and when I woke up Barnabus was growling and stretching, saying, "*That was* one nice nap! *Pointless* not to enjoy the fresh breeze and sunlight!"

I didn't want to worry Barnabus again, but I thought angry thoughts at the voice, hating it with all of my guts, for spoiling the day. For taking the image of Gessa away.

"*Yes, that's* enough napping though. We gotta get to Gessa and Edgar before they bite *it*!"

I thought that I would kill that voice. I would kill it and get Gessa back.

"Let's not *kill* ourselves worrying about *them*, though. I'm sure Gessa is safe enough, being with Edgar and *all.* That man's a wild man!" Barnabus said.

I sighed, and followed Barnabus. He was joyful as all hell, and I was beginning to get very miserable.

We kept on walking, and I kept silent most of the time. The voice was using Barnabus's words, contorting his voice and making me hate. I was so angry, and hate filled. I couldn't blame Barnabus, though. He sounded like he was having a fantastic day, and I thought it would be a shame to ruin it for him. He hadn't acted this happy in a long while.

We finally went to camp in the night, and I let my coyotes run around, and fed them some beef from our provisions. They made me happy. They seemed like little furballs of joy, playing and rolling around for us. "They're Aphrodite and Nickels." I said to Barnabus, when he asked me what their names were. He then played and laughed with the little coyotes, running around. He really did seem happy today.

He went to sleep in his tent snuggled with the coyotes, and I took out the book and read the page again. So this was Gerich, the first. I wondered who or what he could be, what led him to be bound in this book, and was now tormenting me to all hell. I thought of just burning the book, but I thought of Gessa. I at least could still remember her name, and I said it over and over again. I had to get her this book. I knew I had to, I just couldn't remember who she was... Was she older than me? Was she one of the friends of my pops? Who was this "Gessa" whose name I kept on saying? I knew she was important, and I had to remember that name.

I looked at the picture of Gerich, and I wondered why I kept it, as I hated him so much. Maybe I kept it just to remember that I hated him. Maybe he would be the thing I would kill eventually. My long lost hate. I thought of crumpling the picture and throwing it into the fire, but... I looked at him again, and furiously let out tears of anger, holding the image and staring back at his hate filled eyes. He stole Gessa away, whoever she was. He stole my love.

But then I remembered... The book said I could summon him. Perhaps I could kill Gerich. I wanted to kill him so badly... like no one ever before.

I went out further away from Barnabus on the plains, and said the words, "Asta Terro."

Nothing seemed to happen, but then I heard the voice, far away, seeming to laugh at me. I heard it speaking in the growing winds, taking every syllable from every sound around me and turning it into words. Gerich said, *"Welcome to Hell, Zach. Welcome to hate. Don't you love hate? Doesn't it fill you with strength? Doesn't it make you stronger, stronger than anything imaginable? You can thank me, for I hate you the most, you worthless, petty worm."*

"Show yourself!" I said, brandishing Skull.

"You know where to find me, Zach. You know where I am. I am in you. I am HATE."

I took out the picture, and saw him laughing at me. He said, in the picture, moving with the words, *"This Gessa of yours... didn't she steal from you? Didn't she fuck you and leave you to the wolves? Forgot you? As you did her. You probably forgot her for a good reason."*

"No!" I yelled, "I love Gessa! GIVE HER BACK TO ME!!"

"You lost that love... you lost her. Fuck, you even abandoned her! Like she did to you! Don't worry about her... If I was you, I'd kill her for all the things she said about you, and did to you. She wouldn't give you the time of day. She was some random woman, who never cared about you. She's as worthless as you are."

"You're lying! You're some demon, who is lying!" I yelled.

"You know I'm not, Zach... You know the truth."

I thought about Gessa, this woman whose face I couldn't even remember. I hated her then. I hated her as much as I did Gerich.

"Here's what you do, Zach... You go with that idiot Black Knight who's always hurt you, you follow him, and then you kill Gessa... Make her sorry for hurting you so much. She hates you too, you know." he said.

I looked at the picture, and I tore it in half.

Gerich laughed, and said, *"I'll still always be here... Zach... I'll always be here..."*

I then looked at the picture... and I saw a girl on it, and the tear had ripped her face down the middle. Feeling saddened by all the hate I had for this Gessa, I held the pieces and went back to Barnabus.

14

Everdick

I said to Edgar, "Well, at least I'm not afraid of you anymore."

"You were afraid of me?" he said.

"You raped my mother. You kill and eat everything. You are a barbarian, who I don't know what will do, and may lose his mind if he doesn't take his pills." I said.

"...True..." he said.

"But I saw you in your moment of weakness, sacrificing all to try and save your friends. Friends who are almost animals. You protected me over and over again, even though you wanted nothing to do with my life, and I wanted nothing to do with you. And... I could kill you as easily as wave my hand. Do you see that grave, over there? It's whispering something, but we shouldn't disturb it. *I* don't even know what it could do..." I said, as we were walking over a burial mound.

"...These... These are all graves..." Edgar said, following me slowly, taking his time because of his wounds.

"Yeah, but only that one over there is whispering." I said.

"...Let's... Let's find somewhere with a little more life, to camp at..." Edgar said.

So we kept on walking, and Edgar hurried a little more. It felt good to have *him* slightly frightened of me, instead of the other way around.

But I was also a bit frightened of the whispering.

We got a few good miles away from those mounds, and found a stunning waterfall in the early evening. We sat down next to it, and all of a sudden, a *gorgeous* black haired, muscular, naked woman surfaced from the water! She was washing her hair in the water, and then noticed us. She quickly went to the other bank and grabbed her sword, she spoke, asking who we were, and the voice sounded familiar... then it came to me! She was the woman knight!

Edgar was a bit nervous around the naked woman, and I could tell he was a little shy around such a woman, and he said, "We are two travellers, wanting peace for the night."

"Oh! I know you! You're the so-called son in law and granddaughter! I've been looking for you!" and she went back through the water, stood up in front of us, water dripping from her naked body, pointed the sword at us, and said, "I am Sister Patricia Starflight of the Order of the Falcon! I put you two under arrest and questioning for the murders of the men of the village of Tenborough!" Edgar's eyes were as wide as saucers staring at her... I sighed, and I knew I had to do the talking.

I stood up, and said, "Patricia whatever, we didn't do a goddamned thing. And if you want to keep your head, you'll put that pointy, phallic looking sword of yours down."

She seemed to falter a second, surprised someone so much younger than her was talking to her like that, but straightened up again and said, "My sword is Everdark! It isn't phallic in the least!"

"Well, maybe... but it does sort of curve, and get a bit wider at the tip. Are you sure it shouldn't be called 'Everdick?'" I said. I was beginning to feel a lot more courageous nowadays, and if anyone like those bullies of the past spoke to me like they did, I would mess them up six ways to sundown, either with my words, my fists, or my necromancy.

"How *dare* you!" she said, "I am an anointed knight! I have slain dragons and fought against corruption! I single handedly brought down the Curry Group bandits!"

"Well, I don't know about those bandits with the silly name, but dragons have been dead for ages!" I said, "You're not a knight, you're just a bully picking on travellers!"

"The Komodos are alive and strong, and roam the land in strength." she said, and gave a haughty laugh, "You should really learn your history, young lass, and maybe you would know of my many deeds, and the plights stalking the kingdom."

"It's not a kingdom! It's a democracy!" I said.

"...I meant land. Plights stalking the land." she said.

"My father is a *real* knight, and he knows more about the world and has helped more people than you ever have!" I said.

"This man? He hardly looks the part... He is not even armored!" she said.

"Well, neither are you..." I said.

She blushed a little bit, and said, "Well, erm... Don't go anywhere! I will proceed to interrogate you as soon as I am dressed!" then hurried to some bushes and began clothing herself and putting on her armor.

We waited for a while, Edgar all the while staring at her. I told him it wasn't polite to watch a lady while she is dressing, and he said, "Oh! Er, my bad." and quickly looked in the opposite direction, and began humming. I laughed my ass off at him.

Finally, Patricia was dressed, all armored in stunning, polished armor, and said from beneath her helmet, "I know you are not who you claim to be! You are two murderers, on the run from the law! I know this, simply because of my tricky questions to that lumberjack! He couldn't tell me who you really were, and gave these ludicrous names, saying you were from places that don't even exist! Who ever heard of 'Holland' anyway!"

"Holland is a real place, inhabited by the elves! It's also called the Netherlands! Look at a map!" I yelled at her.

Frustrated with me, she said, "Dear, this will be a lot easier on you if you confess your crimes."

"I'm not your dear! I'm not your honey, your sugarmuffin, or cherry-blossom! My name's Gessa, and this is Edgar, and my father is Marcos the Blunt Knight!" I said.

"*The* Marcos the Blunt Knight? He is rumored to be dead! Or secluded... or retired... one of the three!" she said.

"He's just been raising his daughter! Me! What the *hell* do you want? Because we're not going with you, not on your life!" I said.

"...Well, I know you are not related to those old folks now! Ha ha! I have deceived you, and you have shown your true face! Be prepared to face justice, be ready to duel!" she said, and pointed her sword at us again.

"Oh, I'll duel you... but I don't know a thing about swordplay. I challenge you, on your honor as a knight, to duel me with fists!" I said, smiling. These sorts of knights always took "challenge your honor as a knight" as a surefire way to do whatever you wanted. Zach's father told me that, when he had to fight for his life against many knights in the past, who fought him either because he was a rogue knight, or because people wanted the glory of beating him in a fight.

"Little thing you should know, Gessa." he told me, "Honor is all well and good, it would be hard to live if a lot of people didn't have it, but some people are so stuck up in it that they have to shove it waaaay up inside themselves, just to respect themselves. It's like a giant stick up their ass! Best to help them remove it."

"You?? I would assume this 'Edgar' would fight me instead... come now! I don't want to have to hurt you." she said.

Edgar was still humming and looking in the opposite direction. I told him she was finished, and he quickly swiveled his head around, waved his hand and said, "Go on, Gessa. I'm sure you can handle this beautiful..." and he sighed as if he was in love, "Patricia... on your own."

"Very well!" Patricia said, "But in honor of a fair fight... I will remove my armor." so she went back into the forest, and now began undressing. Edgar quickly turned his head again. I laughed and said it was fine, it was only armor. Although he probably got satisfaction from her removing that, as well... Men!

Finally, she was ready, and put her fists up. I put my hands up in the style of judo. "I will allow you to swing! But I warn you! I will counter strike!" she said. This made me giggle.

So, quickly, before she knew what I was doing, I grabbed her arm and her oh so wide collar, stepped in between her legs, fell back, put my foot on her waist, pulled her over me, and threw her over me, pushing her with my foot! This was a tomoe nage, and she went flying, making a sharp "eep!" sound. It was sometimes a dive bomb if you didn't do it right, but I thought it was so cool! I practiced it endlessly with my father. I got up laughing, as she was stunned with surprise on the ground. I didn't put her in a pin, I just wanted her to know I could throw her all day through the forest. I caught Edgar smiling, and he quickly put two fingers to his eyes and then pointed at Patricia. I turned back to her, and wham! She struck me hard across the face. "Fuck!" I yelled. I usually never swore in pain, but that really hurt!

I shook my head, shaking off the pain. This was starting to piss me off! Thankfully I remembered all the times Zach beat up bullies with his fists, so used his fighting style, at least partially. I clenched my right hand in a fist, and had my left hand open in the style of judo.

We circled each other, and as she swung I grabbed her wrist, pulled her towards me, and whacked her across the cheek! I was holding onto the wrist, preventing her from striking with that hand, and we kinda jumped back and forth, not wanting to get in each other's sights with our fists raised.

She whacked at my hand holding her wrist, downwards, breaking the grip, after trying to overpower me with that hand for a while, but I knew my grips, so it remained held for a good while, and when she broke it, I punched her again! Right in the eye.

She swung the freed hand at me in an arching backwards swing, and I quickly backed away. She was walking towards me, and did this most spectacular, absurd jump and punched me! She was in the air before I could swipe at her foot! This Patricia was a bit flashy, but damn! She knew how to fight! But she never fought a Blunt Knight before.

She struck at me, and I circled around her, right by her side, put my foot behind her, and fell with her! We went down, and quickly I whacked her in the stomach, but her abs were as hard as rocks! But at least I had her now in my element. I pinned her.

I held her down with a scarf hold, and kept her head up and my legs as far apart as possible. She struggled to stand, to get me off her, and said, if a little muffled because her throat was slightly constricted, "This will not do! Fight like a warrior!"

"Yield!" I said.

"...I cannot! On my honor as a knight! I will not strike you in this... position!" she said.

"Then I guess we're at an impasse. Do you promise to not take us prisoner? Do I have your word?" Having knights give their word was another way to make them do what you want.

She gave a frustrated little noise, and said, "Fine! You have my word! I will not try to take you prisoner..." so I got up off her, and smiled at her. She was frowning at me. She said, "That was unfair, little lady. Although you fight well." and got up, dusting herself off. Edgar applauded. Patricia said, "You have my word to not take you prisoner... but I must know the truth! I will follow you, until you reveal yourself, either as the murderers, or not! Those families must know peace!"

I sighed, and after Patricia followed us around as we were making camp, kind of looking over our shoulders at whatever we were doing, I told her she may as well be useful and start a fire.

Edgar didn't mind her looking over his shoulder, in fact, he seemed to like it more when she showed him the most attention. It's weird to think that I'm sort of related to him.

"What... What are you doing?" Patricia asked him, as he began taking off his clothes.

"I am bathing! I don't know what it is about ladies, but I as a man don't really mind if women watch me undress! I don't really mind if *any-one* watches me undress, actually... Actually, I feel more comfortable when naked! Watch as much as you like!" he said. Patricia turned red.

He dove in the pool, and began doing these absurd flexes, showing off his naked body. Patricia was wide eyed staring at him. I couldn't take it anymore after a few seconds, and walked away, bursting out laughing. Patricia was either in shock, or enjoying the show, and didn't follow me.

I walked off for a while, simply enjoying the scenery, and saw a huge mountain in the distance. That was Mount Olympus, home of the dwarves! It was breathtaking. To celebrate my fight, I decided to smoke the joint, and made a little fire of my own with my flint and tinder, and lit a stick, then put the burning stick to the joint in my mouth and inhaled. I coughed so much, and tears went down my face from the coughing, but inhaled deeply again, and then one more time. I decided to save the rest of it for later, and put it out, and shoved it back into my bag, in a pouch on the side.

So I just thought about life, that big ass mountain, and what strange people inhabit this world. I sat in the sunshine on a big rock, kicking my legs, enjoying the high. I felt pretty happy, and thought about the world, and wondered if Venny will ever be able to see it all, all at once. I wondered if even such a thing was possible. I took a picture of Mount Olympus, just so he could see it when I got back. Maybe... if I climbed to the top of that mountain, and took a picture? Would it show everything? That would be so cool! I just had to get far up enough to see the whole world! But then there were the clouds. Wouldn't they get in the way? Oh, who cares! I wanted to climb that mountain, one day!

There were rumored to be all sorts of gods on top of that mountain, doing all sorts of strange things. I wondered what a god would do? Would they even have time to do anything amidst answering all the prayers? I'd be swamped, like Jacob was in the Wheel, if I had to answer *every* prayer from every person. I suppose that's why gods are so quiet nowadays. In the stories they used to be everywhere! Doing all sorts of things, as men and women on Earth! I wondered if that was real or not... I've already seen so many strange things, I suppose seeing a god wouldn't be that different.

Unlike meditating, getting high and thinking was enjoyable! Most of the time I would sit and try to push back the oppressive thoughts, which only made them stronger, but now they just seemed unimportant. Like even if I had a bad thought, I would think around it, or through it, and it wouldn't seem so bad, and would actually seem pretty funny! I sighed, content, and decided it was good to go back and see how Patricia and Edgar were doing. Given Edgar's "history" with women, I didn't think it would end too well, but Patricia could probably handle herself against a wounded Edgar.

I walked back, and Patricia was sitting down with one hand under her chin, watching Edgar. I could tell Edgar was getting a little tired of flexing, but if he saw her looking, would get back his enthusiasm and do another one. Only after he curled up in pain and said ow a bunch did he realize he should probably quit. I told him to get some rest. He thanked me and dried himself off with a spare cloth, clothed himself, and then sat down besides Patricia. She looked at him sideways, but I could tell she was a bit curious of him.

"Who... Who *are* you??" she asked him after a moment of silence.

"Well, when I was mad... I was... but I won't tell you about those days. My name's Edgar, now." he said.

"You're a *mad* man? Did you escape from an asylum?" she asked.

Edgar coughed, and said, "Well, I sort of inhabited an asylum for a while... and Gessa's father, mother, and Gestas found me there... It is not a very happy memory for me."

"Then I will not pry. I noticed you are wounded... who did that to you?" Patricia asked.

He coughed again, nervous, and said, "The... hunters."

"Edgar! Shush. He got into an accident." I said.

"I knew you met with them! They must've attacked you, and then fought over the justice of it! Justice will always get those in the end." she said.

"Yeah... they were not very nice people, attacking our friends..." Edgar said. I wanted him to seriously stop talking about it, in case he revealed the whole story to a pretty face, but I suppose it must've been lonely for Edgar for a long, long time.

"Your friends? Who are they? Did you get seperated?" Patricia asked.

"They are in the woods now. They are Barcough and Jillian. Barcough is an old, old friend of mine, and I found Jillian again for him, as the two had been deeply in love once, and wished to respark their relationship." Edgar said.

"I see... Well, that's good of you... I suppose... but it still leaves a lot of things unanswered." Patricia said. Edgar nodded dumbly, a little too vigorously, then clutched his side again. "Here. Let me change your bandages. Lay down, please." she said, and Edgar went a little red, but did as she said.

She took off his shirt, and changed the bandage, saying he should do this every day. Edgar didn't really like being so "exposed" and unprotected, someone at his wounds of all things, but he nervously lay still, and Patricia finished, smiled, and said, "There! If Gessa cannot do this, then I will. I will teach you the healing arts, little lady, as everyone who knows how to fight, should also learn how to heal." I groaned, and said fine.

We slept for the night, and Edgar was tuckered out from his wounds that were still healing, and Patricia and I were worn out from fighting. I kept nervously wondering if Edgar would try something on a sleeping Patricia, but he didn't, and behaved himself. I suppose he really had changed.

15

Tero Sai

I had that recurring dream of Skull talking, but it was saying something in muffled orcish, and all I could think about was my anger, even in my dreams.

In the morning my hate had cooled, but I still asked Barnabus, as the coyote pups were prowling around, why we were going to see Gessa... I said she could probably take care of herself, always has been.

He looked at me in shock.

"What? What was all that stuff about her yesterday, then?? You can't tell me it was just a stupid kid phase! You disappoint me, Zach." Barnabus said.

I grumbled and said that she was old enough to take care of herself, however old she was.

"...What?" he said.

Getting angry, I gave him the picture I had torn in half, and said, "That's what she did to me! She left me!"

Barnabus was staring heartbroken at the picture, and then put his hand into a fist, and punched me hard, right in the face. As I was on the ground, Barnabus picked my head up and slammed me over and over again onto the ground. I quickly drew Skull, hating him, hating Gessa, hating everything, and turned and threatened him.

"Oh... so the big man wants to fight, eh? *The poor little piss drinking barbarian wants to fight? Fucking fight me, you shit eating, twat having, cunt little boy!*" he and Gerich said as one.

"I hate you!" I said, getting up, "You've always insulted me! You've always put me down! Well not anymore!"

"I could just kill you right now... but that would break my heart even more." Barnabus said, pointing his pistol at my head with a glint in his eyes. "Go. Go back to whatever hell hole you want. But don't *ever* come near me, or Gessa, again."

Angry, I told him to fuck off, and walked away. "*That's right, Zach!* Run away! No one will *come* looking for *you!*" Barnabus and Gerich said.

I heard Barnabus yelling in anger behind me, but I ignored it and kept walking. I heard a frustrated yell come out of the wilderness behind me, but still, I ignored it. I forgot about the coyote pups, but I thought fuck them too, they would be better off with Barnabus, anyway.

I decided to make tracks in the forest. The very first thing I did was trip and fall on my face, and Skull cut my hand as I dropped it. I was bleeding pretty heavily, and as I picked it up, it never felt so heavy. I holstered it on my back, and kept walking.

The second thing that happened were all the mosquitos, biting at me, everywhere, feasting on me no matter how much I tried to fight them.

The third thing to happen was finding my food had all spoiled.

The fourth thing to happen was when I stayed in a cave, it was occupied by a she bear, and before I could escape, she scratched me hard on the face.

I washed off the blood in a lake and looked at my reflection. I would be scarred for life.

I felt like everything that could go wrong, was going wrong... Why did I ever leave Mary? But... but... I couldn't remember what she looked like! Frustrated and angry at Gerich, at all the hardship I was going through, I yelled out in the forest, in a hate filled voice. After I thought about the many, many angry words I said, cursing everyone to hell, I realized I never spoke like that, that that was never my tone of voice. Who was I? I knew I was Zach, but what had become of me? I remembered the cigarettes, and I smoked one, and then I smoked the whole pack, thinking about all the anger, fearing what I was becoming.

I lost my voice.

I drank a bunch of water, and my voice was sort of coming back, a hoarse sort of rasping. I wasn't hearing Gerich, but everything awful was happening to me!

But wait! That was something in the book! I took it out, looked at the page, and saw the name Biona Callus, the second. It said I would regret it if I summoned her, but maybe I could appease her? Maybe I could bow down and worship her? Anything! Just so I could have my life back!

I said the words, "Shel Bion."

And a naked demon arose out of the water. She was beautiful, yet terrifying. Her horns on her head made her seem even taller than she already was. Her grey skin was like ash, her tail flicked and was spiked. I stared at her breasts, and she rubbed one, and knew I was looking. I quickly stared up at her horrible, horrible, beautiful face. Her eyes were red, like the blood on my face.

"You would worship me as your god?" she said, in a voice that sounded like thunder.

I said, "I would do anything, to have my life back." bowing.

She laughed, and said, *"So easy. Make it difficult. What about this 'Gessa' of yours? Don't you care about her at all?"*

I thought back on Gessa, but all I could remember was Gerich.

"No! I don't care about her anymore! You are my goddess!" I rasped in my worn out voice.

"Would you lay with me? Would you give yourself to me, body and soul?" she said.

"Yes! Anything..." I said.

"Then you shall have to wait. Suffer some more, and appease me." and she turned, with that beautiful behind, and with that horrible spiked tail, lashed at my face. It cut deep, over my eyebrow, and as the blood went over my eye, I could halfway see her submerging, and laughing at me.

"Please! Please, no! Biona Callus!" I said.

She was gone, down into the water. I said the words to summon her over and over again, but no one came out of that water. I thought maybe she wanted me to go in after her, and was about to dive in... but I was stopped by the sound of a gunshot behind me.

I turned and saw Barnabus stumbling towards me, drunk as all hell.

"*You shit eating... ungrateful...* Come here, boy. I won't hurt you." he said gently.

I had almost forgotten his face. I slumped down and told him to kill me.

"No. You *suicidal...* little guy. I care for you, you *fucking...* good hearted kid. I know it must not be easy for you. Please. Tell me what is going on." Gerich was trying to change his voice, but didn't seem to get the right words to do harm.

I told him I was reading the book, and I was possessed by demons.

"Here... That's alright. Let's start a fire. You can use my tent if you want. Just sleep it off." Barnabus said, and we started a fire. And I cried next to him, as he drank, and drank, and drank. He cradled my head, and drunkenly said, "Shh... it's alright, little Zachary. I know that's what your mom calls you. I only ever insulted you because I thought we were having fun. Just fun. I never knew it hurt you so much."

"I'm just so angry! I'm just so mad at everything! I don't know what to do... I tried to fight them, I tried to appease them, but they laugh and become worse!" I said.

"Here. Give me the book." Barnabus said. Sniffling, I did.

Then he threw it on the fire.

I suddenly remembered I needed to give that to Gessa! That was the one thing I had to do!

So I reached in the flames quickly, burning halfway up my arms, as Barnabus yelled in shock trying to drag me away from the fire. I got the book, but my hands... my arms... they hurt like the fires of Hell. I thought I heard Biona Callus laughing in the crackling of the fire.

The book was cold.

"Fucking hell, Zach! Just get rid of the fucking thing!" Barnabus said. I dropped the book to the ground, and he quickly dragged me to the lake and submerged my arms into the water. He was crying, saying, "Fucking, fucking, fuck! Goddamnit... I told you adventures are shit!"

I heard this, and laughed. I couldn't help myself! He was so right! I laughed and laughed, and Barnabus started laughing, too.

"I need... to give the book to Gessa. Whoever she is. That's the one thing I have to do in life... That is my purpose, even if she may be worse than all the demons put together..." I said.

"What?? You don't remember Gessa?? Fuck... This is bad. *This makes me so angry!!"* he said, and his words were all Barnabus. "Listen. I'm going to bring you home. I'm going to get Gessa back, and you can stay with Marcos and Daisy." Barnabus said.

"I... need... to give the book... to Gessa." I said.

"I can do it." he said. I shook my head quickly. *I* needed to do it. I needed to do it! That was all I knew... Gessa would know what to do. She must know!

Barnabus let out an angry sigh, then said, "Fine. Let's sit by the fire and I'll tell you of the girl you grew up with, that you love. That we both love with all of our hearts. You bloody kids... This is why I never fucking had any! They're just so goddamned stupid!"

He took me back to the fire, and told me of this Gessa person. I thought she was some sort of monster! But she seemed nice. I trusted Barnabus... I suppose I'd have to trust Gessa. I didn't think of her anymore, because then I would think of Gerich, but his image was a bit cloudy, as Barnabus told me stories about her. I relished hearing her name, it was my purpose. My purpose was Gessa.

"She's blonde, y'know? That golden sunlight kind of blonde. Pure blonde, not bleached or anythin'. She's got the same hair as her mother. I was happy as a clam seeing her born. I don't know why... I hated Marcos with all my guts, but it felt good, in a way. You were there. Do you remember the little baby Gess?" Barnabus said. I shook my head, and he continued, "Ah, well, you were probably too young anyway. Duh! Kids have shit memories. Well, she was playing with you in the street once, and out of nowhere a fuckin' car, one of the rare ones, comes racing down the road, and you grabbed her out of the way, just in the knick of time! I saw it, as I was babysittin' and shouted out, hoping she would notice in time, but I wasn't close enough, as I ran towards her. You were though. I was never so proud of you. She was frightened as all hell, and was crying, but you told her to calm down... and that it was alright, mimicking something your dad does for your ma, when she gets upset and sad about something. I took you both in, and, heh, I was as angry as I was worried. Dumb kids... Stay off the fucking streets!"

"How do I know you're telling the truth?" I asked.

He looked at me sadly, very sadly, like it was the hardest thing in the world for him to hear, and said, "I'm telling the truth, Zach."

I felt sort of sad that I never knew this Gessa, then.

He continued, "She does this god awful... fucking annoying... cute as all hell twirl of hers when she's happy. Makes it look like she's as light as air. I don't think she's ever noticed that she does it. She's very pretty, and nice, the most adorable good hearted kid you'll ever meet. I don't know how she came about from a union of rape. You'd think that would make her angry, and ugly, and awful, but she's not anything of the sort. I suppose a lot of the credit goes to those parents of hers, but I think Gessa's just got a good heart. I can see why you love her, as a man loves a woman. Just take your time, you have all your life to love. Don't worry, you'll get there in time, and I'm sure Gessa's got a special place in her heart for you as well."

"For me?? How... could *anyone...* love me... I'm horrible! I can't even remember my parents! I can only remember Gar... and that I despise him with all my might..." I said.

He sighed, and said, "Let's continue talking about Gessa. I'm sure she loves you, as you love her. Love... is sort of like a mirror. It always reflects back. Real love, not incessant, annoying obsession or lust. Here's a story about you, Gessa, and your parents. I was invited over by them, and Gessa was staying to visit, playing with you. I think you were upset about something, so tried hard to ignore her."

"Yeah... I sort of remember... I was upset that my pops... yeah, I called him pops... tried making me learn orcish again. I just wanted to forget about all the orcs... every one of them. They were nothing like me, and I was an outcast to them..." I said.

"That's right. But your mom came in with that sassy sort of way she has, and made us all speak in orcish for dinner. That's why I didn't say a word, as I couldn't understand what the heck any of them said." Barnabus said.

"My... ma... was always clever, and would always find new ways to make me work harder..." I said.

"But you were stubborn, and tried talking in English to everyone, and they would respond in orcish, so eventually you tried your hardest to speak orcish. They knew you were just making up words though, as your parents actually did know orcish, and practiced it just for you." Barnabus said.

"Yeah... I guess... they do love me. I remember them, but I still can't picture Gessa. She seems like a stranger to me." I said.

"Well, when she was leaving, your dad told her some words to say, and what they meant. She immediately looked happy, and said them to you. Do you remember what she said?" Barnaubus said.

I thought hard, and then the orcish seemed to flood back into me, and I said, "T-Tero... sai... Zach. Tero sai, Zach! I can remember her! I can see her face! It means goodbye, heart! She does love me!"

Barnabus smiled and said, "That's a good boy. Hold onto that feeling."

I was just so enthusiastic! I couldn't even picture Gerich anymore! I just had Gessa in my heart, in my head, in every feeling in me! I could practically jump for joy! I stood up, then fell over, as I felt very woozy, and very, very tired.

Barnabus caught me, and brought me to his tent he had set up. I said wouldn't he need somewhere to sleep too?

He said, "I'm going to stay up for a bit... to look at the stars and campfire. And to watch you. I don't want you doing anything else fucking stupid. Don't worry about me, you've had a rough day."

I thanked him, and as I looked up at the beautiful, gorgeous stars, I thought I could see Biona Callus... but then I remembered the words Gessa told me, and I saw Gessa instead. I fell asleep almost immediately, but as I fell asleep, I heard Biona Callus say, in that sort of half dream sleep of almost being asleep, *"I will still always be here... Zach... I will always be here..."*

16

Don't Fuck With the Wrong Birds

There was no sign of Jillian or Barcough, but as Edgar went out, as he boldly said, "to take a shit" he came back, and said there was someone else running to us! Very quickly! Patricia said she would meet with them, but I told her to stay, just in case. I didn't really trust her very much, and I hoped it wasn't more of her buddies or anything...

But it turned out to be Jacob. He came up to us, panting, saying we should really be easier for trackers like him to find! I said, "Well, that would defeat the purpose. Hi, Jacob!"

He went over to me, and tried patting me on the head again, but I quickly gave him a hug. He didn't really know what to do at this, so sort of hugged me back, by patting my back with a hand.

"I have a letter for you! And being deeply... ahem... sewed in with this trouble, I had to see if it was good news or not... but I think you should read it for yourself."

"You read my letter?" I asked him.

"I was just so worried! And if I had to read anybody's letters, it'd be you guys'! Marcos sure didn't look well after he gave it to me... no sir, fuck.

"My father?? Give it to me, please." I said, and Jacob quickly reached into his satchel and gave me the letter.

Edgar was asking him how he found us... as he never had anyone sneak up on him quite like this, and Jacob said, "Oh, you know. I always sort of wanted to be an explorer, go new places, see new things. But I got too drunk, and sort of lost that ambition... or maybe it was all the whores? Those whores fuckin' make life worth living again, I'll fucking say!" I read my letter.

My father had said that he uncovered the truth, and that the detective had verified my story, but they were still angry that the body they found was seemingly brought to the hospital. They blamed my father for trying to cover up the murder! He had to fight back a whole mob, and some of their true colors showed, as they called him a witch fucker. My mother had saved a lot of people with her necromancy in the past... but some people will never forget the horrors in the dark, even if those horrors saved all their lives! He said he is on the move with my mother and a few of the Blunt Knights that were in the area, and that our home... was burned to the ground. I didn't understand this! They proved it was self defense! It made me furious... but he said he would meet with us with Zach's mother and father, who just sent a letter that they were on their way home. I felt depressed that my home... was gone. I was now officially homeless.

He told me that people were looking for him, and for me. He needed forces in numbers, and the Chariot would be able to do that. The government quickly sent some authorities to calm everyone down, and take people prisoner if they needed to, but as my father tried to take justice into his own hands, the mob had killed the detective, burning his report and findings. This was definitely a blow to the Blunt Knights, as it seemed like they weren't trusted anymore, but my father said he would whip them back into shape, and finally, get back to work.

My father had always been sort of a silent protector of the village, just training and improving his skills, and helping to raise me in his off times. He solved fights, he imprisoned someone who came back to the village to murder their wife, and he was all in all, a most upstanding citizen. I suppose the Blunt Knights really did need him... but they were scattered to the winds! They were adventuring, roaming paladins! My father said it was finally time we had a real base of operations for the Blunt Knights, and said he and my mother loved me with all their hearts.

As Edgar was talking about tricky ways to evade capture, and Jacob was pointing out the flaws in each one, I interrupted them and asked Jacob, "Can't you *do* anything? They burned down our house!"

"I... uh... have contacts with an assassins guild, but I don't know how we could assassinate everyone of the entire village... I mean, we *could...*" Jacob said.

"No! Damnit... I don't want to have to kill anyone else!" I quickly remembered that Patricia was listening, but she remained quiet, so far.

"Then it's up to us at the Chariot to help you. I'll be sending messages to all the troops we have, and ask the others if they can get any more aid." Jacob said, smiling. Jacob was part of the Wheel, the courier service, the Hermit, the thieves guild, the Tower, the assassins guild, and also the Chariot, Zach's father's mercenary company.

"Maybe we should just knock on Simon and Melissa's door... as we're homeless now..." I said.

"That's really not a bad idea." Jacob said, taking out a cigarette and smoking it, "I don't know how many friends and family I had to hit up just to have a place to sleep when I was on hard times. That's not a bad idea... I'll be telling Absinthe and my asshole superiors that my time with them will have to be put on hold... I'll just tell them it's a family emergency, that always does the trick."

"But go to one of Simon's countries in the Empire?? It's so strange over there!" I said.

"We'll go wherever they're located currently. Melissa and Simon have numerous palaces, and always stay in a country for a year, before taking residence in the next one. They've gotten into some trouble with a few rebels, as there will always be rebels wanting more, but their holdings are much vaster than Jericho and the Militant put together." Jacob said.

"The Militant? That's Gregory's country, right?" I asked.

"Yup." Jacob said, "You could also stay there, as I doubt anyone would come looking for you in their harsh land... although I hear they have had a good year of prosperity, though that may be propaganda."

I got sort of sad at all of this, and said, "I just want to be with my family..."

"Hey, little dude, it's alright... I'll go and get everything in order. How about you go visit somewhere safe? See some sights? Just go traveling for a bit." Jacob said.

"Do you know anything about Zach?" I asked.

"I got a letter from Mary saying they had split up... Barnabus and him were going to meet you, actually. But as far as I know, they've disappeared off the map." Jacob said, "Mary has sent me a list of all her new recruits, and I sent it to the King, who should just now be crossing the border."

"He'll know what to do. Him and his whole army. They'll fight back anyone who tries to hurt us." I said.

"Yup! Don't worry about it. Now that formalities are out of the way... Who is this stunning, black haired babe? Wanna get somewhere nice and comfy with me, sweetie? I can tell you of my adventures! Yeah..." Jacob said, turning to the armored but helmetless Patricia.

"Hmph." she said, "Based on your words, you are either a bandit or a cutthroat! You are one of the vile no good doers! You must be some sort of villainous assassin! I will arrest you."

Jacob stepped back from her, just as he was trying to lay an arm around her shoulder, and said, "Hey now, don't you know who I am? I'm fuckin' Jacob! I saved everyone's lives, with my quick wit and skill! I'm *the* fuckin' Jacob!"

"I have never heard of you, no matter how many *thes* you may be. I am Sister Patricia Starflight, of the Order of the Falcon, a bringer of justice and good!" Patricia said, taking a step towards Jacob which Jacob stepped back at again.

"Oh! I've heard of you guys! You're one of those lesbo, chick orders! Damn... I'm sure you could tell some stories! Who was your first love, eh? Was it a sexy redheaded teacher babe of yours? Made you get better grades by showin' off the goods?" Jacob said.

Quickly, she hit him.

On the ground, Jacob rubbing his face, he said, "I was only bein' polite!"

"He's harmless, Patricia." I said, as she was looking at him in fury.

"Very well. You people are strange to me. I don't know if you are innocent outcasts or malicious villains. I would very well like to meet with Marcos the Blunt Knight, to discuss our orders, however." Patricia said.

"Don't... Don't you have somewhere to be? Dragons to smite or something?" I said.

"I go wherever the winds lead me, for true good cannot be found by seeking, no, it must come to you." Patricia said.

"Great!" Edgar said, "I'll make some breakfast. It's the last of the moose, though, and I think we'll have to go hunting some more... although I fear if I hunted a boar or moose these days, my side would kill me..."

"I have restocked my provisions, but it is not enough to feed you people. But as you are all homeless, I will give willingly." Patricia said. This kind of annoyed me, but I still ate her food with the last of the moose... I was learning that sometimes it's better to think with your stomach, rather than your pride.

Jacob had food of his own, but he still snarfed up the bites of moose we gave him.

We looked at a map to see where Zach could be. I told Zach that I was last in Burlington, so he'd probably try traveling there... so I drew a straight line from the library to Burlington with my pen, saying they must be somewhere down that path. Jacob shook his head, and drew a zig-zagging, squiggling path, saying, if they were lucky, they'd be on *that* path. This depressed me.

We couldn't wait around at Burlington though, if they were looking for us. We had to keep moving, so decided we'd try to meet Zach on Jacob's path. Jacob's skills at tracking would be helpful, but he had to go back to work and get everything in order. I wish we had Barcough with us to find things... but Edgar could, if he couldn't. I was just worried about Patricia. I hoped she wouldn't get us into any trouble.

I smoked my joint with Jacob, before he left.

He was kind of a drug user, doing anything he could get his hands on, and Zach's dad had to straighten him out once when he was on a horrible drug binge, not showing up to work and even getting lost! I thought I shouldn't be giving someone like this drugs, but I just wanted to thank him for helping me, and Jacob had said he relapsed so many times it was almost like second nature, and that moderation is the key really.

Edgar and Patricia were chatting about moose, and how to hunt one, while we sat around the fire and Jacob and I smoked the joint. "Wake and bake... Always nice." Jacob said, taking a hit.

"You hunted a moose... *with your bare hands??*" Patricia said.

"Well, with Barcough, too. He used teeth!" Edgar said.

"...You people get stranger and stranger by the minute." Patricia said, not knowing that Barcough was a dog.

"Barcough always finds animals before me, and knows which ones to stay away from. He's very intelligent." Edgar said.

"I can imagine all you people are. Which makes you so much stranger. Did you ever go to a hunting school? Were you a ranger?" Patricia asked.

"Nah. I just got lost, and couldn't find my way back, because there was nowhere to go back to! I'm better at being lost, than knowing where to go." Edgar said. Jacob passed the joint to me and I puffed on it.

"I have been lost many times, but always, I listen for the sounds of hardship and suffering, and go to save those who are hurt." Patricia said, "I saved an injured bird when I was a child... when I was lost... and this stunning woman knight found me and brought me home. She was a member of the Order of the Falcon, and she said, like the bird, I was injured and lost, and all I needed was the right care to be able to fly again. I nursed that bird back to life forever... but finally, it was healed enough to fly away. This strengthened me, and led me to the Order of the Falcon, and was the turning point in my life."

"I've eaten a wounded bird before... because I was starving. Birds are hard to eat, if they're small, but the bones are crunchy..." Edgar said.

"I've brought a dead bird back to life." I said, taking another hit. Shit! I wasn't supposed to say that...

"You both mock me. There is nothing more important than to save those who are hurting. I can understand we must all eat, Edgar, but Gessa, you should know better than to joke about death." Patricia said. I quickly nodded.

Jacob said, "This one time... my brother, hooboy... fuckin' killed somebody who spit in his drink. The fuckin' bartender! He just fuckin' spit in his drink! They were both fucking the same woman, but he should've known better than to mess with my brother like that. Never saw such a ruckus... I mean I have seen worse, but not from a bartender! My brother snapped his neck, as his woman came in through the door... Man, he apologized day and night to her, but that bird... she just flew off! Took all of my brother's things too, with all the other men she was fucking...

just goes to show you! Don't spit in drinks and don't fuck with the wrong birds!"

Patricia was shocked, and looking at her face, I burst out laughing, which led to Jacob laughing too... Edgar gave a chuckle, but stopped laughing and looked at us inquisitively, as we just laughed and laughed.

I gave Jacob a hug as he said he had to go, and he finally did hug me back. A real hug. "Let's smoke again sometime, dude." he said, then waved as he walked off.

We left to find Zach, and I never felt like I missed anyone so much. I just wanted to hug, and hug, and hug him... to squeeze him to death!

17

Teck

Skull was talking to me again in my dreams. I struggled to understand it, as it spoke in orcish to me. It said something about the goad, the dead. The last word I caught was "teck," meaning blood.

I woke up to Aphrodite nuzzling my head, wanting to get fed. I took her out to Barnabus, and he was slumped down sleeping sitting with his head against his knees. I woke him up and asked him if he had any food for the coyotes.

He quickly unsheathed his sword and shouted, "Demons! I'll kill you all!" then looked up at me, and said, "Oh... Zach. Here, in my bag. You should just let the things free, though... I had this awful dream of Jack coming back from the dead, with all his dead friends in Hell... Your spooky demons put me on edge..."

I sat down with him, and I was glad he took it seriously... as seriously as someone could who didn't have to deal with them, but I was sad and frightened about what was coming next. The next one, the third, stuck out to me, being Teckus, and it mentioned he was a jokester... I told Barnabus about the two I had... the two I *saw*... and knew were biding their time, waiting for the third to approach.

"*I'm here* for you Zach." Barnabus said, with a hint of Gerich.

"Well... the one I just heard... who sort of came from your mouth, just said he was here. His name is Gerich, and he made me forget, and hate." I said.

"Fuck! I never liked supernatural shit... not as much as Dismas, but still, if I can't understand the fucking thing, then I don't want to have to deal with it... and I don't understand demons." Barnabus said.

I showed him my bear scar, and the gash from Biona Callus's tail, it was hard to not show it, and said, "I got this from Biona Callus, who brings suffering and hardship."

He looked at the scar, and said, "Besides the bear claw marks, it looks like you cut *yourself* with a knife, kid..."

Surprised, I took out my knife, and it was crusted in blood. I dropped it in shock.

"Maybe... you need some help from Daisy... maybe she knows what's going on..." he said.

"Can... Can you look at the book for me? Please?" I said, frightened that I actually *was* losing my mind.

"Ok... It's such an ugly looking thing... with such horrible stuff in it... I can't imagine how anyone could have written it..." he said.

"It was made of real people. That's what the librarian said." I said.

"Well, I suppose only someone so demented would write such a thing." Barnabus said, as I gave him the book.

"It was written by the Lich." I said.

He looked at the cover page, and said, "I see that... Only that bastard would write something so evil, on such an evil subject. Although it could be a pseudonym, someone who wanted to take the 'glories' of the evil legends of old..."

"The demons are on the next page." I said.

He turned the page, and looked a little pale, and said, "I see me, being killed by you. It looks like it is drawn in blood... from the edge of a knife..."

"What?? No! I would never do that!" I looked at the book, and the demon names were there still, but on the next page... was exactly as Barnabus said. I felt very faint.

"I... I think we need to take you to get some help..." Barnabus said.

"Look! The names are there!" I said, showing him the book.

"Yes... and I feel like it's something that you took a little too seriously... The writer is just trying to scare you, Zach. I see your name is there... I just want to scratch it off..." Barnabus said.

"Will that work, you think?" I asked.

"If it'll make you feel any better, I'll try." Barnabus said. At first Barnabus tried ripping the page out of the book, but it held fast, even though he was grunting and pulling with all his might. "Must be... some sort of super special adhesive or some shit..." then he tried scratching my name off with his own knife, but as he did, I felt like my insides were being scratched to ribbons, and I quickly told him to stop. He did, as I nearly fainted from the pain. "I just don't get it... Well, you know what, let me tell you about a god I know, and a saying from your father. She'll help you, even though I don't really believe in her, and is sort of a joke god, but sure, maybe she'll help. Let some gods help you instead of demons."

I nodded, sitting down, still feeling the pain, although it was passing.

"Well... the first thing you know already. Do you remember it? Means good luck and love..." Barnabus said.

"Figaro, Fadaro, Pigaro, Padaro." I said, nodding and smiling.

"Yup! Good, silly, lucky words. Should help you change that down and depressed mood of yours." Barnabus said, "I will tell you about the God of Luck. I don't know if she has a real name, and has been called many things in the past, sometimes God of Cheaters, or Dice God, but I always called her my Fiona, after a lucky girl from my past."

"Maybe... I should learn of a really strong and holy god? One that can smite demons and devils?" I said.

"Bah. Those are all bullshit anyway, and people take them too seriously. Gods should stay where they belong, and not cause people to kill each other for petty things. That's why I always liked my Fiona. She's a good gal, who just gives you a little extra confidence when you play poker." Barnabus said.

"Ok... I really hope her luck can help..." I said.

"Now, where was I... Fiona was a call girl somewhere, and when she gave herself to a very well paying man, she decided to stick with him for a while. Now, whenever they did it, the man would win every game, no matter what it was, or even if he knew how to play, and he gave all his winnings to Fiona. She quickly became very rich, but still, stuck with this man. But one day, she saw a beggar on the street, being kicked at and scorned, and with that big heart of hers, decided he needed some luck as well. She gave herself to the beggar, and the beggar's luck turned around instantly. He was accepted into a knighthood order and soon became very well off for himself.

"The man she was with became furious, and tried shutting her in a cage, to keep her for himself, but she would always escape with the greatest luck. You see, it wasn't only when she laid with others it gave them luck, but when she fingered herself, she would get luck as well! So she would do this every night, and go out and bring luck to any man or woman who needed a helping hand, and give them a fuck when they were out of luck. She did so much good, with that lucky twat of hers, that eventually she was called on by the gods and given a place with them. So if you're ever feeling down, depressed, and unlucky, remember Fiona's lucky twat, and maybe, just maybe, you'll have that luck again."

"...Are you the beggar who became a knight in the story?" I said.

He laughed and grinned, but was silent.

"Well... ok. I'll remember Fiona. She sounds like a nice god." I said.

"Good. Well, I think we should get moving. Let's go find Gessa, and give this accursed book to her." Barnabus said, so we packed up, and got walking.

We walked, and it was uneventful. I thought of Gessa some more, feeling happy, and I prayed the words, Figaro, Fadaro, Pigaro, Padaro for awhile, and they made me think of my parents, and made me feel happy, and I thought of Fiona's lucky twat, which wasn't that bad. Gave me strength, and made me think that I could find love again, besides people who steal from me. I imagined this Fiona to be someone beautiful, holy in her own way. I imagined laying with her would be the nicest thing imaginable, kind, sweet, and lucky.

But while I was imagining her, I had flashes of battle, and the sight of blood. They were intrusive thoughts, violent thoughts, that I couldn't get rid of. So I would keep saying the lucky words, even though I felt like I wanted to punch somebody! I felt like fighting! It had been awhile for me since I fought, and I just thought I needed to stretch my muscles. I didn't feel like fighting Barnabus though... I didn't want to accidentally hurt him or anything, after all he did for me.

But I didn't have to fight him, as some riders approached us.

We stopped and waited, wondering what they wanted. I said, "Figaro, Fadaro, Pigaro, Padaro," hoping it wasn't something bad.

An ugly sort of woman and men stared at us from atop their horses. "What's this? A fucking orc? And it looks like he's got a Black Knight with him... We told your kind to stay out of our land." the woman said.

"We don't want any trouble, we're just travellers, and this is my charge. He wants to be a Black Knight one day!" Barnabus said.

She spit at him, and said, "We don't care about Black Knights or orcs. And you need to leave. Go back to wherever you came from, but if you step one more foot in our land, we'll kill you."

I thought of Gessa, trying to calm myself down, and I imagined strangling her! I quickly tried to shut out the image, but I couldn't get rid of it!

The hands that were choking her weren't my hands though. They looked like an orc's hands, but they were a different shade than my own... and far more muscular. It was a horrible image.

"*Kill them.*" The woman said, as Gerich was commanding me.

Immediately, one of the men shot at me with an arrow, and it stuck in my chest, which thankfully my armor prevented a deathblow. The pain... was unimaginable. I grabbed at the arrow, and it looked like Biona Callus had stuck it in me instead. She obscured my vision! She was huge! She said, "*Imagine a dick being stabbed into you. Over and over again.*" and she shoved the arrow deeper into me.

Barnabus was yelling at me, telling me to stop shoving the arrow into myself! Biona Callus left, and I looked down at my bloodied hands. I can't really remember what happened next... but when I was done, the people were all dead, and Barnabus was panting next to me, our weapons bloodied.

I dropped Skull in shock.

"What the fuck happened?" I asked him.

"Yeah... first time for me taking a life sucked too. You'll get over it. These people were no good." Barnabus said.

"I... killed??" I said.

"You took out almost all of them! I only shot one of the fucks and gutted one who was trying to stab you in the back! Where the hell did you learn that! I could've sworn you were another person!" Barnabus said.

"I..." I started, and trailed off. Teckus must've done this. Teckus! Not me! I... didn't really know. Was that what killing was like?

I had the image of those hands strangling Barnabus. I told him I couldn't travel with him anymore, that he wouldn't be safe!

"Now, now... It's alright. We'll get your evil sorted out. Marcos taught me some ways of subduing, even though I thought I'd never use them, I guess I will on you." Barnabus said.

We kept on walking, me in shock. I still imagined Fiona, but just imagined what she looked like, smiling at me or something. I imagined Gessa, and tried with all my might to keep those hands away from her.

We finally got to a river, and I found an old, cracked mirror. I thought I could give it to Gessa... but it was kind of trash. I looked into it, but someone else looked back.

I dropped it in shock. It was an orc. It looked sort of like me, but I knew it to not be me.

I looked again, thinking that maybe my new features were just shocking, and I saw just me... and not who I had just seen.

I took the mirror, and we set up camp by the roadside.

But not before those hands got to Barnabus.

When I came to, I was on the ground and Barnabus had my arm on my back in an armbar. He was yelling at me to snap out of it. I said, "I... I'm alright now!"

"You better not be fucking bluffing! You just roared and made sounds like an animal just a second ago! Where did I meet you at the start of your adventure?" he yelled, pushing my arm harder.

"The Black Dragon! We drank seven beers! You called me a mongrel who humps his mother!" I yelled back.

He released me then, and said, "Fucking hell, Zach... I knew orcs have a thing for bloodlust, but seriously... I never knew it was like this!"

I stared back at him, on the ground. The images were gone for a while.

"I need to summon the next one. I need to somehow fight it." I said.

He growled in anger and said, "Fucking fine! We'll go through every fucking demon on your list! But after that, I'm through! You're not getting sucked up in anymore of your fucking devils and bullshit! I'm not gonna see you turn into some sort of satanist goat fucker!"

I sighed, shaking, and sat beside Barnabus. I told him to be ready in case anything happens. I took out the mirror, and I knew the orc was there, because his hands were around *my* throat now.

I said the words, "Sinful Sake."

"What kind of bullshit demon words are those?" Barnabus said. I turned to him and told him to shush, and looked back at the mirror, and was shocked to see a bloody orc grinning at me. He looked like he had just been through a great battle.

"You called? Son of violence?" he said.

"I need you to stop this. I don't want to hate, or suffer, or kill. I want this to end."

"You do not even know our language... You are a shame to me." he said.

"I... Are you Gar?" I asked.

He laughed, and said, *"I am the father of all orcs. I am violence. We were brought into this world for ONE purpose. To kill."*

"We can have peace. Not all orcs are like you." I said.

"You are me, son of woe. I am you. We were brought into this world together, with blood. Yes, the blood of a bus. With pain." he said.

"Bus. I know that means vagina... I know that is also an insult to many women." I said.

"It's really not so bad. Women bleed all the time... either from bus, or from us." he said.

"No one needs to die." I said.

"You do. You are on the path to our lord. You and your bus... Gessa." he said.

"I would never hurt her. I would never hurt her like people have to her, like people have to her mother." I said.

"Come now... A small, teenage bus. Join us. Join your heritage. Kill, rape, and destroy. It is the pleasure... You won't find anything like a teenage bus! The wheels on the BUS go round and round..." he said.

"Why can't you be civil? Be kind, and nice, and peaceful? WHY ARE YOU ALL TORMENTING ME!!" I yelled.

"Because you are a bus. If you will not take her... then I will. And then she will die. Perhaps when she is dead? It'll be the same either way... Although you won't get the pleasure of having her fight you..." he said.

I smashed the mirror, and it cut my hand, and blood trickled down.

I saw him in the shards, laughing at me... saying, *"I'm gonna always be here... Zach... I'm always here..."*

I put my face in my bloody hands.

Barnabus said, "I don't know what the hell you saw in that mirror... but it sounded like you were having a one sided conversation."

"I... I need to stay away from Gessa... I can't go near her..." I said.

Barnabus sighed again, and said, "I'm going to stay with you, Zach. I'll be here."

18

Meaningless Suffering

I wanted to ask Edgar a question... even though it may seem kind of off, and the past is the past, but I had wondered about it for a long time. It was the basis of the fear I had of Edgar. I wanted to know why.

I talked to Edgar, while we were in private and Patricia was further out in the woods, as she was having a rough day, with "cramps," I asked Edgar, "Why did you rape my mother?"

He immediately turned pale, looked to the ground, sighed, then looked me into the eyes, and said, "I thought I loved her."

"That's no excuse." I said.

"I know. It will never be enough, and it can never be justified. I heard her in my head... sort of nice, different than my previous love that turned evil and horrible. At first I thought it was her, the old love, but she was not like her in the least. The voice that mimicked her was the same one though, the old voice of hate."

"But... why?? You just wanted to be with a pretty woman!" I was starting to get a little angry. I wanted him to say because he just wanted to, because he was just evil and a horrible person. I could tolerate that. I couldn't tolerate a confused schizophrenic.

"I suppose she was very pretty... she tried to understand me, unlike Marcos and Gestas. She tried to care. She talked to me, like a person, and not like I was a beast, or a demon, or some sort of monster." he said.

"So the first person who showed you kindness you showed horror to." I said.

"I believed in all the horror, I was horror, I actually thought I *was* a demon. I thought that I was in Hell, literally and figuratively, and that I deserved it, too. I cannot tell you what was going on in my mind... but I tried to fight the voices, as I tried to do what they said."

"What? You can't do both! That sounds like you flipped a coin and got heads and tails at the same time!" I said.

"In a way, that's exactly what it's like. I flipped a coin, wanting to know what I should do, and in a way, it disappeared. There was no right path for me. I was lost." he said.

Frustrated, I walked away. Why couldn't he just be a monster? *Why* couldn't he just hate everything! He never showed a hint of wanting to rape me. He never looked at me funny, not even when I was naked! If he attacked me, I could've just killed him, and be done with this feeling... I didn't want to have to make peace with a man who was my genetic father by raping my mother!

For a while, it was sort of like he was my pet monster. A beast, even less than Barcough and Jillian. But... he was just a man! He was just struggling to live a life, trying to fucking make heads or tails of living like we all did! I just wanted to swear and shout at him, to get some sort of evil reaction, and I did just that when he followed me, because he was fucking worried about me!

"You fucking rapist! You're a monster! I don't want to fucking have two fathers! I don't want any of this shit! I just want to go home, but I don't have a fucking home! I don't even have a life! I bring people back to fucking life! You're worse than me! You must be worse than me! You... fucking... fucking..." and I started crying as Edgar was looking at me, after he flinched at every insult thrown at him.

He didn't know what to do. He didn't dare to try and hug me. He just let me cry, and cry, and cry.

When I had finished, and he was sitting on the ground in front of me, he said, "If it makes you feel any better, I've killed more people than you ever have, even without necromancy."

"Yeah... and you ate them too!" I yelled.

"I did." he said.

I screamed at him, "You're not supposed to admit it! You're supposed to try to cover it up, and I'm supposed to figure it out, and then beat you to a pulp!"

"You don't even care why I ate them?" he said.

"I... I guess... I don't know! Why? Why, then??" I said.

"I thought they were going to eat me." he said.

"So you're eating cannibals. Great. Just great. You're just a serial killer! You enjoy killing and eating people!!" I yelled.

"No. I don't. I was terrified of everyone, of everything, I thought that surely they would try to kill me, me and those I cared for... but then it turned out it was the people I cared for who hated me the most. I thought this... and then later, it was also true. I lost everyone." he said.

"Why? Why? What was the point?" I said.

"It was my illness. There was no point. There was never any point. The suffering I endured and caused was meaningless." he said.

This made me cry again.

I was created because of meaningless suffering.

I took off my shirt, as Edgar averted his gaze, and yelled, "You're a rapist! You gonna rape me, too?? Rape your own daughter??"

"No... Gessa..." he said. He was looking very sad.

But I kept on yelling.

I said, "Look at me!! You created me!! You made me, because of some stupid urge!!"

He looked into my angry eyes, and began crying.

I was angry, shirtless, breasts to the wind. And he was just fucking crying.

I wanted to hit him!! I wanted him to attack me!! I wanted to feel what my mother felt, and hate him all the more because of it!!

But he was just crying, staring into my eyes.

"I'm a bastard, Edgar!! Marcos was more of a father to me than you could ever be!! He loves me! HE CARES FOR ME!! You don't care about anything!" I said.

"I... lo-" he started saying.

"Don't fucking say it! Don't you *ever* fucking say it! Go fucking die!!" I yelled.

He sighed, got up, and walked away.

I followed him, wondering where he was going, saying, "Ed-Edgar... I didn't mean it..."

He took out his knife, and I screamed as he rammed it into himself.

"PATRICIA!!" I screamed.

She came sprinting through the woods to us, she was fast, and she didn't need to be called after the first scream. She quickly went to Edgar, removed the knife, and began bandaging him, keeping pressure on the wound. It looked like he stabbed himself close to the heart.

I was next to her and Edgar, and Edgar was wearily holding onto consciousness. I stammered, "Ed-Edgar! Please don't die! Don't die! I love you, ok? You care for me too, right? I care for you! Don't fucking die!"

He smiled, and tried saying that it was ok, but all he got out was "ok."

"Don't die or I'll bring you back to life!" I said, "If you die, I'll make you kill everyone for me! I'll become a murderer, even worse than you! I'll kill the entire world!!"

He sort of blinked, and looked kind of sleepy. I slapped him! I wanted to wake him the fuck up! But he was slowly closing his eyes. It felt like I was stabbed in the heart too. I told Patricia to kiss him!

"Huh??" she said, then quickly went back to work, holding in the blood.

"Kiss him now!!" I yelled.

She quickly did, and I could see him sort of waking up in surprise. I helped keep the pressure on his wound.

"Kiss him until he's better! Just... Just kiss him!" I said.

So she did, and Edgar slowly put his arm around her head, and she stroked his.

The wound was bad.

But he didn't lose consciousness.

Patricia quickly told me to start stitching up the wound, then kissed him some more.

It was like sewing, right? I could sew, right? With hands shaking, I stitched his wound closed. Thankfully Edgar wasn't a wimp when it came to pain, and Patricia distracted him from the pain that he undoubtedly went through because of my inexperienced, nervous hands.

He lived. He fucking lived. And I cried and cried next to him, Patricia looked at me, but I just yelled at her to keep kissing him.

I let them kiss for a long while, even though there wasn't any point to it anymore, and I had stopped crying. "Let's take him back to camp." I eventually said.

We carried him underneath his arms, and he was stupidly happy. "Am I dead?" he said.

"Fucking shut up." I said, "Or I'll make Patricia do even more things."

She stammered protests, but I told her to shut up too.

We sat him down by the fire, and he seemed sort of out of it, and just grinned into the flames.

"What... What was that about bringing Edgar back to life?" Patricia eventually asked me.

"I'm a necromancer. The hunters attacked our friend, a mountain lion, and I made them kill each other after Edgar killed one of them. All I need is one corpse, and I can kill." I said.

"Oh... kay... um... This isn't some sort of joke?" she said.

"What do you think?" I said to her seriously.

She looked deep into my eyes, my eyes that held no lies, and she quickly looked away.

I thought about making her fuck him. But I figured he was alive, and that was reward enough. We sat in the firelight, and stayed awake all night. Patricia was now very nervous around me, and made sure to not turn her back on me, and I wanted to make sure Edgar didn't die.

But Edgar fell asleep, and I hugged him goodnight. Fucking schizophrenic.

Patricia said, as Edgar was sleeping, making loud, heavy breathing sounds, "Are you going to kill me?"

"Fuck no. You saved Edgar's life. Without you, I would have a dead father person. I don't really know what to call him, so I guess I'll just call him Edgar." I said.

"How... How can the daughter of a Blunt Knight be a necromancer?" she asked.

"I don't have a clue. I guess I just could do it, while pretty much everyone else can't. My mother could, but can't anymore. Maybe it runs in families." I said.

"*Would* you kill me? If I asked you to admit your crimes to the families whose fathers are dead?" she said.

I said, "Yes."

She became quiet for a good while, but eventually said, "How can I trust you? How can anyone trust you?"

"You can't. Just know that I don't want to kill, and have only ever killed in self defense, or to save my friends." I said.

"What if someone fought you to save their friends who were attacking you?" she said.

"I'd kill them." I said.

"That's... an unfair approach. This is not like what I have heard of the Blunt Knights at all!" she said.

"I'm not a Blunt Knight." I said, "I always sort of thought that I kinda was... but I now know my ideals are different. I don't want my friends to die, no matter what the cost. And if I had to... I would bring them back to life to kill their killers."

"But that is meaningless vengeance! The ones who loved them would try and kill you, and it would never end!" She said.

"They better not have anyone who loves them then." I said.

"Gessa... I don't know what to say to you! This is not right! I will tell your father immediately!" she said.

"Do it." I said.

Frustrated and angry, she said she was going to sleep, and said I would be lucky if she was still here tomorrow.

I really wished I had some weed. I thought of the kiss she gave Edgar... I wanted a kiss like that. Maybe I could make her give me one like that...

I suddenly heard myself. I was saying make her do something.

Like raping.

I quickly went over to her and said I was sorry. That I wouldn't kill her, and that I didn't really know what to do. She was packing up to leave actually, trying to get away from me before I tried something crazy.

She said, "I can understand that seeing your father figure try to kill himself has brought some hard emotions on you. I will not leave, but I will have a long talk with your father. With both of them."

I sighed, and said that was alright. She was very attractive, and I didn't know why I was thinking of having her kiss me... I guess I was just lost and confused, like that bird she told us about.

And I was a dead bird brought to life by a necromancer.

19

The Force of Death

I heard Skull talking to me again in my dreams, and he said one word in orcish, for it was undoubtedly a he, "Heor." Run.

I was terrified of the fourth. The force of death, nameless. My pops was nameless for a while, for a vow, but my ma figured out his name, and I think he told her as he lay dying, and lived again. It was a revelation for each of them, a way to fight the death of their family members. A way to remember them. But I thought about the death I was fighting. How could I fight something nameless and could kill me? Was it some sort of poisonous gas?

I heard Gerich talking through Barnabus, hating me... I tried to not give into hating him back.

I found some cut marks on my wrists... and I knew it was Biona Callus's doing. I bandaged them and covered them up.

When I went hunting, I blacked out and found rabbits torn to pieces shaped in a smiley face around me... I knew it was Teckus. I decided to bury the rabbits, as all the meat was shredded and messied.

I had never bled so much as when I had been possessed by demons. I felt very tired all the time, and Barnabus often had to stop with me to rest. We decided to not go to Gessa, but we still walked, as Barnabus said it would be better if I kept my mind off things.

I wondered how many minds I had. I was losing the one I wanted.

Maybe... it was some sort of sickness? Some mental condition? Perhaps I was like Daisy, and had schizophrenia. Daisy... never mentioned anything like this. I did hear voices, I did see things, did she black out too? Did it make you forget, and hurt yourself, and kill? I wanted to take a bunch of pills and end this. One way or another.

I realized that was probably what the fourth wanted me to think about. But I couldn't help it. I thought about death. If Barnabus wasn't with me, I probably would've ended it. He always joked with me, and told me stories, and tried making me happy. He really did care for me.

I made him bind my hands so I wouldn't hurt anything else, but after I blacked out, he said I still managed to bite through the ropes and he quickly tried to stop me, but I bit him. Barnabus was rubbing his neck when I came to, and I could taste the blood in my mouth.

"B-Barnabus! A-Are you ok?" I said

"Yeah... Just a little scratch... Fucking orcs, do you fucking put a grindstone to those teeth of yours?" he said.

We kept walking, and Barnabus bound me even tighter, all the way up my arms. Gerich didn't even need whole words anymore, he could take syllables of every sound, of every sentence, and hate me all the more.

"You like it? Being a bound rag doll? Easy for someone to fuck you this way. I'd probably just hate fuck your bound and useless corpse!" he said.

I tried focusing on talking to Barnabus.

"You really should just kill him. The one that comes after us is nothing like us... Hell, we're even afraid of it! You should be afraid too. Don't give in to that fear. Fight it! Hate it! Or you will die. I only want what's best for you, you ugly little mama's boy." Gerich said.

"You seem *kind of out of it? I* don't *know what to do...* I wish I could just get someone to help you, but I don't trust leaving you alone... *There's nowhere safe for you."* Barnabus and Gerich said.

I wish I could just cover my ears, and be deaf.

I saw Biona Callus whenever I tripped, and I'd always be tripping, not focusing on my feet or through her will. It looked and felt like she pushed me to the ground. Barnabus always had to help me up.

We went to a small, harmless stream, and when I went down to get a drink, Biona Callus arose again, and grabbed my face and brought me into the water, and she was kissing me, but I couldn't breathe. My lungs felt like they were going to explode, and Barnabus struggled to pull me out, but Biona Callus was pulling me in with her, kissing me. Finally, she let go, and waved goodbye with a horrible, evil smile.

I sputtered up water and gasped for breath.

"Listen, Zach... drowning is not a good way to go... Don't fucking kill yourself!" Barnabus said.

I saw Biona Callus, rubbing herself around and around behind him.

I wish I could just shut my eyes, and be blind.

We made sure to stay away from everyone, after I told Barnabus about Teckus. Barnabus looked at the book, and even looked at a few other pages, but he said it was just gruesome pictures and descriptions of evil. I only saw blank pages. "So *you're a* little *fucking joke*ster, eh, Teckus... Well *how's this* for a joke? *You* get out of my little guy and go fuck some more of those orcish sluts of yours! Yeah, I've fucked plenty o' orcish sluts, I'll just *call* them *Teckus* from now on!!" he yelled at me.

Gerich had told me to call Teckus.

I was wary of listening to anything Gerich said, in fact I tried my hardest to ignore him, but Teckus was an orc, at least he looked like one. Was he the one talking to me as Skull in my dreams?

"Sinful Sake." I said.

"Fucking goddamnit! Don't ever say your demon words! I don't want to hear them!" Barnabus said.

I immediately felt like someone was beating me up, and Barnabus was surprised, as I bounced back and forth, from hits that only I could feel. Wham! In the face. Wham! In the stomach. Twisting my arms, attempting to break them, but Barnabus held me down, but I still felt like I was being kicked over and over again, in every part of my body, even in the balls... It hurt like the worst beating ever, and after it was over, I shook on the ground, fearing to be hit again, and in so much pain.

I wish I couldn't feel that pain.

I wish I couldn't feel anything.

Barnabus was crying over me, saying he's never been this worried about another human being. "Well, orc being." he said, "I've never seen you like this! You look like you're barely alive!"

We stopped for the night, and immediately I noticed something in the dark... It was nothing. No sounds of Gerich, no sight of Biona Callus, Teckus wasn't trying to hurt me... It was just silent, and dark. I quickly started a fire, but that made everything around me seem even darker, quieter, and scarier. There were no sounds of night birds, even the insects left me to peace. Except for the moon, which was full, it was completely silent and dark. I was thankful for that big shining globe in the sky.

But a cloud passed over the moon, and it was dark again.

Immediately, I felt a very intense feeling of paranoia, listening to the quiet. Barnabus was out taking a crap, said he hadn't taken a proper crap in awhile, since he always had to watch me. I desperately wanted him to come back. I didn't want to be alone in this... silence.

I started imagining things in the darkness around me. I saw the outlines of a figure in the corner of my vision, turned to look, but there was nothing there. I thought I heard scratching, coming from behind me, and I turned and looked for the source of the sound, but it was gone. I imagined all sorts of things that the fourth could be. Was it the Grim Reaper?

Was it the dead come out of their tombs, to bring me back into the earth with them?

I immediately heard rustling coming out of the forest, and in horror, unable to move, I looked at it... and Barnabus came out, swearing. I breathed a sigh of relief.

He sat down next to me, and said, "This sure is a spooky night. Would be a great time for ghost stories, but I think you're afraid enough as it is. You're shaking! No one... else... is trying to hurt you, are they?"

I shook my head.

"Good. Maybe it was like some sort of fever, or somethin', that just needed time to heal... yeah... that's it." Barnabus said.

I saw a shadow from the fire, that wasn't Barnabus's or mine, moving, of someone or something sitting down right beside me. It felt like my heart stopped because I was so frightened.

"I do love the night..." Barnabus said, "So peaceful, dark. As if the entire world's gone to bed."

I stared at the shadow moving with the flames.

Then the shadow was all around me.

Everywhere I looked, it was there, in the dark.

Nothing, darkness, and shadows.

I ran from this thing that seemed to have trapped me. I ran down the road, and I could feel it chasing me, trying to subdue me. TRYING TO BRING ME TO HIM!!

I kept on running, but it would try to corner me, appearing before me, behind me and in front of me. I shut my eyes, but I had flashes of a giant skeleton, beckoning me.

So I kept them open, even though all I could see was darkness around me, and it was night.

I just ran and ran, I didn't know where I was going to, even what I was running from, but I ran.

I got on top of the hill, and the moon shone again. I looked up at it, and it looked like some sort of dead thing, some threat of death. And then I knew the words.

I said the silent words.

And then I couldn't hear.

I couldn't see.

I couldn't feel my body.

I didn't know who I was, or what was happening, but I knew I would die.

Maybe I was dead.

But in the darkness, I felt something... something marvellous, I felt someone holding my... my hand. That's what that feeling was.

Then I heard something. I heard Skull talking in orcish to me, shouting at the demons, warding them back. And I heard a woman say my name.

And then I saw an orcish warrior, noble and proud, leading me back to the land of the living. And then I opened my eyes, and saw Gessa over me, holding my hand, crying.

"G-Gessa?" I said.

"Zach! You look terrible! Are you ok?? You didn't answer! You looked like you were dead!" she said.

There was a man and a woman behind her, one looked sort of like some wild barbarian man, and the other looked like a black haired woman knight.

Barnabus was yelling out, looking for me. Gessa said, "Barnabus! Over here!" and Barnabus ran up to us.

"Fuckin, fuckin, hell... Don't scare me like that, Zach! I thought I'd lose you for good!" Barnabus said.

Gessa just hugged and hugged me, and boy did it hurt. I thought about the demons.

I felt death.

I felt the pain of death.

I felt the suffering and the pain of death.

I felt the hate of the suffering and the pain of death.

And all I could think of was Gessa, of my family, of love and joy to be around the living. And I knew how I could get rid of the demons. Not totally... Not completely. For each one represented something of life and death. But I knew where to start.

I handed the book to Gessa.

I could tell the demons were furious. I heard Gerich shouting at me, hating me, but I had heard that all before. All of my wounds felt like they were reopened, Biona Callus lashing at me and hurting me, me bleeding and hurting, but I had become used to it. I felt Teckus, trying to get me to kill, I felt his wrath, but I calmed myself, and didn't black out. I felt the horrible fear, consuming me, forever, for all time, but I lived, for now, with what was right in front of me.

I kissed Gessa, and she kissed me.

20

Sickness of the Soul

Zach looked horrible! He was wounded, and bloody, a walking wreck! He had scars all over his face, all over his body! His hands were bound, and I asked Barnabus what the hell he was doing to him! Zach quickly said it was alright, that he asked to be bound, then looked at me strangely, like someone else, but shook his head and was Zach again.

I looked at the book that was whispering to me.

I didn't want to open it.

We sat there for a while, and I just hugged Zach over and over. We were both crying. I wiped off my tears with my shirt, and his as well. We got caught up in everything that happened to each other, but Zach had a hard time listening to me, he seemed to be hearing someone else when I spoke and would sometimes ask for me to repeat some things. He looked absolutely terrified! But as the sun was coming over the horizon, he breathed out a sigh of relief and said he just wanted to look at it for a while. I sat with him, and held his hand. He didn't want to seem to let me go, and I held him fast.

"Who... Who hurt you? Who did this to you?" I asked him.

He paused for a second, and said, "Gerich, Biona Callus, Teckus, and the nameless."

I didn't know who in hell those people were, and I asked him who they were.

He said, "I don't really know... I think they're demons. Maybe not. They're in the book."

"How can something in a book hurt you?" I asked.

"I don't know." he said.

I slowly opened the book... Necromancy, Life After Death, by the Lich. I saw the names Zach had said, and that horrible picture drawn in the next page... but underneath the drawing, looked sort of like some sort of seal, with strange words. I read the page on the demons, and saw Zach's name, and so many other people's names on the page. It looked like the page was drenched in blood.

"All... All these people... Why did they write their names here? Why is the page stained with blood?" I asked Zach.

"Huh? Only my name is there..." he said, "Maybe you can read the words while I can't? The pages are all blank to me, besides the first one." This spooked me.

I turned the page, and the first thing I saw was a picture of a woman, with black hair, commanding hordes of the dead. It said she would bring the world to ruin. Making it die, and live again, and the cycle of Life and Death will be overthrown. It called her the Lady of Life and Death. The Queen of All.

That's what the bird called me.

I read the writing on the next page, and it said, *"Welcome, you are the chosen one. The one who has accepted the sickness, and has died and lived again. Welcome, my child, to life after death. You may command the dead, subjugate the living, and have complete control of the flow of the world.*

But always remember who your master is.

I am the Lich, and I have created the very first instance of necromancy. It is a sickness, and very soon it will infect the entire world, maybe even every world, and allow me dominance over death. Now, finally, I have complete and everlasting power. You may worship me as your god, if you wish, but I advise you to cast down idols and gods and worship yourself over all others, for all gods must die, and you will never die, for you are already dead."

I began to get very fearful of this.

The organism that causes necromancy is practically invisible, masking itself in the body, in the bloodstream, in growth and decay. It works very well on organic tissue... but I have found difficulties having plants accept the organism. I created one tree, one seed out of very, very many, which is dead but still alive. It is a useless specimen, as it does not fruit, does not seed, and looks to all like a burnt and withered tree. I fear it is simply a dead host for the organism, and cannot sustain the life needed for necromancy, unlike every living animal.

The dead are curious to me. After a while, they cannot remember anything, and it is simply the organism acting as if it is alive, but I have had conversations with the recently dead. Is it the human soul, grasping onto their remains? Is it the organism trying to continue the shadow of life? The brain is dead, cannot think, cannot know, although does stay alive for a little while after death. Is it just memories of a life gone? Or is it more? This has led me into research on souls, and how they may be dominated. I am making great strides in this work, but I must ask myself if my labor will fruit. For what is a soul?

I have never believed in souls, in fact I thought they were fairytale nonsense, a way for religion to control your mind and actions. My work would be considered blasphemy to all but the most disdainful of holy men, but I take pleasure in the fact that if I cannot have their souls, I will have their bodies and minds. For all must meet me, in the end, as I walk the earth immortal and omnipotent. It is too bad that true knowledge, like souls, is impossible to grasp completely... As no matter what you know, there is always more to know. So learn, and strike down those who would claim to know all.

This is why we have books.

The souls of my generals are trapped in these pages, their bodies used to make the leather, the paper, the bindings, so that they may live on and continue to work, for all time. A sickness of the soul was all that was needed to bind them... And if it is not the soul, then it is their mind, their body, and their will, and what is more of a soul than that?

I envision that many will take on this sickness... to try and learn the secrets that are in this book. They will all die a complete and everlasting death, their names only remembered on the first page."

I frantically told Zach to stay with me, that I would save him. He asked me to repeat that, saying he heard someone telling him that he was doomed. I asked him how he could stay so calm when someone was telling him such horrible things! He said he didn't really believe them, and that he was just happy to be near me again. I kissed him again.

The book made my head hurt, after I tried reading more pages, and I couldn't get past the next sentence saying, *"Take your time. There is always more to learn."*

I shut the book in anger.

I didn't want to wait! I wanted to cure Zach *now*! I had to! I had to... I needed him to be alive! I didn't want him to turn into a corpse I would have to have conversations with! There must be a way!

But we took our time, and found a sheltered area where we could be in peace for a little while. I wanted to take the bindings off Zach, but he said someone else would try to rape and kill me! He looked so frightened when he told me this! This made me angry. Whoever this Lich guy was, he already brought my best friend into Hell. No! Not Hell! He was alive... Yes. He would still be alive.

Edgar was worn out from his near death experience, but Patricia made sure to take care of him if I couldn't. She had a long conversation with Edgar, telling him to be a father to me, to lead me on the right track, and even if he said I already had a father she forced him into being one for me, so he promised to be a real father in my life.

I think Patricia's beautiful face made him keep that promise.

I could practically take care of myself from now on, but Edgar strove to care for me in other ways... feeling ways. It made me so angry! But he sympathized with my anger, and told me stories about the past, and that he couldn't even remember his real name. "What??" I said to him.

"I think it was Jacob? Or... Barnabus? Oh... no, I know those people... All I am now is Edgar. That's the name that stuck, after being lost for so long. I was... Balthazar. Maybe that was my real name, but I'm pretty sure it's a character I created, that was my pseudonym. I sure don't look like a Balthazar! I get shivers when I hear that name..." he said.

"Balthazar, Balthazar, Balthazar." I said to him.

He laughed and said I was right, it was just a silly name. He really did try to step it up a notch, even though I just tried to get on his nerves.

I remembered the Lady of Life and Death's midnight hair... and I looked at Patricia suspiciously. She sure didn't look like any queen of necromancers I've ever seen, maybe a queen of something, but not a queen of necromancers. She was very nice with me, even though I snapped at her sometimes. She tried to understand me, and teach me, like my father has, peace and mercy. This made me sad that after being a daughter of a Blunt Knight for all my life, I still needed teachings of peace and mercy...

She said, "We must always learn of peace and mercy, lest we forget and cause evil." I bet her and my father would get along swell.

I still just wanted to kiss her! The more I thought about it, the more frustrated I was! I was a girl though! I'm not gay! I said this over and over... I wish I could talk to Zach's mother about it, she was a bit of a bisexual. Her and Zach's father have even gone to strip clubs together once! And they enjoyed the same things! This drove me nuts in the past, and I was sure they would end up regretting it, but still, they remained faithful to eachother... but still, I wondered who all those friends of theirs were, who I never heard of before, who told Zach stories about their sex life! Were they cheating on each other together?? At the same time? Maybe they were swingers?? I would have to get the truth of this from them, one day. I quickly looked away from Patricia's bottom, embarrassed and frustrated.

At least I had Zach, who I kissed endlessly.

He was a different kind of love.

I didn't even think that he was older than me, that it would be sort of weird, I just cared for him with all my heart. He told me stories of his adventure so far, and he'd been through so much, just for that fucking book.

And now the book was threatening to consume his soul.

"What??" Zach said, when I whispered something in his ear, "I can't! That would be... I don't know!"

We agreed we would wait for a while.

At least until Teckus was gone, and Biona Callus wasn't tempting him, and he could hear my words over Gerich, and he didn't have that awful fear of his.

So I tried to calm my mind myself. Meditation was very difficult for me these days, but I tried in a peaceful clearing a bit away.

I gave up after I remembered Patricia's naked breasts, like a real woman's.

No! I had to try! Even if you have sort of positive thoughts, you can't let them suck you in! You gotta just let them pass! Let them pass...

And I listened to the birds, let the clouds pass in the sky, heard the insects making buzzing noises, and breathed in... and out...

Over and over again.

Like how I wanted with Zach.

Goddamnit!

I was walking back to the camp, swearing under my breath at stupid meditation, fucking Buddha and all his goddamned wisdom, and all that crap... Barnabus heard me and said he never knew I had such a shit mouth.

"What? My mouth is clean as all can be! You fucking bum!" I said, a little angry.

He laughed and said, "Hey, you little cunt, you got a stick shoved up there? Take it out, before you start growing a tree like a man!"

"Fuck you! You drunk old... *Komodo dragon!*" I said.

He looked at me for a second, and then burst out laughing, and said between laughs, "You... you..." and laughed again, "Don't take it seriously! I guess you're a grown adult woman now, with insults and everythin'! Komodo dragon! Never heard that before! Is that an insult to my breath, or my hygiene?" and he laughed and hooted some more.

I angrily stalked away.

Even though I was kind of salty at Barnabus for a while, he took me by the arm and said, "Little lady... you should know to never take an insult personally, because if you do, you let other people's words distinguish who you are. You need to tell yourself who you are, but I don't mind being a Komodo dragon. Actually, it's sort of a compliment!"

"Don't let compliments distinguish you either." I said.

"Very wise, little Gess. Very wise." he said, nodding his head. He told me of all the trouble he went through trying to figure out necromancy, trying to learn about it to help me get rid of it. I thought I didn't want to get rid of it... it was sort of like protection. But what if it made me lose my soul? I thought hard about that, and thanked Barnabus, saying we'd find a way.

So, this was my family now. All that was left, as the rest were scattered to the winds. Barnabus, the drunk old uncle, who really was very wise, and very kind, but didn't show it off to everyone, and prefered everyone to think of him as a foul mouthed drunk. Edgar... my new father, who I'll still always call Edgar, no matter how much he's changed, and no matter how much Patricia told him to try and be my father. Patricia, the good hearted knight, who was bound to get me in trouble with my real father... and she was absolutely gorgeous, stunning, and graceful... and Zach, my best friend in the world. I sort of thought of him as my boyfriend, but didn't tell him yet. I never had a real boyfriend before... and he was going to be my boyfriend whether he liked it or not. So there.

21

Remember Love

Gessa had talked about wanting to have sex! But I gave an excuse, that really was a very valid excuse, that the demons would end up causing harm if we got intimate. She was too young, my best friend, and I don't think it would be very pleasant, with my hands bound because I didn't want Teckus to kill her, hearing Gerich ruining every nice sentence, seeing Biona Callus who made me think differently on gorgeous women of late, and... whatever the last one was.

But I would try to get rid of the demons. It was just a puzzle... a horrible, evil puzzle that wanted to kill me.

And bring me to him.

I saw him whenever I closed my eyes for a long period of time. That would be my fate, a skeleton, dead, and somehow warped and twisted, a servant to the Lich, if I didn't figure this out... I had a long conversation about it with Gessa, because she sympathized, feeling very sad for me, empathized as she also had strange creatures talking to her, like the birds, and understood what I was going through, to an extent. No one can know what it's like to have these demons. Except... for all the other people on the page, whom I could see now. They showed up one by one, seeming to splatter the page with blood after every name, until it was completely red. I wasn't alone. I wasn't the only one. But I wondered what had happened to those people.

I wondered if they were anything like the nightmares I had.

Each name would stick out to me, each name would paint a person in my mind, either how the name was written or how it sounded in my head. Each one was brought to ruin by the demons, brought to the Lich and snuffed out eternally, and each one died a horrible death.

So I decided to start with Gerich. I told him... I loved him? Would love be the opposite of hate? He knew I was lying, and laughed at me for trying something so stupid. He said many people had tried that, and they were all idiots.

It was hard to focus on Gerich, though, whenever I tried to figure him out... because Biona Callus's naked body would be in my sight whenever I was hurt. I ignored her, no matter how much she tried to get me to do what she wanted. She tried taking me out into the woods once, like Shekinah had, even saying nice things to me, but I ran for it, tripped and fell, and then I would have to deal with Teckus.

He seemed to be able to hit me, even if I hadn't summoned him. I felt his foot on my back, pushing me hard into the dirt. He wanted me to kill, and I could tell was angry with me because he sort of lost that "humor" he had, like stacking dead animal heads or painting a picture with blood. It made me sick, whenever I found something he had done with my own hands, and I fought him with all my might whenever we were by the others.

I realized I was starting to call the demons and I "we."

I just wanted to be I again, but it was always a we. Gerich was the most prominent, like the book said, Biona Callus was horrible, like a pretty woman who really has a heart of coal, Teckus always tried fighting me, and the other... I just feared for my life whenever it would turn night, and I would "see" it, watching me... Something. I don't really know, but it was most associated with the Lich.

I decided I'd start with Teckus then, if Gerich was being so impossible.

I thought of peace... but immediately, he hit me. I couldn't subdue him, he used my own body against me, making the pain with invisible blows.

I tried over and over again to think of peace, and didn't put up a fight back. I could've sworn I could hear him laughing...

So after I was beaten to a pulp by an invisible demon, I tried to figure out Biona Callus. She beckoned me into the woods... But I was terrified! I wasn't about to willingly fall into her hands! Probably if we had sex, I'd end up shoving my dick into a bear trap! A real one! She seemed to hate men...

I wanted to be with Gessa, and not Biona Callus. This would make Biona Callus furious, and would slice at me, clawing at me with her long fingernails. She said she would rape me then.

I tried being gentle to her, even tried giving her a hug... but it turned out that I almost fell off the edge of the cliffside we were near. I looked down at the drop, and quickly walked back to the others.

The others had finally unbound me, and it felt nice... I realized I couldn't live my life in fear of demons forever.

I tried thinking of courageous thoughts, whenever it would turn night, but I just thought of the shadow of death, and I'd always see monsters in the shadows, my own imagination playing tricks on me. In a way, the last one was the hardest, because it could be anything, it was nothing, and I didn't know what to do for it. I thought maybe the force of life? How the heck could I show something so dark, sinister, and frightening, life?

I still felt very paranoid, as if something was watching me, and unlike the others, was just waiting. Just waiting for me to die. Maybe... there was no fourth? Maybe it was just the writer playing tricks on me? Whenever

I'd think this shadows would move around me, seemingly on their own, with no source...

It was maddening! All of this! I just sat with Gessa, taking a break from trying to figure them out, but there was never a break! But at least Gessa would kiss me, and I'd feel better... I wanted to figure out a way to let her down, too... She was my best friend in the world, and I didn't ever want to ruin that friendship. But I think she didn't *really* want to have sex, I think she was just grateful to me for getting her the book...

But then she let it slip that she thought I was her boyfriend.

"Gessa... You're my best friend. We don't have to be boyfriend and girlfriend."

"Too bad. I'm not losing you. I love you."

"And I love you, too. But..." thinking of Barnabus's words, I really did have to think about it before I tied it in with someone. I really did love Gessa, but I didn't want to hurt her by accident... Was I already hurting her?

"But what?" Gessa asked.

"But... but... You're four years younger than me!" I said. That'd probably do the trick.

"And Barnabus and Mary are ages apart. So what? We don't have to have sex... I'm just curious, is all, and I never had a boyfriend..." she said.

"I..." this made me sort of sad, and I figured what was the harm of it? "Ok, Gessa. I'll be your boyfriend."

"Good. Because if you want my help, you're going to have to be. I don't want to have to bring you back to life just so I can be with you." she said. I guess I could see the logic in this...

But still, I made sure to let her know that she meant a lot to me, that I would never hurt her, no matter how romantic we were. But that would just make it worse! I wasn't about to say something mean to her, to push her away and hurt her... but... I didn't know what to do!

At least I didn't fear, and hate, and suffer, and feel pain around her.

I was thankful for that... I just felt happy to be around her. I tried talking with her about the old days, but that just made us both sort of sad. I showed her the coyote pups instead.

"Awww! They're just so adorable! What are their names? Where did you get them?" she said, cradling Nickles.

"They're Aphrodite and Nickels. I... was hunting... and I hunted their mother... and we ate her..." I said.

She was shocked, but sort of seemed to remember something, and said, "Well, I've done a lot of bad things too... I even ate meat! At first I felt like some sort of monster, but I realized that's just part of nature, and I *was* starving..."

"I wish I never had to kill to eat again. I wish I never had to kill." I said.

"But... But what about the people who hurt you! Who want to kill you, and the ones you love!" she said.

"I don't care. I would rather have people live, than have to kill them. I would do anything to bring them back to life."

"As I would... As I can." Gessa said... but also with Gerich. This was a different tone than what I normally heard... I wondered if there might be something there.

I told Gessa to play along with this, and just say whatever that came to mind, even if my words didn't make sense. "I wish I could talk to the woman that birthed me, my birth mother. I will never know her, and I desperately want to know who she was." I said.

"That's alright... I wish there was some way *to be with* my father and mother... *all of my family..."* she and Gerich said.

"Where did they go?" I asked.

"Huh? I told you. *They have gone* to see your dad and ma! *They went* to get the Chariot back *together*!"

"All... All at once?" I asked.

Gessa was looking a little confused, but still talked, saying with Gerich, *"Maybe* mashed potatoes taste good with a hint of gravy, *I don't know*! This game is difficult... *He* had a she who *took* a wee on the tree, with *them* and a hen, *away* from the barn! I'm just going to *look at the book...*"

"That's good, Gessa. I need to see it first, though." I said, and took out the book. I saw four names underlined with blood, Hannah, Indigo, Paul, and Naomi, amidst the other names which seemed fainter, in a way.

And then more, and more, and more names would be underlined, all of them, every single one.

I asked Gerich, "Are... Are these all your family?"

"Everyone is family." I heard him say in the wind.

I took out the torn picture of Gessa that Barnabus had given back to me, and looked at it. Gessa was still in the middle, torn in half, but Gerich was on one half, and four people were on the other.

"Asta Terro." I said.

And the pictures moved. The four people were trying to reach Gerich, and Gerich was looking back at them, just looking, resigned in his fate. Gerich turned to me and said, *"She will bring everyone to him."*

"I understand your hate now." I said.

Angry, he said to me, *"How could you ever. How can you ever understand my hate. You will never know the people I cared for, you will never love them. They are names in a book now."*

"You're right. I can never understand that feeling. But I will remember their names." I said.

"Say it! Say their names!" he yelled at me.

"Hannah, Indigo, Naomi, and... Paul." I said, without looking at the book.

He seemed to grow calmer at that. His hate filled eyes didn't seem so angry anymore, and he turned back to the people on the other half. I put them together, and they struggled to reach each other, but Gessa was in the middle of them.

Gessa was staring at me, wondering what I was doing. I told her that I needed her to take another picture of this picture. "Ok... I don't really see the point, but ok..." and she took out her camera and took a picture of it. It was still only a picture of a fragmented picture of Gessa...

"TRY AGAIN." Gerich said desperately.

I asked Gessa if she had a pen and a piece of paper, and she did, but when I tried to draw the picture of the people right, it wouldn't come out right from my hand. They looked all wrong, and I couldn't draw very well.

"TRY AGAIN!!" Gerich yelled.

"I can draw, if you want." That's right! Gessa was good at drawing, she could draw them! But she couldn't see the people, so I described them to her, telling her exactly how they looked, down to the minutest detail... and what came out of her hand... looked exactly like the picture of the people.

"Now. Draw Gerich. He is a thin man, sort of like Jacob, with an angular jaw and dark, furry eyebrows, an aquiline nose, very shallow cheeks, combed hair but not slick, has a muscular body with one bicep bigger than the other, a thin waist, powerfully built legs, and has these steel tipped boots on."

"I loved those boots. A gift from Naomi." Gerich said.

"What else is he wearing?" Gessa asked, as she drew the outline of Gerich.

"Doesn't matter." Gerich and I said.

Gessa seemed to notice the change in my voice, and was a little frightened, but drew Gerich with an arm over his family. When she was finished, he was moving with them, they were hugging and kissing him, and he never looked... so loved. So loving. "Remember me. My name is Rich." he said to me, and then the family resumed their poses and looked at me, happily as Gessa drew them. I kept the drawing in my pack, and remembered the names, Naomi, Hannah, Paul, Indigo, and Rich.

22

Kissing Wizards

I cried that night, thinking that Zach didn't want to be my boyfriend... that he thought I was just some dumb kid, even though he kissed me after I drew his demons, but quickly backed away, as it felt like someone else was kissing me, forcefully, not like Zach... He said he couldn't kiss me anymore.

I wanted to get rid of Teckus.

I wanted to fight Teckus, to kill him.

I thought it was strange that I believed Zach so wholeheartedly, but I knew there was something dark and sinister about that book, about necromancy. He thought he maybe just had schizophrenia, but he didn't act like my mother in the least, or even Edgar. He had asked Edgar for some pills, but Edgar said that it probably wouldn't work on him right, and that each case is different, anyway, and needs different medication. This made Zach sad, and made me sad that I found him that night...

Cutting his wrists.

I told him to stop, that he shouldn't hurt himself! That it was alright!

I wanted to go near him and hug him, but he quickly backed away. He said, "I see Biona Callus when I hurt myself... I don't know what to do for her... I think if I felt her pain, then I would be able to appease her. If I could only understand whatever she went through, I could get her to leave..."

"*Don't* you *ever* fucking hurt yourself again!" I yelled at him. He looked at me surprised, and I continued, "That's what she wants you to do! She wants to be just some dumb broad who wants to be figured out, and make you hurt yourself trying! She's... just a stupid bitch!"

"O-Ok..." he said.

I told him to come with me back to camp, and if he wants to stare at someone pretty, he could stare at either me or Patricia. He got a little embarrassed at this.

He tried telling me that he would never stare at me like some lustful idiot, but I told him to get help from Patricia, that she would fix his wounds.

I let out a tear. He did think I was pretty, didn't he?

I never thought like this before... I never felt so... unwanted, even when I was alone. I never tried to get the people at school to like me, I actually tried my hardest to leave them be... but I wanted Zach to like me. I angrily punched and kicked a tree, thinking why must boys be so difficult! Why did they think such stupid things!

So in the morning, I angrily didn't talk to or even look at Zach, and he could tell I was frustrated by something, and left me be. He's supposed to try harder then! Not leave me alone! It made me angry, so I stared at Patricia instead, imagining her. She caught me looking at her, and tried making conversation about good and all that stuff, so I ignored her too...

So instead I talked with Edgar and Barnabus, as we went to the next town as Edgar was getting low on medication. He usually never went into town, but he had to to get his medicine. He said it was worth it to be able to think clearly, even though he was always nervous around large groups of people. He always got a large supply of medicine whenever he did, and could go for months and months on end without ever having to approach civilization. Barnabus said he was a wack job, and Edgar said that a job at whacking would be fun.

There was a carnival in the town, and Edgar was very, very nervous, with all the flashing lights, drunken people, and roaring music. Patricia saw him as he fearfully didn't want to traverse through it, and gently held his hand, saying it was alright. She sort of dragged him through the carnival, and Patricia told us to enjoy ourselves, and they would be back later, as she was curious of Edgar's condition and the pharmacies around the country that the Wheel had set up.

Barnabus was getting drunker and drunker these days, and slyly bought a whole bunch of alcohol from a vendor, saying it was for a party. A party of one, I thought... He said he was happier when he didn't drink, sort of, a different sort of happy, but he always got more work done and was more focused when he was drunk. I didn't understand this at all, so thought I'd try some booze and see what all the fuss was about.

Zach didn't want to drink, and said it would screw up his focus, even though he desperately wanted the courage of being drunk so that whatever was behind that booth would go away. I asked him if he was high, as I also felt very paranoid when I smoked weed. "What? No! Of course not! I've only ever been drunk, and I always made mistakes when I was! If I got drunk... one of the three demons left would find some way to make me regret it..." I said he was missing out on not getting stoned, and said he should try it with me one day.

My anger was waning at Zach... and I realized I was just frustrated, confused, lonely, and miserable, and that I was probably being too harsh on him. That book didn't help in the least to relieve these feelings.

It said, after I read it some more, *"There will come a time when my nemesis will try and prevent me from dominating the world. He is a passerby, a no one, but he will be the tipping point for life, either for its destruction, or saving. He will, like the rest, come into my command however, and I am confident that no matter how forceful he is in life, he will die, like the rest.*

I have taken many cities throughout the continent, secretly, until they must all show their naked and dead flesh to the world and rise and bring its corruption. The animals are the easiest to subdue and work tirelessly to spread the organism. They show me the world as I wait, and as I slowly corrupt the Shazians. They are easily corrupted, they are corrupted themselves, thinking themselves uber humans and the ultimate race. All they need is someone to guide them in their faulty life.

You will have someone like this. Someone who believes themselves pure and incorruptible, you may have many. You will eventually have all. Call them your love, call them to your side and deceive them. The fragilest minds are the ones who are most pure, who believe in a good and evil, and try to walk the fine line between the two. And those who believe in love.

You will know that the only good and evil created is with your own will.

That love is a construct and a way to dominate.

That kindness is suffering."

Buddha had said sort of the same thing... that happiness is suffering... but not kindness.

"The others that have come to this planet have already been infected with the organism, and I am happy to know that soon it will spread throughout the stars and the many planes of life.

You may read more later. Your love is trying to get away from you, and you must catch them, control them, and enslave them completely. Have fun."

I looked at the last words, trying to read past it again, but all I could get was it telling me to have fun, over and over. I looked at Zach, and I felt terrible. Like I was the writer of the book, trying to control, dominate, and deceive.

So I decided to drink. I didn't want to think. I didn't want to have to love, to feel like I wanted to make love, and I stumbled around the carnival with Zach. "Tell... meeee about... sex! Yeah... what the fuck makes people want to dooo it? Do it... Do it... Do itttt... Is it, like, some sort of animalistic way to prevent ourselves from death? It's genes, and reproduction, and changing... It's evolution! Sex... is evolution! That's why it's so weird, because everything evolves!" I said to him, drunkenly, spilling the beer in my hand.

"You... haven't really drank at all, have you?" Zach said.

"Don'tttt worry, honeymuffindear... I can handle meself..." I said, hiccupping.

"It's... probably not very good for you..." he started.

"Zachariah! I am a lady! I can handle anything! I could *kill* the entire..." hiccup, "World! I am the Queen of theeee Universe!" I said, laughing.

"Is it something with the book?" he asked.

"Nononono... don't worry... I'm just so horny! Allll the fuckkkking... time! All the fucking time! Fucking time! I want... Patricia..." I said, getting sort of sad.

"What? But she's a lady knight!" he said.

"Yeah! She's this glorious... lesbo! That's what Jacob said... Am I lesbo, honeymuffinsugarpie?" I said.

"I... I don't *think* so... Are you? That's alright, if you are. You'll still be good ol' Gessa to me." he said, giving me a nice smile. I just wanted to kiss him! Dumb fucking orc.

"Ooh! Oh, oh! Let's get our fortunnnes told! Maybe it's really a naughty kissing booth!" I said, looking at a fortune teller's carriage.

"Ok... I have some money... just don't throw up everywhere, kay?" Zach said, and we went inside the carriage.

The fortune teller was this hooded man, and I couldn't see his face. Zach nervously handed him some money, and the fortune teller tried taking out some cards but I said, "Youuu gonna kiss? Or tell? Kiss and tell!"

He looked at me surprised, and coughed a little bit, and said, "What is it you wish to know?"

"Whooos this fuckin'... passerby! Are you him?" I said.

He shifted in his seat.

"I am Draziw." he said.

"That's a stuuupid name... You look like a Floyd!" I said, laughing.

He coughed again, and asked who we were.

"Yooouuu don't know? You're a bum fortune teller. I'm Gessa! This is my daaarlllllinnngggg Zach!" I said. Zach waved at him.

"Well, Zach and Gessa, I could tell you the past, present, and future, but perhaps I should tell you that alcohol always has negative effects, and is a very dangerous substance, especially to someone so young." he said.

"Hey! Why's hisss name first! I'm just as important as my sugar-muffinheart!" I said.

"I'm not drunk." Zach said.

"Yet something is still at your mind, at your heart, at your soul." he said.

"Hearts and souls! I hadddd a heart... and a soul? Do I stillll have a soul? They're trying to eat Zach's! Like he's a moose!" I said.

"I believe you know the answer, Gessa, to releive Zach of his suffering." Draziw said.

"Sufffering... is kindness... but that's not right! Kindness is good! Everyone likes kindness! No one wants someone to suffffer! That's bullshit! Shit, shit, shit..." I said, and Draziw quickly offered me a bag that I threw up in. I felt a lot better after that, after I threw up all over into the bag, getting a little bit of it on my hands that I wiped off on the bag. I was still drunk, but I felt better, still drunk. I handed the bag back to Draziw, and he quickly put it to the side.

"You must purge others of their suffering. Show kindness to them. It is all anyone can do." Draziw said.

"Fiona was kind... I wish I could talk to her about it, she would know what to do..." Zach said.

"Hey! Who's this Fiooona? She one of your girlyfriends?" I said bluntly.

"N-No... she's the God of Luck." Zach said.

"Wellll you'll get lucky, one day... I'm sure I could help you get lucky! What is it you want lucckk for, anyway? You want luck to fuck!" I said and laughed.

Zach coughed and said, "You can never have enough luck..."

"Or enough fuck! Fuck, fuck, fuck... Heya, fortune teller dude! Wanna come with us? I'm sureeee you could help Zach... He's possessed by demons created by the Lich! And I'm a motherfuckin' necromancer!" I said.

The fortune teller, Draziw, looked very surprised, and said, "Um... What? Necromancy has been destroyed, and the Lich was imprisoned ages ago..."

"But my lover has a demon problem! It's like periods, but all the time! And I keep raising motherfuckers back to life!" I said.

"Uh... ok... I will meet you on the outskirts! You must tell no one! Good day... I must prepare..." he said, and bid us to leave, packing something, getting ready for god knows what. I thought he was silly.

"You shouldn't tell people about us." Zach said, as we left the carriage. I just kissed him, which he was surprised at. "Gessa! You are not yourself. Let's take you back to the others." he said.

I giggled and said, "Fiiiineeeeeeeeee."

So we found Barnabus, who was smiling a lot, saying he just went to a belly dancer, and never knew they were so flexible!

We found Edgar and Patricia on the edge, talking about sickness and suffering. I just wanted to slap them! Slap them both! I cared for them, dumbass beautiful Patricia, and my idiot half father Edgar.

We went back outside the town, and I finally, sneakily kissed Patricia, when I said I wanted to tell her something. She quickly backed away, and said she would talk with me later. Her and her long talks! Maybe if she was naked that would be fun.

I hugged that dumbass Edgar, saying he shouldn't ever try to kill himself, saying it made me the saddest I ever was when he did. Edgar said he wouldn't, and that I should probably sit down.

And we found Draziw, with a huge backpack, saying he needed to talk with me and Zach some more. I laughed and laughed at him, but he was so serious! What was he so serious for? Barnabus talked with him, and he seemed to be satisfied with Draziw's answers, but kept a close vigil on him.

Then we finally set up camp. I gave everyone a kiss, because I felt like they all needed one, even that weird old wizard, and I passed out immediately in my sleeping bag.

23

Thank Kindness

Kindness is suffering.

I just had to show kindness.

There must be a way to stop Biona Callus from hurting me.

There was this strange old wizard invited into our camp by Gessa. He seemed odd, like he was even older than he looked, but gave me good advice when me and Gessa talked with him, even though it sort of came from a drunken Gessa.

She's never drank so much! I had to protect her from all the people staring at her, even though she didn't notice them. I thought surely some trouble would come out of it, but nothing happened thankfully, even though the demons were tormenting me the entire time. Rich had gone though, giving up on his hate, happy and loved in the picture. I'm glad Gessa and I could offer him some peace. I stared at the picture, and I remembered the names, and I felt happy.

"Tell me about the demons, Zach." the wizard said, sitting down next to me.

"I'm sure you wouldn't believe me... *I* don't even believe me..." I said.

"You should always believe in yourself, and others will too. I will believe you, Zach." he said seriously.

"Well... one, the one who I showed love to, I showed his family and promised not to forget, is named Rich, used to be Gerich. He used to make me hate and forget, but he seems at peace now." I said.

The wizard seemed to be taken aback, and said, "R-Rich? Richard Fox? He was my oldest friend... my best friend... he... he can't have been taken..." I was confused at his response, and said I'm sure it was another Rich. He said, "Yes... May I see that picture you are looking at? Just to make sure."

I handed him the picture, and he sighed, looking at it for a long while. He handed it back and said, "Keep that safe. Rich has suffered enough."

I paused for a second. Who was this strange man? Then I told him about Biona Callus. "She is this stunning, horrible demon woman... who makes me suffer, and I see her whenever I am suffering. I thought back on your advice, and I figured I should show her kindness somehow."

"Good. Even those who are wrapped in suffering, who are enveloped and consumed by it, can be shown kindness. Never forget that." he said.

"Teckus... is an orc, who wants me to kill, and hurts me with physical abuse, beating me. I feel him trying to attack you, but I have gotten better at controlling him... although I fear for everyone else's lives when I am near them." I said.

"The orcs have been at war their entire existence. You must figure out a way to show peace, to even those who would kill and destroy you mercilessly. There is always a way, although it may not be easy." he said, "It is never easy... when you must not fight, and show peace."

He sort of stared off into the distance, and I wondered what he was looking at. He looked back at me, and asked if there were any more.

I said, "Well... there's one more, who I'm not sure is even real, or just my mind and fear playing tricks on me... It has no name. It is the force of death. It is shadow, and cold, and darkness. I know it is there, but I cannot see it, hear it, or feel it. I just know it is there."

He seemed to clench his fist in anger, and said, "That... should never have been. That is not death, that is the most evil perversion of death. Do not believe it, do not fear it, and always, always, fight it. You are living yet, and the living will always strive to be alive. To fight death. Remember life, bask in it, become it. And you will defeat this death and darkness."

I thanked him for his advice, and he nodded at me. He went to talk to Gessa, but she said her head hurt, and snuggled up in her sleeping bag.

I thought of cutting myself to have Biona Callus show herself... but Gessa didn't want me to hurt myself anymore, and I could understand that. The suffering almost made me feel more alive, gave me feeling from my numb existence... But I knew there was more to life than suffering. My wounds hurt, I looked like hell, and all I wanted to do was make more of them. The people at the carnival stared at me like nothing else, and stayed away from me, fearful of this wounded orc who had been through so much suffering. They thought I must've deserved it somehow... that it was somehow my comeuppance for being some sort of despicable orc. I didn't hold it against them... I was starting to believe it myself. I summoned Biona Callus, saying "Shel Bion."

"That's good of you... They will always make you suffer. You will become like me." Biona Callus appeared in front of me, bending over to me, with her breasts in front of my face.

"We... are alike, in a way. Although I've never been a demon..." I said to her.

"We may be more. You must give yourself to me. You must suffer with me. Forever." she said.

"Yet you will make me suffer more than you, if we are together. Forever. So that I may not suffer as much as you. That... hurts me, to see you suffer. I would do as you say, lay with you, but I would fear for my life..." I said.

She became furious, and grabbed through my pants, at first rubbing, then bending, and bending, and making me hurt. *"That's a man, for you. Always thinking with his dick. You must hurt. You will hurt. There is no other way... and you will love me all the more."* she said.

Gessa was drinking a whole bunch of water, and noticed me clenched over in pain, and went over to me quickly. Biona Callus was still hurting me, and I could see both Gessa and her.

"Wh-What? What's happening?" she calmly but quickly asked me.

Biona Callus was crushing my balls, and it hurt like hell. I couldn't talk, and just felt the pain.

Gessa tried waving her arms in front of me, tried punching at the air, but that just went through Biona Callus, and Biona Callus didn't seem to notice.

"Would you have her instead? Would you have a little girl?" Biona Callus asked.

I struggled out, "She's... my best friend... I would never hurt her, to make her suffer physically, or emotionally..." Biona Callus let go and grabbed at my arms, pricking my skin with her nails, and Gessa struggled to stop me from cutting myself again, because that was what I was really doing. I still managed to cut BC+Z in my arm, surrounded by a heart... Gessa screamed for someone to help her.

"There... now you will remember, and love, the pain..." Biona Callus said.

"I will always remember you, Biona... I will always care for you..." I said, trying to hold in the blood.

She laughed a haughty laugh, and said, *"You should know, we're not as simple as Gerich was... the fool had it coming. I WAS AN INNOCENT!!"* she yelled in that horrible, booming voice. I thought my eardrums would burst.

I let out a laugh, and said, "And look at you now."

She slashed at me, over and over, and Barnabus and Patricia were the only ones who stopped me from almost taking my life through Biona Callus's horrible will. I would've sliced myself to ribbons, if not for Barnabus's strong hand. I probably would've bled to death, if not for Patricia's first aid.

They laid me down, and took away my knife, and Skull, and anything sharp I had on me. I thanked them for that... but still, I didn't need anything sharp to hurt me for Biona. I could use my hands, crush my balls, break my arms or fingers... it was up to Biona Callus how I would end up suffering. I laid down by the fire, exhausted.

But still, I wondered why she didn't just kill me. She seemed to want me alive. I thought there was something to that.

So I thanked her for saving my life.

"You thank me??" Biona Callus appeared on top of me, laying on me very erotically, *"You thank your tormenter?"*

"I thank you, Biona, for all the kindness you've given me. You could've killed me a thousand times over, but only warned me with suffering." I said.

"I could kill you now! Make you take your own life. You could do it, all I have to do is make you!"

"Yet you won't, because really, no matter your actions, no matter your image, you are kind. I thank you for that kindness." I said.

She picked me up, despite my horrible pain, and led me into the woods while the others weren't watching. I thought this would be the time... I would suffer the most. But at least I wouldn't die. Gessa noticed and followed me and her, and Biona Callus said she wanted her to see this.

We stopped at a clearing, and I stood watching Biona Callus as she took a few steps forward. She turned to me, and was a different person... a different being. An angel, beautiful, clothed in white, and she looked kind, and generous.

She said, "Thank you, Zach. I have never received a thank you, no matter how much kindness and good I had offered. Never. I never strove to be thanked, I never worked so tirelessly for good just to be, but I thank you for that kindness to me."

Gessa was astounded. She could see this angel, and stammered out something, "Wh-Wh-What??"

"Gessa. You are the most intrical in his plans. You are the key. Be kind to those who would make you suffer, and be generous to those you love." the angel said.

"Who are you??" Gessa asked.

The angel smiled, and said, "Call me Fiona." I opened my eyes in surprise, as the angel turned and seemed to walk up an invisible stairway to the sky. She paused, turned back, and said to us, "Oh! And have some luck." and she lifted up her skirt and showed us... her twat. I stared at it for a second, as Gessa was, then looked up to her smiling kindly, and said thank you. "Don't you forget it. You will always have luck if you show kindness." she said, and turned and walked up the invisible stairs, disappearing as she did.

We looked to the sky for a long time, looking where Fiona had disappeared. Gessa said to me, "I-I will care f-for you. I don't want to hurt you w-with my whims, either. I-I just want t-to love you, and w-won't push myself on you."

"We have the rest of our lives to love, Gessa. We can love whenever you want." I said.

"I think I'm good for a while. Whoever that Fiona was, she was magnificent. Thank you, Zach." and she kissed me on the cheek.

We went back to camp and Barnabus was telling a story, "Let me tell you about the cock and the pussy..."

Patricia said, "No! I do not need to hear any of your filth."

"It's really a very gentle story, of love... and stroking. There once was a rooster, a big cock by the name of Julio, and a wee little pussy cat named Romi. The cock would rise every day in the morning, and do what cocks do in the morning, crow and doodle doo. The pussy roamed in the evening, and loved to be pet around and around, purring and feeling oh so happy when she was. Although Romi wasn't the normal cat, and was a pussy that loved getting wet, and Julio wasn't the normal rooster, and was a cock that loved going in and out of dark holes. The wetter the pussy got, the tighter the hole for the cock, the happier they would be. They were such strange animals! Their owners didn't know what to do with them. The pussy's owner thought she should just throw the cat in a river, and be done with her, and the cock's owner was getting hungry, and thought he should just chop the rooster's head off and be done with him, too. So the two ran off, and were miserable! One hid in a cave, and the other swam away across a lake.

"But the cock and the pussy met one day, and stroked against each other. The pussy and the cock were so happy! They both loved to stroke and play with each other and themselves! They were happy, but they were so strange to each other! But they began to understand each other, one as a cock and the other as a pussy, and the cock and pussy even had a growing friendship! So each night they would get together and do what they liked best, the pussy got wet and the cock went in and out tight holes."

"Enough, please." Patricia said.

"You didn't even hear the end! It goes like this, ahem... They went on like this for many years, but Julio and Romi were getting old, and they couldn't stroke each other as firmly and fondly as they liked, and decided just to remain good friends, and each went their separate ways. They then each went and had a family of little pussies and cocks! This is the circle of life, and no matter how much your pussy likes to get wet, or your cock likes to go in and out tight holes, treat them well, and just don't let them run off before you can have some fun with them first."

Draziw laughed, Patricia scowled at Barnabus, and Edgar was looking strangely bashful. Patricia turned to me, and quickly went to me, telling me to get some rest... but then she seemed to notice I looked a lot better, even though the scars on me were everywhere, but that was all they were.

They were only scars. Patricia examined me, checking each wound, and asked me if orcs could regenerate. I told her no, and that I had just gotten very, very lucky.

24

Down the Rabbit's Hole

All I could think about was the angel. Fiona. She was the most gorgeous woman alive, and I realized I wanted to be just like her. She was the most gorgeous woman that was an angel, anyway. I just... remembered her lifting up her skirt! I... I didn't know what to think of this. Was I a bisexual? Was I gay? I didn't really know, but I did love thinking of Fiona.

Zach noticed I seemed to be lost in thought more, and I just told him I loved him, and wouldn't touch him, or kiss him, or try to fondle him. I gave him some space, was generous to him, like the angel said I should be. I didn't even mind if he blushed a little bit when Patricia gave him a physical, because she was just so astounded that he wasn't wounded. She wanted to study this, to figure it out, because she said this healing could save many lives. Zach just told her to say, "Figaro, Fadaro, Pigaro, Padaro."

"So... it is nothing but a placebo? Goodwill and happiness? That does not make sense! Let me hear your breathing, I want to make sure the insides are healed as well..." Patricia said. They continued, and Patricia was very professional towards Zach's naked body, and I just stared up at the sky... wondering where in Heaven that angel went...

But, I thought I should get back to business, and learn about necromancy. I accidentally brought a rabbit to life that Barnabus shot, and it ran off into the forest. I was looking for a quiet place to read, and I found the rabbit staring at me, bleeding from its head, with only one eye. *"How's the studying going?"* the rabbit asked.

I didn't want to talk to dead animals any more.

But I said, *"It's going well... I'm learning a lot about this Lich guy."*

"The Unholy Father? Yes, anyone who can speak our language should know of him." the rabbit said.

"Are... you the organism? The necromantic organism?" I asked it.

"I am many things. What is it you imagine when you think of dying?" the rabbit asked.

"I... uh, I don't know... sort of like meeting all my dead relatives? In Heaven or somewhere?" I said.

"That could happen. The brain secretes a serum that makes you... almost dream. To aleviate your passing. You become numb, go into shock, and the pain quickly passes, as you fall asleep, and dream."

"Is... Is that what you felt?" I asked it.

"Not anymore. I cannot dream. I cannot sleep. I am dead, but alive. Think hard on those who you would steal this sleep from." it said. I told it to go to sleep, but it ignored me, and hopped off.

I looked at the book. I felt like I had gone down the rabbit's hole.

Down into its grave.

I sat down, opened the book, and read, *"The angels fight back my forces that wish to destroy this world. The angels are beings created, or perhaps trapped and bound, by the Shazians. They fight the dead, and bring healing to all who are hurt. They are a nuisance... but I have resurrected a few, after they have passed, and brought them to my servitude. The dead angels bring fear and misery to all who encounter them, and it is symbolic that the old gods are dying, that they all must die, live again, and come under my command.*

My world, my universe, my everything, will have no gods, no life, and no will. It will only be me.

I must wonder if that is a lonely existence, but if I can make my wishes true, then I will do so. Simply because I have the power to make them true. The living hate, suffer, kill, and die for foolish, despicable purposes. They need a wise and all powerful hand to guide them. They need me.

I do not believe that I am a messiah, or a savior, in fact I believe quite the opposite. I do not wish to live a lonely, futile existence forever, in truth I believe that would be a hell even worse than the one I concocted for the Shazians. Perhaps I just enjoy the thrill of conquest. The joy of killing, the command, the power to shape worlds with a wave of my hand. It isn't as lonely as you might think, for who needs friends when enemies are far more enjoyable to have? There will always be new enemies, for as long as life grows and prospers, I have an enemy. For I have become Death.

I always thought the Grim Reaper was a little crass, but I am beginning to look more and more like it... although I abstain from wearing a long black cloak and wielding a scythe. I have always had an ugly physique, and it is pleasing to see it wash away from me. Wash yourself of beauty and ugliness, cast off the chains of the body, and bring glory unto Death.

As soon as you realize that the body is meaningless, you will learn how to control it completely. Others', your own, all and everyone's. I'd advise cutting off your hair first, then any other appendage that seems malformed and displeasing to you, that is useless and a burden. Be sure to use a strong, sharp knife."

Sighing, I knew the drill that the book only showed me what it wanted to show me, and couldn't read past the next line. It was frustrating, because I knew the next page was filled with words, but I couldn't wrap my head around them. They seemed to not make any sense in my head, and was as if I was reading gibberish. Less than gibberish, because gibberish at least makes a sound. These were just symbols with no sound and no meaning. But I knew they were words.

Patricia thought I had just been drunk when I kissed her, kissed her in a lustful way that was more than just a kind peck... but still had a long talk about sexuality with me.

She said, "The body can be a pleasing thing. You must always cherish it, yours and others, and treat it with the respect it deserves, for the body is the house of the soul."

Embarrassed, I came clean and said, "But... yours is so magnificent! I wish I could have your body... I wish I could touch it! I... I don't know... am I gay?"

"We all go through turbulent times, trying to figure out sexuality and our body, especially when we are young. Do not be tempted, do not falter, and look past the body. For even if we find ourselves ugly, and weak, and unattractive, we are still all beautiful."

"How... How did you know it was the right time? To... have sex..." I said.

"You will know. When you give yourself to another it will be a wonderful thing, for you are sharing the body that you use every day, that is a part of you, that is where your soul inhabits. Do not throw your body away to one who will not appreciate it. Give yourself, as the other gives themself, in mind, body, and soul."

"Thank you, Patricia." I said, staring at her face a little too long, so perfect, so nice... and she just smiled back.

I'd furiously try to get rid of the feelings I had for her... but that would only make it worse.

So I tried to keep busy instead. I talked with Zach about his demon problems.

"Well, now there are only two... and they seem to be filling in the void for the others. I feel the shadow closing in on me... I feel Teckus, trying to get me to kill... and... rape. My body feels as if it is on fire! I wish to fight, to kill, to choke the life out of someone! And it makes me furious! All I do is keep hacking at firewood, trying to burn off the energy, but it will never leave!" I *had* noticed the giant pile of chopped logs by the fire.

"Well, at least you aren't hurting yourself anymore. The scars you have now look quite dashing, in a way." I said.

"But... I wish to hurt! I wish to hurt others. I try to fight this feeling, but it seems as if all I can imagine are my enemies, and how I want to destroy them... like Gar. Like the Lich. Like fucking Teckus!" Zach said.

"Maybe you need to think gentle thoughts?" I said, and I slowly held his hand. He immediately turned to me, looking like a monster! He grabbed at my arm, grunting, and I said, "Z-Zach... you're hurting me!"

"Bus. Tero sai..." he said in a strange voice, and laughed, a cruel, heartless laugh, that wasn't Zach's, which was nice, and kind, a good laugh.

He grabbed my other arm, and held me down! I tried to fight him, to get him off me! He was twisting my arms, bruising them, and he ripped down my pants, and I screamed.

Edgar quickly went into the secluded area we were at, and bashed Zach's head with a log. He struggled on top of him, fighting him, but Edgar would just keep beating and beating him! I told him to stop! "Stop! *Please, stop!!"* and Edgar seemed to wake up, in a sense, and Zach was unconscious on the ground. Edgar looked very frightened for a second, looking down on the blood on his hands. I went to Zach quickly, to make sure he was still breathing... and he was.

The others followed, and told us to *never* leave their sight again. "Always have a fuckin' buddy. Even if you have to go to the bathroom, you're not going out alone anymore." Barnabus said.

Barnabus was swearing under his breath, as Draziw and Patricia dragged Zach back to camp. Barnabus said it was fucking pitiful that he still had to babysit grown adult babies. Edgar trailed along behind, and I thanked him.

"He... He was going to do... what I had done..." Edgar said.

I cried, thinking that Zach might've. He wasn't himself! He didn't even want to have sex! And the words he said... as if it was a joke! Good-bye, heart! I was going to get my heart back, and Teckus wasn't going to stop me!

Maybe... Maybe if I didn't look attractive! Maybe then Teckus would leave me be! I asked Edgar to give me his knife. And nervously he did, when I said I just needed to cut my hair. He was shocked as I cut it all off! I ripped and cut at it! It was all going to go!

When I had finished I handed the knife back to Edgar, and he looked sort of surprised and sad. He said, "That... is... different..."

"Am I ugly? Do I not look feminine anymore?" I said.

"I... you look like a boy, yes." he said.

But then I noticed my breasts. I thought of cutting them off, whittling them down to nothing, and I asked Edgar for the knife back. He quickly took me back to camp, set me down, and I stared listlessly into the fire.

Patricia was staring at me, saddened, and Draziw sat next to me, and said, "The book you are reading has no knowledge."

"What?? It's about necromancy! I need it to control it, to get rid of it! I don't want to bring the world to die, to live again!" I said.

"Yet it is like turning on a lightbulb that emits no light. It absorbs light and goodness, instead of creating it." he said.

"...F-Fuck you! It made Zach possessed! I... I need to read it to cure him!" I said.

"A great man once said, 'Beware the whispers of the dark.'" Draziw said.

My father had said that. How did he know who my father was?

"*Who* the *fuck* are you?" I said.

"What? You don't know? You already said my name, and who I was. I really am a bum fortune teller... but I do know of magic. At least what looks to the inexperienced like magic." he said.

I... had said something about a bum fortune teller... What had I said? It all seemed kind of fuzzy, and all that I remember was inviting him, because I thought he was silly. I said, "No..."

"Perhaps it was a coincidence. If it was, then know this... you've won the lottery." Floyd said.

Yeah! I called him Floyd!

He continued, "I have fought for millennia against the Lich. I have imprisoned him, subdued him, and as long as I breathe he will continue to stay in that prison. I am cursed, like the Lich is, with immortality, power, and knowledge, for I am the Lich."

25

Learn History

I woke up to Gessa screaming at the wizard, trying to hit at him but being held back by Patricia. Gessa's hair was gone. I don't remember what happened to me, and the last thing I felt was Gessa hold my hand, and then Teckus rising within me.

It was night, and I looked at the wizard sitting calmly by the fire... He looked at me, and I could've sworn I saw a skeleton looking back at me under his dark hood. But it was just a trick of the light... he was just an old man.

Barnabus was watching me closely, like he had been. He and I had thought I was getting better, but after he told me what I almost did... we realized I was only getting worse.

Teckus was tricky, and if I wasn't focused on him for a second, he would either hit me... or control me. The shadows seemed denser than they ever had been, and sometimes I felt as if certain senses were numb, sensationless. This didn't bother me so much, until I started going blind... well, not really blind, because I could always see the Lich in darkness.

He was a skeleton, and always wore something different... looking like people I've loved corpses, decayed and still. He even was wearing my armor once. But now, he was getting closer and closer to me... and I noticed the sword he was holding. The huge, black blade of midnight, and if you stared at it, it would suck you in for what felt like eternity, consuming your mind, your soul, your body, completely, forever. Though, this wasn't as bad as looking into his soulless, empty eye sockets, that seemed like... there was something there, or maybe absolutely nothing.

For I would feel true terror then.

They would haunt my dreams, they would obscure my vision, and I was unable to look away if I stared into them. It would be impossible to turn my head, my will would be gone and forgotten, and I felt... like nothing. The void. Like all life had disappeared forever from my body.

Just like him.

Barnabus helped me up and we went to Gessa and Patricia. Edgar was watching, but didn't seem to want to intervene. As we passed him I asked him why he wasn't, and he said, "Some people have evil in them, past evil, but still evil. I am one of these people. Your wizard is another."

We tried to calm Gessa down, and she was screaming something about a passerby, "The passerby will get you! I am the passerby! I'm going to kill you!"

Draziw stood up, and said commandingly, "I once held that title. I am the last Shazian. I am Floyd, and I named myself the Lich in darkness. Be still, and calm, my daughter." and Gessa stopped fighting. I wondered if this was magic or just the wizard's tone of voice.

"You're... the monster that's been stalking me?" I asked, as we were all around him, looking at him.

He said, "No. I almost wish I still was, and could change its will... but I have split myself from the necromantic organism, which is now totally and wholly the Lich. I lost a lot of my memories of the evils I had done, and gave them... to that creature. If I didn't I would've lost my mind, lost the focus for my eternal vigil, killed myself, and then it would have risen again, to stalk creation and bring nightmare and death to all. I know I wrote the book, Necromancy, Life After Death, but its words are shadows to me."

"You made Zach possessed! You're evil! You're trying to kill my best friend!" Gessa said.

"I... Yes. I created the sickness of the soul, as a protection for the book, so that only the one most worthy could read it. I am saddened to know that... everyone that has died for the book has been my friends of the past... and that I killed and bound them in darkness. They are now a part of the Lich." Floyd said.

"Wawawawait..." Barnabus said, "You're just some kook who's off his rocker. The Lich was never real, and the Shazians are all dead."

Floyd said, "The ones who kept the rubemeralds are." The rubemeralds were these cursed gems that kept the Shazians alive. My pops had one, and it cursed him. He actually got the one he had from Barnabus, and that was the reason Barnabus was once cursed. The Shazians all seemed to die... at least that's what my pops said, and the rubemeralds were all destroyed.

"How do we know you're telling the truth? If you are... then we can trust you even less." Patricia said.

"As I believe someone in this camp said... you cannot. I thought my business with this world was finished, but I was brought back, unsure of my purpose. I know now that my purpose is to aid Gessa and Zach, and if I can, destroy the Lich completely. I could not destroy it, for it is like death, although not really. It is a monster mimicking death, clinging to death as if it was life. I showed it mercy, and imprisoned it, although not willingly. The only way was to split myself, lose half of my being, my evil, and hold on to what was good. We are bound together."

"Then really, we should probably just kill you... and be done with you." Barnabus said.

"I wish it were that simple. I would gladly die, if I knew that the Lich would as well. But it would break its bindings... and I fear it tricked me somehow... for I tried to kill it, as I tried to kill myself... but it is the opposite of life. If I died, it would live. If I live, it will remain dead."

"Sounds like gambler's insurance to me." Barnabus snorted.

"We are both sides of a gambler's coin... and you do not want to know what is on the other side." Floyd said.

"I don't believe you." Barnabus said, then raised his pistol and shot at Floyd. I yelled out, but was astonished that Floyd had raised his hand, and when he opened it, sitting there... was the bullet, harmlessly in his palm.

"You would need to have the power of the gods to kill me... and even still, I would fight against you for life, to prevent death." Floyd said.

Barnabus shot again, saying that that was a fluke, and Floyd threw the bullet at the bullet, and they fell in the air together, hitting each other at the same time, at the same force. We all just looked at the bullets that had melded together from the force. "Like those... the Lich and I are together." Floyd said.

"Fine. You're some super duper god man. Good for you. Now, *the fuck are you going to do for us?*" Barnabus said.

"I will show peace, and not war." Floyd said, looking at me.

I was clapping, but I realized I wasn't clapping. It was Teckus. I quickly stopped clapping. I needed to focus on him... and somehow, show peace.

We sat around the fire, the others very nervously, besides Floyd. Floyd just peacefully looked into the fire. The others were all looking at him. I thought if anyone could help get me out of this evil, it would be the creator of the sickness, or half creator or something.

We had been hunkering down for awhile, just waiting, but we decided it would be a good time to try and see if we could contact Jacob or Mary. Barnabus had asked Gessa if she could use her contact with the Wheel, but she said she wasn't going anywhere with Floyd, and didn't want to talk about it. I tried telling her that Floyd was one of the good guys, but she said if I read the book then I would think differently. Floyd remained silent at this.

I felt sad that Gessa had cut off her hair... to try and prevent Teckus from trying to rape her... but I knew that wouldn't stop Teckus. It made me furious! *I nearly raped my best friend!!* Because of someone else!! Some sort of... weird... fucking demon! I just thought about Shake Spear and his life. He gave me courage in the shadows, and reminded me of the many times he showed peace instead of war.

I prayed to Fiona, thinking of her lucky twat, and her neverending kindness. The generosity that she must've shown, the luck that she gave. I found a red rock that looked like a heart, after I said my lucky words and was thinking of Fiona, and I gave this to Gessa, telling her no matter what, she was my heart. She thanked me, and stared at the rock for a while. I quickly backed away before Teckus could take advantage of her.

I thought of Rich, and said the names, Indigo, Paul, Hannah, and Naomi, and stared at the picture. I could've sworn he winked at me, but I'm pretty sure it was my imagination. I just thought of my own family, all of them, even though I was adopted and none of us were related. We were family, and we loved and cared for each other.

Teckus wanted me to kill them all.

So I told everyone to watch me, as I summoned Teckus.

"Sinful Sake." I said.

Immediately I felt flashes of an orc, a great warlord, greater than every orc. He looked down on me, and said, *"Shasta terom, Zach."*

I didn't know what that meant. I said, "I offer you peace."

He laughed and said that is what he just said... but only if I would forsake all of the humans, walk the earth as a true orc, and kill for my food, fuck for my continuance, and bleed in his name.

"And if I do, the Lich will get me, as he did you." I said.

He hit me.

He said, *"The Lich is the enemy. I offer you peace... and you spit in my face. You may live, you may continue, but only if you do what I say."*

"You've submitted yourself to the enemy! You've become a pawn! You are nothing like an orc, for an orc will never submit! Shake Spear would kill you for your traitorism!" I yelled, angry that such a false orc, a halz rek, could talk to me so.

"I AM NO FALSE ORC!! You would bow to me, you would worship me, if you knew me... But I do not even know who I am. I am Teckus, the God of Blood." he said.

"Catta sero te!" Never forget who you are.

He roared at me, and said, *"Who are you, to command me? Who are you, Ren we Gar?"*

"I am Zach!" I yelled.

He laughed, and said, *"You are me, Zach, and not Zach. Remember that. Who am I? You will never know, for even I do not. I HAVE BEEN SHROUDED IN SHADOW!! I HAVE BEEN IMPRISONED!!"*

And it felt like Skull was talking, telling him that he had his allegiance... if he knew who he was. I saw Athunhel before me, a great orc, not bloody or violent like Teckus was, all in flashes, almost imagined, as if the pictures struggled to reveal themselves to me.

"I am I! You are I! I am orc! I am rek!" I and Athunhel said.

Teckus roared in anger, saying, *"You are NOTHING! You are less than the blood of a bus!"*

Shake Spear would never talk so crudely.

And then I remembered that Shake Spear lost his name, was shrouded in shadow, and was cursed to be risen again.

"Samay somon samay, Teckus." I said. Athunhel laughed, and hit Teckus, and Teckus fell back.

Teckus said, *"No! You are nothing! I am the truest of orcs! I have killed thousands! Millions!"*

"And you cannot remember the one you killed for your name. Your father, who threatened to slay all of his children. You do not remember your many deeds of peace, your life, and the good you strove for to save your people. You were the greatest of orcs, and you do not even know who you are. I know who you are. You are Shake Spear!" I yelled.

This seemed to make Teckus fall back, and Athunhel hit him again.

"YOU ARE SHAKE SPEAR!! THE NOBLEST OF ORCS!! YOU FOUGHT, BUT ONLY FOR PEACE!!" I yelled.

This made Teckus roar in pain, and Athunhel bound him, with ropes coming from his hands.

"I... am not! I wish to be nothing! I wish to die!" Teckus yelled.

"Yet you are dead already. You will meet your fate! You will meet the Mother! She will take you! Athunhel will take you! YOU ARE SHAKE SPEAR!!" I yelled.

"I cannot be! I would not be! I have caused evil! I would never! I am lost! Let me be nameless!" Teckus said.

"My father was nameless, a human, and still, he fought for good." I said.

Teckus seemed to clutch at his head, seemed to hate the roaring of the dead orc millions who arose before me, who called him by his true name.

Shake Spear.

He was bound and dragged by the dead orcs, taken to their afterlife. I do not know of it, I have never learned of it, but he yelled out his name, Shake Spear, and he told me to remember his name, the truth, and the good he had done. And to always strive for peace. "Remember your name, Zach." he said to me.

I collapsed, unable to deal with the visions of the dead orcs.

26

The Split

I went to Zach as he collapsed. I checked if he was breathing, and he was.

He said such strange things, and I never knew an orc could go through so much for his heritage. But I suppose that's an orc for you. I wondered when he would eventually break down for his identity. He was my best friend, and an orc, and people despised him for that. Just because he was different.

He seemed at peace now. I wondered who Shake Spear was. I had read stories about him, given to me by Zach, but I wondered who he really was, besides legend. I suppose he must've been Teckus.

I wondered at the evil that Floyd had created.

I sat next to Zach, until he regained consciousness, and looked at the heart rock he gave me. He really did love me. It wasn't only his words and demeanor... it was his actions. He cared for me like no one else. We've been through such horrible times, and still, Zach cared for me, like we were kids, like we were teenagers, trying to make sense of love. I figured out pretty quickly that being a teenager was a hard time for love, but I ignored it, and just held Zach, cradling him, wishing he would wake up. He had been through so much suffering.

And as soon as he blinked his eyes open, I kissed him.

I felt wonderful.

There wasn't really an age difference, we were just different, and thought about that difference. I told him he was my love.

He said, "I-I love you too."

I suppose he didn't really know what else to say, and couldn't offer me an excuse. I was thankful for that.

We were all we had.

He didn't care that I tried to look ugly for him, that I cut my hair, he said that was fine. I wondered if maybe he had gay thoughts too...

But I realized he just loved me as Gessa. Not somebody else, and no matter what I looked like, he would still love me.

I cried and said that he meant more to me than anything... than life itself... and he cried too. He couldn't say any sort of excuse, I had revealed myself to him, and he had revealed himself to me.

Oh, he tried to say I was too young...

But I just kissed him, and he thought better of it.

I would have him no matter what. I wasn't some innocent, idiot Gessa anymore. I was Gessa, the necromancer, maybe the Lady of Life and Death. I was a woman. And if he didn't respect that... well, I won't tell you what I promised myself I'd do.

Although I looked angrily at Floyd, and thought about what I'd do...

I danced with Zach, slowly, even though there was no music. He laughed and cried. We were two. One and one... and we were always together, through the worst of times, through the best of times. I danced with him and made a silly face he laughed at, and continued dancing.

Barnabus saw us, and started up a tune, "Oh there's nothing to knowww...

There's nothing to be...

But one and one, but two make three...

That love is life, and all is strife...

For even the best, must know the worst...

And find their love, amidst their life..."

I asked him if he had anything more cheerful.

"Er, ahem...

I once was a chicken, called myself Bob, had a crazy wife and ate corn on the cob,

She was my darlin', we were married too, she was named Sue who struck always true,

And would make me bloody, black and blue...

She could move a mountain, I could move a cat, I whistled and spit and wore a cowboy hat,

Drank whiskey all day, even though it's hard to say, how much work you can get done that way,

If my Sue caught me drinkin' I'd be beaten 'til the next morn's ray...

But we'd fuck all night, and there was never any plight, if I held that troll just, just right,

The hag brought me children, don't know all their names just call 'em all Ken an' sometimes Dave,

I lost track how much she gave...

Oh she'd beat up the horse, she'd beat up me, we're one and one and a billion birds and the bees....

There was this old, old cat, never ate a thing, didn't know how, but she made me sing,

I drank all the booze, there's nothin' to lose, so I walk down the street, in my cowboy shoes,

Before Sue catches me, and makes me sing the blues...

Cuz she'd beat up the horse, she'd beat up me, we're one and one, and Jill makes three...

She was my woman, and I paid her fee, I don't really know, but I think she loved me,

But she wasn't as nice as Dee...

The horse was dead, I nearly was too, so I ran from that woman, until I met you...

You make me happy, much better'n Sue..." and Barnabus continued his silly lyrics that Zach would always laugh at. I wasn't paying attention to the song anymore.

We stopped to rest, and Zach kept on looking at something in the distance... that he was frightened of. I'd move in front of him, as he didn't seem to be there, obstructing his vision, and he snapped out of it.

I held his hand, and he said he couldn't feel my hand. I held it harder, but he said thank you, and that he just felt very cold. I gave him a blanket and put him near the fire, but he just shivered.

There had to be a way to stop the fourth from taking him.

I read the book, ignoring Barnabus telling me not to. Floyd said to be cautious, and I told him to go to hell. Patricia cut my hair as I read, and fixed some of the parts that looked a little off. Edgar just sharpened his knife.

The book said, *"These barbarian mutants, that people have been calling orcs, fight to live the strongest out of all. It seems like while humans fight each other and squabble for petty, insignificant differences, that the orcs have a distinct pride and goodwill to each other. They are scorned by all, but still, they fight the hardest for life. Well, if anything, at least life will have a different colored skin when I am through, for the survivors may only be orcs.*

One of their many heroes, their greatest, has already fallen. He is a good slave.

I realize that I am no better than a slaveholder, but eternally, taking the will and life of my slaves forever. I have been feeling pangs of regret, and wish I could purge myself of these feelings. My work has consumed me completely, eternally, and once it was brought into motion there was no way to stop it. I look back on my countless friends and family, who are now corpses under my servitude, and I have surrounded myself with them, hopelessly clinging to the memories of the past. I have decided that I will split myself, so that I may eternally focus on my work.

I do not mind if others hate me, in fact I relish their hate, although I am beginning to hate myself. I have never loved myself, or hated myself, I simply was. But as I trudge deeper and deeper into my work this new feeling distracts me.

I make others suffer for the joy of it, for the happiness it gives me. Although the more I make others suffer, the more I suffer. I thought I could remain unfeeling forever, but as I kill men, women, and babes, I feel their suffering. I have experimented in grafting the dead, making the omega zombies, and I notice each wound of the dead, and I wonder how it felt to die that way. I have begun to feel what the dead have felt, have asked the dead to describe it for me. It is fascinating, although it is a pointless fascination, and needs to be put to a halt. My work is death, and not suffering and torture. Some pleasures are self consuming and a needless waste of time.

I have committed countless atrocities in my war, and it is the most thrilling game to play. It is the game of life and death. I realize that once I am finished, the game must end... and I will be left with only the dead, peace through destruction. I need to complete my goal, and not prolong my victory. I must ruthlessly and completely finish this game. I must finish it, and not enjoy it. That is my purpose in death.

The worst feeling is feeling that I could've been alive still. That I didn't need to die, and no one needed to die. I do not have the same senses as I did before, actually I have senses that no one has, that are only revealed to the dead... I was blind, deaf, and dumb in life, and everything is now opened to me, but it is a different feeling. Instead of feeling the joy of each sense, I simply know. Music does not sound so sweet, the pristine bodies of the dead do not look as pleasing, my body moves as I command it, and it is wasting from me even now. I have begun to sit in lonesome dark and silence with the dead tree, meditating and planning, even if I should traverse the worlds and command my kingdom firsthand. There is no point... I am dead, and the dead can finish my work even without me. I feel as if the necromantic organism has conquered me, instead of me it. The master has become the slave.

I will begin the procedure of the split. But before I do, know that the best way to get someone to do what you want... is to offer them a challenge."

I wanted to fucking continue reading! I couldn't even look at the next page! My eyes would just swivel around it! It had to have the answers, it must know, but it was keeping it from me!

Floyd was deceitful, a manipulator. I thought that he was acting, and was really the enemy... but he looked like the epitome of goodwill, kindness, peace, and even of life. But... that's what he'd want me to think! That he was a good guy! But good and evil wasn't real! It was only a way to categorize, to feel your conscience! I had been making my own conclusions from reading the book... and I feared it was sucking me in, and subtly affecting my mind.

But it was fascinating. Whoever Floyd and the Lich were, he was an evil like nothing else, and I was reading his life, his history, his mind put on paper. I thought about writing an anti-necromancy book, but I feel that would be kind of boring... there's already a Bible anyway. No one is really interested in something without conflict, at least I'm not.

My mother always reads kind stories, like vets curing puppy dogs and kittens. She likes the good stories, the ones where people help each other out, and the antagonist is just bad, random things happening to people.

My enemy was the Lich.

My enemy was Death itself.

I wondered if Floyd tried to bring people back to life, at the start, just so that they may live. I had thoughts like that in the past, but everything I brought to life wasn't really alive, and seemed to prefer to have stayed dead. What was so off putting about life that the dead didn't even want to be a part of it anymore? Was being dead even better than being alive?

So I asked Edgar why he tried to kill himself. I thought it was just the shame I put him through, the hate that I doled out on him, but maybe it was something else?

"I... don't really know what to say to that, Gessa. Are you having thoughts of suicide?" Edgar asked.

"Um... no. I don't think so... but... if anything happened to my family or friends, I had thought that I would kill myself... If... anything happened to Zach, I wouldn't know what to do!" I said.

"I thought that I should die many times, either to end the voices, or because of some hidden evil they told me. I thought I had no reason to live. I had asked a friend to kill me once... but he didn't. I learned that my life's purpose was now to make amends. To do right to the people I've wronged. When you told me to die, it felt like I could never do that. It felt like my life's purpose would never be fulfilled, and the only way for me to make amends... was to die." Edgar said.

This made my heart sink. I told him that he was doing fine! Just fine! I realized I didn't hate him as much as I used to, and that... he was trying. Why the hell did he... why did he... I didn't really understand any of the things he did, and worse, I don't think he did either.

"Take heart that all life is special, and even if you do feel terrible, and awful, you are a part of that life. We are all." Edgar said.

"How can someone who believes that want to kill themselves?" I asked.

"...Well... it is difficult being alive, it is confusing, it is painful. There may be no right answers, and we may just only be like bacteria, trying to survive and reproduce." he said.

"So you just gave up?" I asked.

"I had ruined life, with my existence. I had killed. In a way... I loved life so much, I thought it would be better without me." Edgar said.

"That... That doesn't make sense!" I said.

"I have been lost, confused, and paranoid, because of my illness... I thought everything was something else. I still get feelings of distinct paranoia, which is why I do not drink or use drugs, as they would counteract the medication I take. If you ever feel like there isn't a reason to live, tell me, and I will help you." he said, trying to be a father. He usually said he would help me with something when he tried to be a father.

"Can... Can you tell me about some of your fears? Are they irrational, completely? Or do they come from real danger?" I asked.

"A little bit of both. Think of it like this... There is someone watching you. You don't know why they are watching you, but they are. This person could be a killer, sizing you up, in reality, but he could just be curious about a silly hat you are wearing. And then you hear him talking to you in your head, wanting to know where you live, what you are doing, and threatening you. This is just the voices, correct? There is no real reason to fear... but then you notice the person following you home. You think about confronting him, you think about running, but perhaps his house is just down the road. He turns, and goes the opposite direction. Did he notice you watching him? Perhaps he would save you for another day, or perhaps he simply was going in his own unique direction, and didn't even think about you. You could never know, but having him telling you your worst fears in your head, accentuating and embiggening them, does not help." Edgar said.

"How... How can you ever feel safe? How can you not run from everyone and everything?" I asked.

"You learn how to fight. You learn how to kill... and sometimes, you do run. There is real danger in the world." he said.

"Thank you, Edgar." I said. He smiled and said you're welcome.

I realized I never wanted to cross my genetic father.

Even if I could raise a thousand corpses from the grave, he would still probably find some way to kill me. But I snapped out of it, he didn't want to kill me... did he? Was he like the man in his story, saving me for later? How could I trust anyone! I didn't want to have to learn to kill everyone with my bare hands, like Edgar had!

I calmed myself down, thinking that the man in the story was just lost, and was going home. That had to be it.

I started to understand his paranoia.

27

Live Life

The day looked like night, but... darker. Like I was in a pitch black cave, and the only things I could see and feel were those who were close to me. It felt like the living seemed to emit a faint light of their own, the more energy they had, the brighter their lights were, only if I was close enough to them. The horizon, the things in the distance, could not be seen. People looked like ghosts to me, almost, kinda blurry. Gessa stood out the most.

I wondered why the hair that Gessa had left was black.

Like darkness, sprouting from her head.

Like the darkness coming from the Lich's skull.

He would always be following us, watching and waiting for us when we stopped. I noticed that Floyd could see him, as I could. I felt so cold, and with death literally stalking behind me, I felt terribly, terribly frightened.

I stuttered out to Floyd, "Wh-Why i-is he w-waiting??"

"It is not part of this world. I am the light, and it is the shadow. It is always near me, and I fear the sickness of the soul is drawing it to you." Floyd said.

"C-Can we f-fight it?" I asked.

"I have only known one man who has survived its blade." Floyd said.

"C-Can we get him to help us?" I asked.

"We are traveling to him now. You know him and love him." Floyd said.

"We're going to see my pops and ma... Is he a member of the Chariot?" I asked.

"When I met him, he was nameless." Floyd said.

Huh? My pops fought the Lich? *And lived?* I didn't dare turn to look at it, in case I accidentally tempted it to attack me. How could you fight something that was dead? That exuded death through its every being?

Floyd was trying to tell me something... but I couldn't hear him. Instead I heard someone whispering to me... right behind me. I didn't dare look. I just prayed Figaro, Fadaro, Pigaro, Padaro, until it stopped. Gessa was trying to say something to me, and I just stared at her, frightened.

I was wrapped in a blanket, but still felt so cold. Gessa went underneath the blanket with me and hugged me, and led me away from what was right behind me. I heard it walking behind me, its footsteps making crunching sounds in the dirt.

Crunch.

Crunch.

Crunch.

Almost as if it was its maw, chomping on my corpse.

Crunch.

Crunch.

Crunch.

Naomi. Hannah. Paul. Indigo. Rich.

Crunch.

Crunch.

Crunch.

Fiona's lucky twat.

Crunch.

Crunch.

Crunch.

Remember Shake Spear.

Crunch.

Crunch.

Crunch.

I thought of running, fleeing it, for it undoubtedly wanted me to die, as the shadows lengthened even more. But I had to be brave. There must be some way to fight this darkness... but was the fourth the Lich?

Crunch.

Crunch.

Crunch.

I heard it snap its teeth at me. If it breathed, I could've felt it breathing. It was more like I felt the opposite of breathing, on my shoulder, on my cheek.

Hahhhhhhhh...

I couldn't hear anything but it. It was the only thing in my senses, as the others faded, and faded, and faded...

Like it was only me, and it.

And soon it would only be it.

I could feel it reaching for me, and I ran.

There was nowhere to go. There was nothing. It was only darkness, and I ran through the darkness.

In a clap of thunder, Rich was before me. He said, "Love your life! Love life! There is nowhere else to go, and you must fight for love! Say the names of your family! Tell me you love them!"

"Matt! Melusine! Marcos! Daisy! Barnabus! Mary! Jacob! Dismas! Simon! Melissa! Gessa! I love you all!"

"Good. Floyd was my brother, my best friend. He is this... thing, now. Or part of him is. I was warped, I could not remember over my hatred.

Go." Rich said, and I ran, and could hear a blade swing at Rich. I just kept running.

Fiona flew down from Heaven, down to whatever horrible hell I was in. She said, "You need luck most of all, Zach. You do not have time. I offer kindness to you, and give you this." and she touched my head, and a path was illuminated before me. "Go. My kindness could not save the lives that were taken, and I suffered for them, for all the worlds that I traveled to, to bring kindness and healing. Be kind, generous, and do not fall into your own suffering." I thanked her, and I ran down the path, and the blade swung at Fiona, and I knew she was gone.

I ran and ran, and from the shadows were figures, trying to get me to fall off the path, trying to reach at me and grab me, but also from the shadows arose the orcs, fighting all the many shadows. Athunhel and Shake Spear walked before me. Shake Spear was cleaned off, and looked at peace again. Shake Spear said, "Remember your heritage, fight to keep it alive! Fight for it, as we will fight for you. All my peace was meaningless in the end, and all I could do was war."

Athunhel said, "We will fight for you, and we live on as you do. In your axe, in your blood. You are rek, Zach."

And the two charged at the thing following, fighting it and fighting it, but ultimately, falling.

And I ran down the path.

And I ran down the path.

And I ran down the path.

The path came to a halt, and then it was in front of me. The force of death, and I saw it, and heard it, and felt it. It didn't seem believable, but it was real. It was madness and woe! It was darkness and death! But I could see it! It was before me! I could hear it speaking, in many tongues and many words, and none of the words I heard made sense, but I understood what it was saying.

It wanted to die.

To be still, motionless, and not able to feel the pain of life.

"Y-You're alive?" I said.

It told me it was still alive, but dead. It was the beginning, and the end.

It was all, and it was nothing.

"Live! You must live! Come back to life!" I said.

It told me that was what the Lich said to countless millions.

And here we are.

And I was about to die.

"I will not! I will fight you for all that is alive! I will live for love, kindness, and peace! I will breathe, and I will feel my heart beat! I will see the trees, I will walk the earth! I want to feel the sun on my face, the breeze in my hair, and hear the roaring of the sea! I want to love and cherish everything! The people, the animals, and the plants!"

It seemed to sigh.

And asked me to tell it about the sun.

"I-It's the force of life. It is the energy everything needs to live. It is this giant roaring ball of gas, ignited, like the greatest fire in existence. The sun, water, and oxygen created life on this planet." I said.

Tell me about water.

"I-It is a liquid that our bodies are made of, and keeps us alive. It filters us out, and cleans us, both on the outside and the inside. It is partially made of oxygen, that we breathe in and out from the air." I said.

What is air?

"It is an important part in keeping us alive. Our lungs breathe, our heart beats, and the oxygen in the air is transmitted throughout the body through the bloodstream."

But we couldn't talk anymore, as it seemed to look over my shoulder, and said that its master was here. I asked it to help me! Anything!

It told me to breathe in and out. I did.

It told me to look for the sunlight. The sun shone down in the darkness, everywhere, filling it with light, blinding me.

And it told me to be submerged in water and to live again.

I arose from a lake, awoken to reality before me. The others were all missing, but soon, Floyd found me, and the others ran up to me, asking if I was alright. "You just disappeared! Poof! Seemed to fade away!" Gessa said. The sun shone down on me, and I breathed in and out. I felt so warm.

I felt like... everything was alive. Every sense seemed sharpened, to a point, I could see far off into the distance and notice every single detail, I could hear every sound around me, everyone's worried breathing and a blue jay squawking miles and miles away, and I could feel the smallest, littlest things, like Gessa's fingertips, the very fingerprints, on her hand.

And her kiss, feeling like my heart was exploding. I wondered if my pops felt that way when he kissed my ma.

But I noticed the figure behind her, and stared at it. It was my foe. The Lich. It waved me goodbye, and walked off to whatever hell it inhabited. I could swear I heard it laughing at me, resting its sword on its shoulder and walking down the road.

28

Unfinished

Despite Zach just being... gone, when he came back he looked and felt like he was the happiest man on Earth! Had the most energy, the most will! He looked taller than he already was! Every flaw of his seemed like it was a strength! He had no flaws! Every ugly scar he had was incredibly dashing, and his frame seemed perfectly proportioned for him. I just stared at him as he led us down the path, saying he knew where his pops was... the bum was at the Black Dragon. It was impossible to not look at Zach. I was terrified of kissing him, but my heart led me over my head. He seemed like the greatest person in the world! He was loving, kind, peaceful, and full of life!

I just felt like a little, decrepit, teenage girl necromancer. I felt sort of pitiful.

But Zach would immediately dispel my fears, that I was ugly, and wretched, and a monster. He seemed to notice whenever I got wrapped in my feelings of self-doubt and self-hatred, even if his back was turned! He said I breathe a bit sharper when I was thinking those thoughts, and then that I breathe too slowly when I tried to hide it from him. How could he tell the exact rhythm of my breathing?? He said, "We are all on the path to death. We must all meet it in the end, living can only go on for so long, but we can live life while we can. Do not feel hatred, or doubt. It is a meaningless feeling, that is only a distraction to the wonders of life." and showed me a sly stick insect, hiding itself on a branch, which he gently picked up and showed me, then gently put back down again. He walked gently on the grass, but like he was firmly planted in his base, and if anyone tried to shove him over, he would never fall.

We all just stared and wondered at him, and he didn't seem to mind. In fact, he'd look us in the eyes and smile! The person behind those eyes made you feel like you should look away... but you didn't, and felt even better looking into them. It felt like he could see through your eyes, to the person on the other side, and he was kind and gentle to that person, and loved you, no matter how much you felt like you were unworthy of that love.

Barnabus asked him if he was feeling alright, if maybe he needed to sit down? Zach said, "We have so much road to walk! I could walk forever! It feels great to move my muscles, to walk down the road and see each new thing! But let's rest. I've been trying to slow my pace, and I know all of your bodies are strong, but I feel that something else is on each one of your minds." It was hard to keep up with him, physically, emotionally, and mentally. Spiritually? Was he baptized in that lake and given a new purpose?

So we sat down, and Zach played therapist for each of us, asking what was the matter, letting his coyotes play around with us.

First, Barnabus said, "I don't get it. You were pissed off and hurt as all hell. What the fuck are you so happy about? You just have a good lay with one of your demons? Or are you and Gessa doing something we should know about?" I felt embarrassed at that.

He laughed, and said no, he never felt this way, even when he was with Shekinah. Fucking Shekinah... I'm sure she just led him on a string, taking his body for herself and then even his gold! I realized I never wanted to be like that...

Zach said, "I'm sure that bodily pleasures are magnificent, and with the right person are even better, like the lock and key of your heart and body. Mary will come back to you, and you don't have to worry that she will love someone else and will forget you. She will always remember, no matter how your relationship plays out. You also don't have to force her into being your woman, and she will still come back to you. Like Fiona, the more you grasp at a relationship, the harder it is to keep it." I thought about the lock and key, and sex... He seemed like he said what we were all thinking even without being crude, like Barnabus was.

"The fuck are you giving me relationship advice for, kid?" Barnabus said.

Zach said, "As one looking at it on the outside, I can feel what is going on inside. I know you have felt jealousy, and anger, but you should leave those feelings be. The more you think about them the harder it is to get rid of them." Barnbus seemed a little frustrated at this, but said fine, he sure looked chipper today, so maybe he wasn't just a dumb kid anymore.

Patricia said, "You seem to have gone through the worst evil that is possible, but you are still alive and have even cast off this evil! How can I fight the evils of the world if I don't even know what I am facing? Your plight is a mystery to me."

"It is the force of evil that was against me. The corruption of the soul. I have seen the beginning and the end, and I know now that you must alway learn of... good, instead of evil. If you look at every angry, evil thing, if you strive to counter it in every possible way, it will eventually consume you. Now, this is not like your excellent medical skills. Always learn of maladies and sicknesses, but do not be sucked into them. Keep a distance from yourself and the evil."

"How then did you heal?" Patricia asked.

"My wounds were healed by an angel. They are beings of the past, or perhaps spirits. There are powers unknowable to us, for good... and evil. All we can do is to learn, of the past, present, and for the future if we are ever able to fight unknowable evil. Always learn, but remember to take a break every once in a while. Others will continue your work when you are passed." Zach said.

"That... brings sort of a relief for me. I was burdened that I would never be able to finish the good I strive for." Patricia said.

"As long as you live, are peaceful, kind, and loving, you are already doing good." Zach said and smiled. Patricia looked at him, and wondered.

Edgar said, "Are you magic now? Can you cure the voices? Can I ever make the proper restitution for my evil?"

Zach looked sort of sad, and said, "I am not magic. I was simply brought through the worst trials of the soul. Perhaps one day we can relieve you of your suffering. I will look into the matter, but do not fret. You are already healed, as far as I can tell. You do not believe the voices. You do not give into them, and from what you've told me, you do not hear them very often either, so the meds must be working. Remember to take your meds. Sometimes it will be impossible to make amends, and all you must do is learn from your mistakes and never fall into them again."

"Thank you, magic man." Edgar said. I couldn't tell if Edgar was joking or being serious, but Zach just smiled at that.

Floyd asked him, "I cursed all the people who had tormented you. I caused evil, I am the Lich, but I know... I am not. It has left me, for once in my life, and I am worried about this."

"Yes. It has left. It will rise again." This made Floyd sort of shocked, and the rest of us too.

Floyd said, "Are... you sure? How can the shadow leave the light? How can it exist without life?"

"It has cast off the chains, as I have. All it needed was somebody to play its game. Gessa knows more about this, and she will be the turning point for life, either its saving or destruction." Zach said.

"The passerby. I believed I was him." Floyd said.

"Yet you are only a man, a wise and powerful man, and are not the Lich. Whoever is the Lich's enemy is the passerby. He wished us to believe that there was only one other who could defeat him, but really, there is all of us. Everyone who lives is a passerby."

"How... do you know this? I have traveled all of creation, everywhere, and learned all that there is to know. I am surprised someone so young could speak with such wise counsel." Floyd said.

Zach said he guessed, that he took intonations and words from our sentences, and made the conclusions.

"Then you are clear headed, and not corrupted. I will teach you anything you wish to know, all you need to do is ask." Floyd said. Zach thanked him, saying there is always more to know.

I asked Zach, "Did you read the book?"

"I have not. But you still should, even if the last sentence will be a disappointment, and will cause you fear. Gleam anything you can from this monster, and remember it is only a monster." Zach said to me seriously. I looked deep into his eyes. I knew what I had to do.

I opened the book, and read the page.

"I HAVE BEEN FREED! The maggot in me, the last ounce of life, has finally been expunged! I am DEATH! The little man before me is nothing to me! HE WILL DIE!!

I chase him and chase him, and the book is my will, it is me. I write the book, to give you the lasting power of death! I have all the power! And it will be yours. YOU AND I FEEL NOTHING. THE LAST SHRED OF HUMANITY IN US IS GONE.

And so I wish to thank you. For freeing me of this prison.

My true enemies, the heroes that have fought to defeat and bind me are gone. Rich... Fiona... Shake Spear... Life itself... except for one... Floyd. Floyd will fall like the rest, by my blade.

Floyd has escaped me, but he will not forever, as I laid in that prison, as

I was bound in his body, I have thought endlessly on ways to torture and kill him... over and over again, but now I don't have to plan... for I am freed. By you and your love.

The one that I have cursed is my freer. You know who I am talking about, the one you cared for... the one you loved... I thank you and him, for I know you to be the Lady of Life and Death. The Queen of All. I knew it had to be a woman. I knew it!

I know it. Because I am watching you right now.

Forever. We will conquer, and you and I will never be alone. You will be my Queen in the Kingdom of Death.

Have a beautiful rest of your"

And the sentence just cut off. The rest of the pages were blank. It was an unfinished book.

I didn't want that to happen to me! Just cut off, be expelled from existence! I felt terribly frightened, horribly alone, and I couldn't stop reading the page, over and over again. Just say "day," damnit! The bird said the same thing! The Lich was the bird!

But it wasn't a bird.

It was Death.

It was necromancy, and the organism that causes necromancy.

And it was already inside of me.

Zach held me by the hand as I was hyperventilating, telling me to be calm in a calm voice, to just breathe in and out, slowly. "It's in me! If I die, it will get me! I can't die, but it wants to kill me! *Help me, please!!*" I said.

Zach said he would, that he will, that he would do everything that he can to help me. That nothing will stop him.

How can he say something like that!! How can you stop something that is impossible to see, impossible to feel, and causes people to come back to life! What could he do?? I just tried to calm my breathing.

Zach took me by the hand and we kept walking. I could *feel* it... sort of crawling within me... touching me! Underneath and on my skin, inside of me everywhere! I just wanted it to stop! I wanted to kill myself to stop this feeling!

When we stopped for the night. I fell asleep... and the dreams were some of the worst ones I've ever had.

People raping and beating me, so vividly, monsters. I couldn't stop them, no matter how many times I told myself to wake up.

The Lich said to me when he was finished, *"I always liked the color black... let's change some things..."* and he touched my head, and showed me a mirror, and my hair was as dark as midnight.

And he killed me, over and over again, but brought me back to life whenever I was dead.

I felt like my life had ended, and would end over and over again.

Floyd woke me up. I was never so thankful for him, even though he was sort of the cause of this. Was he? Was it always the Lich?

I gave him a gentle hug, and he said he knew my fear.

That it happened to him whenever he fell asleep, too.

I looked in my mirror and my hair was black.

29

Is God a Writer?

I breathed in, and out, savoring the feeling of my lungs expanding and contracting. I walked down the road, a new man, a living man. It felt like my life was a blur of confusion before I arose from the lake. Now everything was so clear.

This didn't stop me from worrying about Gessa, the others, about the Lich coming back from the grave.

But I would deal with it one step at a time. One foot forward, then the other. Gessa looked actually very stunning with her new black hair, and I told her it was just hair anyway. Even if it was a gift by the Lich. It was just a subtle way for the Lich to try and scare her, to claim her as his own. I wouldn't allow that to take Gessa's peace of mind, her heart and will. Her body may change, but she was still Gessa, and no one could take that from her, or us.

She already looked like a woman, her body changing with her mind. She was an adult now, and I respected her as one.

The others all were a little confused at my change in demeanor, as I thought I should've been. But I wasn't, in fact, it seemed natural that the change in my mind and body should take place. It felt like being alive, as everything evolves and changes.

I laughed at them, wondering what to do with me. Even the other forces of the world were funny to me, the ones watching me, the ones who saw me no matter what I did. That I was showing my life to. They were all the silliest creatures imaginable, and I thought they should know that and lighten up for once in their life.

So I told them jokes, and stories, and taught them ways to do things.

Barnabus had the hardest time dealing with me, as it seemed I didn't need a mentor anymore. I told him he will always be able to teach me things, and if he couldn't, then I will teach him things too. He was frustrated at that, but he grew calm, saying that my father had acted the same way when he didn't need a master, although he just ran off, stole Barnabus's knife, and they never saw each other again until they met at the Black Dragon.

Barnabus still didn't know what to do with me, so decided he'd drink to figure this out. I abstained from drinking. I thought that if my life was a story, the author of the book probably didn't know what to do with me either... I felt like I stuck out, but was perfectly attuned and a part of everything. I imagined the author probably wanted to get drunk, too.

I thought he shouldn't make any stupid mistakes.

We walked for a long while, and I prayed to the gods, whoever was listening, and especially to Fiona. I thanked her for showing me the path.

We decided to rest, and I had a quick nap, just listening to the calmness of nature. The others followed me, and took my lead, and I told them we could take our time.

I fell asleep, and I thought of the story book world... just if my life was a story...

And I talked to the writer.

He was a little peeved that I said the first word.

He decided to take a break from trying to control, and just needed a smoke. For some reason he seemed to smoke constantly.

The writer laughed, and said I was funny.

I thought he was funny, too.

"But... But how can you be talking! I have schizophrenia, and I don't want a relapse! I may have to delete this if I end up losing my mind..." the writer said.

I paused, to let him think, and take his time. He would find the answers if he thought about it. I thought the music he was listening to was nice.

"The musician died from some stupid cause. A young man, who ended his life. Don't die like him." the writer said.

"I won't. If you promise not to, either. I don't want someone else to have to finish writing my story." I said, "Take your break. You don't have to think about everything all at once."

"I'll do that, Zach. I think you should wake up, though. You never know what horrors are around the corner." he said.

"There's nothing around the corner. The Lich isn't behind you, and there is no danger for you but the one you cause." I said.

"Which danger is that?" the writer asked.

"Trying to break the fourth wall." I said. The music changed, and I noticed he was listening to something by someone by the same name of Floyd. I thought he should listen closely.

So he just sat, and listened to the woman pouring her heart out in her music. Pouring her heart out, like Gessa did for everyone. He just sat and listened, and thought that I really had grown a lot.

"You will have a fantastic rest." the writer said.

"Thank you. Remember that someone is probably writing your story, too." I said.

The writer laughed and said that was alright, and would continue to write mine for the time being. He thought about the worlds of books, the history, the emotion and words, the people in it who inhabit it.

And he looked up at the sky.

And finally, was about to take his break as the music was ending.

"We all make mistakes, Zach." he said.

And I woke up.

It was such a strange dream... I promised myself I wouldn't mess with reality again. I don't think the writer would be able to handle that, if I messed with his world.

I just hoped he wasn't messing up mine.

I realized that I was a magnet for all sorts of supernatural things... that everything in creation was now drawn to me, as I was blessed by the four, simply by overcoming their trials. I hoped it wouldn't turn out to be a curse, and I wondered what my pops would think.

I felt like the thin edge of a knife, be careful with me, or I'd cut you.

I felt like the power of life was at my fingertips.

I felt like a god.

But still, just Zach, an orc, and I felt happy being around my friends and family. No one would take me to Heaven or Hell, while I still lived.

"How... How can you feel such things?? How do you feel like a god?? I feel like the Devil..." Gessa said. She had a hard time accepting that she was good these days. She had a hard time accepting her new life. I fear I didn't help, being content as I was.

"No reason, Gessa! I just feel really good, no worries!" I said, trying to mimic my old words and life, but she could tell I was just acting...

"You were never as happy as *that*..." she said.

I laughed, and she seemed to be happier when I laughed. I realized that humor was the perfect outlet to relieve stress and tension. As long as it came naturally.

There was no reason to force anything.

Although... with my newfound peace, it felt harder to grasp at humor.

Gessa always made me laugh though. I suppose humor was especially a way for people who felt bad to feel good about their life. I hoped I wasn't losing myself... but I felt more like myself than I ever had. It's strange... so I just talked with Gessa.

"You were always the funny one, Gessa." I said to her.

"You always made me laugh, and I like that you're so happy. I wish I could have that happiness." Gessa said.

"I will give you my happiness, then." I said.

"But... But you're not *really* happy! You never seemed so serious! If you were happy, you'd lose it eventually, but you're not! You're just... like someone else! You're at peace! It doesn't make any sense!" Gessa said.

I told her, "If it made sense, it wouldn't be a very interesting life."

"I-I don't get it... Will you just hold my hand?" Gessa asked.

I did, and we walked in silence. I noticed her hair was growing more, I could practically see it growing. I felt Gessa's fingertips, turned to her, put my palm on her palm, and said, "Do not try to control. Let it come naturally. Let your blood flow to the rhythm of the heart, let your peace come from stillness, and not force. Do not fight against life, simply be it."

"You sound like a Buddha." Gessa said.

I remembered that Buddha was nice. I am happy to think that Gessa still thought of me as nice.

"I want to cry... because you seem like the old Zach is gone. Like a new Zach, and I don't know what he will say, or do, or act like! All I know is that he talks like a Buddha, looks like the greatest man on the Earth, and feels like he would never harm anyone, but if anyone harmed you, they would sorely regret it. Anyone. Even the Lich!" Gessa said.

I thought that the Lich probably thought of himself as a god. He thought of himself as Death incarnate. He would fall, like me, eventually. I couldn't live forever... but I would just let this feeling envelop me, be me, and I would be it. Angrily I thought of Rich, Fiona, Shake Spear, and Life itself. They had all been brought down by the Lich, consumed completely eventually. But they were still all in me.

I am the four. I am Zach.

And I walked in peace, holding Gessa's hand.

I suppose it was just the horrors of the curse which made me change. But I figured it was also just part of growing up. And now, I had a new challenge. To bring the Lich to destruction, completely. And I had all my family to help do that. I talked with Floyd, to see what he thought and if he could teach me anything new.

So, being blunt with Floyd the wizard, I said, "I feel like a god on Earth. Is this feeling simply the peace after hardship? Conquering my fears?"

"All feelings pass. I believe you need to talk with your father and mother about the changes you have gone through. They may offer you insight." Floyd said.

"I... am a little terrified of what they'll say to me, after everything that's happened." I said.

"Don't worry. They love you. I believe you need a long rest, too. As you have said to others, take your time." Floyd said.

"I... thank you." I said.

And... I thought about my family, about the people who hurt, as I had hurt, and it made me sad. I realized this was empathy. If you are feeling down, depressed or lonely, I will listen.

I talked with Gessa. And I talked to her about God.

"So, if the god of everything is just someone who imagined us all up, what's the point? Is he trying to sell his story to other gods?" Gessa asked.

"I think he just felt lonely one day and decided he needed some friends." I said.

"Hmm... I guess, but you have to realize how much control someone can make in their imagination. I feel intrusive thoughts and have horrible imaginations all the time." Gessa said.

"As have I... but, if he could change the world, why couldn't he? Why is everything so terrible?" I said.

And strangely, the world felt light and happy, for each of us. Like there was never any strife, any pain, or strangely... any purpose. I quickly calmed myself down, knowing that there is a purpose to life, and I didn't want to live a life that was devoid of anything. That was just fluff.

"D-Did you feel that? What was it? It felt like my brain was put on... a pillow... and I could stay there forever..." Gessa said.

I knew not to be tempted, and said to her, "That is another aspect of dying. Living will always be difficult, and we must cherish those difficulties and overcome that challenge."

"I... I wish I didn't have... the Lich. By Fiona and her lucky twat." Gessa said.

And it felt strangely like the wish came true, like he really was gone, but only for a second. Was that all she needed to do? To wish it away? But... it was out there, somewhere. I realized that that creator probably didn't know what to do with the Lich either, and it was probably something that tormented him. Maybe the writer needed mortals to help him. Maybe he needed Zach and Gessa, instead of the other way around.

So I vowed I would help him, as I realized not everything is under a creator's control.

For if the Lich was madness and death, then I knew the writer feared it too.

30

Family Reunited

I knew that "creator" of Zach's was frustrated.

I thought it was funny. For if he created all my hardships, he should suffer too.

But... then I felt bad that I felt that way. I wished everyone could feel my horror... and I wished none could. I told Zach that I wish I didn't feel like this... and I thought about everyone who hurt, and I wished they didn't hurt. It made me so sad and frustrated! There must be someone to blame!

But there was no one. Not even the Lich, for he wasn't the cause of all suffering. In fact, he had stayed out of life for a long time, and we still felt ways to suffer.

I couldn't figure it out, so I got drunk, like god must be doing now, as he was such an asshole and fucking with my life. I stole Barnabus's booze and got drunk.

Buddha was at least a man... but he somehow turned into a god! There was no god to trust, all gods sucked. I hated them all!

I had grown a lot, I wondered if I was dying while I was growing.

Jacob and Zach's dad approached us, riding on Zach's dad's motorcycle. The rumbling of the bike alerted us, and the first thing I asked Jacob for was a cigarette. "S-Sure, dude. Don't you want to know how we found you?"

I said I just needed a smoke.

So I thought of that silly writer/creator, and drank and smoked to forget him, like he was probably doing for me. But we couldn't forget each other, we were right in front of each other... in a sense. I decided I never even thought like this even when I was high, and I wanted to get high.

Fucking writers.

Fucking Floyd, fucking Lich, that wrote a meaningless book of suffering. That taught me nothing.

That tortured Zach, and estranged him from me, turning him into some sort of god man. A book that made me feel like shit!

So I drank. I realized I didn't feel sad when I drank... but I still felt so emotional! At least I couldn't remember those emotions...

Jacob and Zach's dad were saying something, but I was too drunk. Barnabus tried yelling at me, but I told him to go to hell. I wanted to think of nothing and no one... and just cause pleasure until I felt better... I laughed at that thought, and just stared at Patricia. She knew I was staring at her lustfully, but ignored me. She tried hard to, but she fucking cared for me, and worried for me... and felt bad for me! She was never going to do what I envisioned her doing! She was a real woman! And I just had some stupid teenage urge...

Zach said I should slow my pace. I told him to drink with me. I just took Barnabus's booze, not even caring if he saw... He was angry at this, but he understood the feeling. I thanked him and gave him a kiss... just on the cheek. I wondered if Zach was jealous but noooo... he thought it was nice that I kissed without remorse. Fucking god man. I just wanted to fuck him.

But he was my best friend, and I realized it would be scary fucking a god. Was he really a god?

I smoked cigarettes with Jacob, not even minding the taste, and just thought about life, barely paying attention to the sentences of our group.

I wondered what they were so worried about.

But I ignored it, and drank. I realized this wasn't healthy, but who am I to judge?? I was a goddamned necromancer who was raped by the Lich whenever I fell asleep. I hated life. And in a sense... I felt like it hated me.

Zach's dad tried to snap me out of it.

Saying I should drink some coffee instead. I just drank and drank. That was all I wanted to do.

We had coffee... but I was too drunk, anyway.

Barnabus drank with me... he was one funny drunk, I'll say.

And Jacob smoked and drank too.

And Zach's dad seemed quiet, as Zach told him all he went through, and drank as well, but not as much as us three.

Patricia, Edgar, and Floyd all were quiet, as we drank and stammered on. We were having fun, but Patricia said she liked sobriety, trying to find peace, Edgar said it wasn't healthy, and Floyd... Floyd said that he knew my feelings, and I would find ways around it eventually.

I cursed them all to hell.

Then said sorry. I really did like them all... I wondered if they liked me? I talked to each of them, as I ate a meat burrito provided by the others. Chomp, chomp, chomp, I didn't care what I ate these days, as long as I was fed.

I began to hate myself, to despise myself.

But I thought fuck that! Fuck those feelings! Fuck them all to hell...

Fuck them all!

And I went off to the woods to listen to the sounds of nature and smoke my cigarettes. Zach's dad smoked a pipe. I wondered why he wasn't smoking marijuana.

I tried to imagine this creator... but he was shrouded to me! He kept a distance! HE SHOULD BE IN MY LIFE!! God should care! But he never did! No one did! So I just smoked, and told the creator I would listen to them if they smoked and drank with me.

But no one answered.

There was no creator. And I realized that's what all atheist's feel. Fuck gods! Fuck them all! Maybe I'd change my mind when sober... but for now, they could all go to hell! They nearly killed my best friend!

Or was it always the Lich?

Could even gods not control evil? Was it always there? Did gods feel evil too? I was angry at these stupid gods... and I showed myself to Zach, as I said I wanted to show him something.

I took off my shirt, took off my bra, and asked him to feel me. I was smoking a cigarette, drunk as all hell, but still, I wanted him to touch me. To make love to me.

He said he loved me, and just hugged me. I thought, shouldn't he at least feel a tit?

But he didn't, and just said he loved me.

I melted under his caress. I wanted him to take me as I was, but I realized I was angry, that I wanted him for nothing but drunken pleasure. So I hugged him, even though I unzipped my pants and told him to feel around.

He just hugged me. Fucking god man.

So I dressed and went back to the others, and made sure to get another beer. I was just starting to have fun... and I thought I would take Zach. He was mine! No one was going to take him besides me! I felt angry that Shekinah of all people beat me to it! That should've never been! I would make him happier, I vowed.

He just thought I was too young!! I was angry at this. I wanted him to suffer, or feel pleasure... I didn't really know. Maybe both! Pleasurable suffering!

This is fucking difficult. I couldn't deal with it. So I just caused myself pleasure. Until I felt better.

Remember that pleasure passes, but enjoy it, while you can.

Like Buddha said, happiness is suffering.

I thought of this, but I still caused it.

And I didn't think of the Lich, or anyone, just the pleasure. I felt happier that way. I just thought of bodies... of minds... of drinking and smoking... and of pleasure.

Don't worry, the feeling will pass.

Especially if you make it.

I passed out.

When I came to, I was in my sleeping bag with the coyote pups. My pants were unzipped, and I couldn't remember what really happened. I thought that Zach... that sly dog... must've fell to my advances and made love with me.

But... I couldn't remember it.

I began to feel very embarrassed and ashamed. I lost my virginity and I couldn't remember it?? I didn't feel any different, so maybe I didn't do it right. I quickly zipped up my pants, and got out of my sleeping bag, knocking over the unfinished beer sitting beside me.

The others were cooking up food, as Zach's dad and Jacob brought a whole bunch of food and supplies for us. "It was the least we could do." Zach's dad said, smiling.

I went up to him and hugged him, apologizing for being so drunk! It was so nice to see him, always armored, flaunting his signature pompadour and grinning that crooked grin.

"We quickly laid you down, and Zach told me about all the things you two have been through. Don't worry, everything will be alright." he said.

Jacob was stuffing his face, and said between bites, "Yeah! Things are looking good for the Chariot! We're going to the Emperor's land and going to fight some rebels!"

"You all are invited to join us. We won't have to be separated again." Zach's dad said, and I hugged him again, and he offered me some food.

I took my breakfast sandwich of eggs and sausage and went to sit beside Zach by the fire. He just smiled and said good morning.

I said to him, "C-Can we do what we did last night again? I p-promise not to be so drunk..."

He looked at me inquisitively, hugged me, enveloping me in his strong embrace, and said, "There. We just did what we did last night again."

I felt so embarrassed.

But in a way, filled with relief.

Then Zach's dad said my father and mother were here, and a bus came from down the road. "My parents got a bus??" I asked.

"Marcos never did like riding horses. They just had to take care of a few things first, before they joined us, so sent Jacob and I ahead to find you." he said.

They came to a halt before us, and Zach's mom, with her thin frame, leather jacket, her glasses, and red hair, jumped out of the bus, saying, "Goooood morning, sweeeethearts! I've missed you all, I love you all! Let's be happy again!" Zach and I quickly went to her, and she rushed me and gave me a hug, kissing me on the cheek over and over. "You poor little Gess! We'll get rid of all your sickness and suffering. I like what you did with your hair!" she said to me and hugged me.

And then my parents came out of the bus, and both hugged me, as Zach's mom was doing to Zach, calling him her little Zachary, over and over again.

My father was the biggest, strongest man I've ever seen, but he hugged me kindly and gently. I told him I was a horrible person now, not fit to be his daughter, but he laughed and said I will always be his daughter, no matter how horrible I felt about myself, and that he would help get my evil sorted out. No matter what, he would always love me, and always care for me.

My mother was the smartest, kindest woman I knew, and she just said she would listen to everything I could tell her, and would help me in every possible way, and understood when I told her I could feel the organism. She said it was like an invasion of the body, but she already had an invasion of mind when she heard voices and saw ghouls, and told me how to fight against it. You just gotta remember who you are, you are not the invasion, no matter how much it wishes you to be. Your body, your being, will reject the invasion, and all you can do is learn about it, and find its flaws and expose them.

My mom was a little disappointed with my hair, and I told her it came from the Lich. She told me, "Don't worry about it. We can always dye it however you like, and I'm sure Zach's mom can make you feel as beautiful as however you wish. It is only an exterior, anyway."

"Alright... where the fuck is Mary, then?" Barnabus said.

We heard giggling from the bus, and Barnabus charged in and the two fought, and swore, and said nice things and loving things, and then walked out hand in hand. "They wanted me to go ahead and train the troops, but we have some of the Chariot's lieutenants holding the reins. It was a family emergency, and we all need to fight this, all together." Mary said.

"What about Dismas?" Zach asked.

"He is around the area... hunting what's been hunting you, Zach." Zach's dad said.

"The Lich?" Zach asked.

"What? No. The hordes of dead rabbits that have surfaced from the area! Never seen something so disturbing." he said.

"I-I made them come back to life." I said.

"Can you make them come back to death?" Zach's dad asked.

"I would need to talk to the rabbits first." I said.

"Hmm... Well, I'll take you out to Dismas. He is in sort of a siege against the rabbits, and they've already killed a lost child, and are on a rampage." he said.

I killed again. Why the hell is necromancy so difficult to control! Was I never in control?

Just like the gods, I couldn't control what I brought to life.

31

Help in the Mundane

My pops took Gessa and I out past the woods, to a hillside where we found Dismas in an entrenchment, smoking a cigarette and waiting. There was a barrow of a rabbit burrow on the next hill over. We crept over to Dismas as he waved us over. "They were encircling you guys, trying to trap you in, but I broke their line with some guerilla tactics. I never knew rabbits were so fast... or could bite so hard!" Dismas said.

"They didn't kill your horse again, did they?" My pops asked.

"Nah. Charlie is doing fine, although is a little spooked." Dismas said.

"So. We have the source of the problem, now we just need to find the solution." my pops said, looking at Gessa.

"I-I could talk to them. I-I could go over there..." Gessa started saying.

"I don't think that's a good idea. The rabbits attack everything, just to kill them. Only rabbits have come back to life, which I'm wondering about." Dismas said.

"Let's try talking to them. The Lich wants Gessa alive, and if I go with her, then they may settle down... as the Lich knows me, and remembers me." I said.

"Yeah... me too. We'll go with you." and my pops unsheathed his sword, Dismas put out his cigarette, wielding his sword and shield, and the two walked on each side of us.

My heart was beating hard, as we walked to the hill.

This was another aspect of the Lich. I felt like he was teasing us with his rabbits, but maybe he wanted us to know that he could turn something as harmless and innocent as a rabbit into a weapon of death.

"Stop." Gessa said, "They're whispering a lot harder now." I couldn't hear a thing.

And an innocent, dead monstrosity of a rabbit popped out of a hole. Its head was completely decayed, and it was just a skull on top of a red, bloody body.

"*Haiaisihaispotlakammerrrr.*" It whispered.

"*Toaksslamooobbreeakennnnen...*" Gessa whispered back, almost trying to calm the rabbit.

And more and more dead rabbits popped out of their holes, watching us with dead eyes.

Soulless, dark eyes of the dead. And I heard them whispering. I never knew rabbits could make sounds so frightening.

The rabbits hopped around us, encircling us. Dismas and my pops were smiling! They were grinning, ready to fight!

And they attacked the two, and I saw an old, old, dead rabbit on the hillside, watching. It reminded me of the Lich, and it had only one eye left. Gessa tried to talk to the rabbits, but they would swarm Dismas and my pops, biting them and trying to get at their unarmored parts. I walked forward to the old rabbit, as Dismas and my pops battled. The rabbits seemed to leave me be.

"Your master is dead, as are you." I said to the rabbit. It hissed at me.

"Zach! Stay away from them!" my pops said, locked in battle with the bunnies.

Gessa was talking to the rabbits, and it sounded like she was arguing. She tried to command them, to force them, but that didn't seem to work.

I said to the old rabbit, "Your life has ended... You don't need to kill." It said something unholy to me.

"Zach! It said it wants all to die! Don't fucking talk to that rabbit!" Gessa said.

I told the rabbit that I was just like it. I had wished all my family was alive, too. The mob of the rabbits swarmed and swarmed, and even more seemed to come out of their barrow burrow.

"ZACH! WE NEED TO LEAVE!" my pops yelled. Dismas and my pops dragged me away, as rabbits clung to them and nipped at them, and I told Gessa what to say to it.

I told her to say sorry.

She popped her head back in surprise, and she did.

The rabbits became still, watching us in that unbreathing, unmoving posture of the undead. They began to file back into their holes, and Gessa said sorry in necromancy to every rabbit. She said she was sorry for eating them, for killing them, for bringing them back to life. I couldn't understand her, but I knew this was what she said. She was shaking when she was finished, and finally all the rabbits trailed into their barrow, to be dead once again.

Finally, it was just the old rabbit, and it chomped its teeth, and fell over, dead.

I thought I heard faint applause coming from bone hands, a skeleton, but it was just my imagination, or something in the wind.

Dismas grabbed his horse hidden a ways away, and we quickly went back to the others.

My pops and Dismas were congratulating us, telling everyone they should've seen us! That Gessa and I worked perfectly together! That we stared death in the eyes, fought back, and figured it out! My pops said that Dismas and him would've just mutilated the bodies of the rabbits so much that they couldn't even move, and that our solution was better than theirs. A lot less bloody.

My pops didn't know what to do with me, and thought I had changed. I told him I was still his son, Zach, and that nothing could change that. He looked surprised at this, and said I only said stuff like that when I was feeling depressed.

I guess I was feeling sort of depressed.

He hugged me, and I just thought of all the shit I went through, and I hugged him back. I was nearly bigger than him now.

"I can't even imagine all the hurt you went through fighting... demons..." he said to me.

"It was all very difficult, but I learned to remember love, thank kindness, learn history, and live life. That's all anyone can really do to fight death." I said.

"I learned from fighting necromancers and zombies to remember the dead, to keep them alive through you, and to always have a few living friends who can save you from death. Friends are the family that we have." my pops said.

"What... What about the Lich?" I asked.

"I learned from him... that you should never trust the words of a monster. And that namelessness is just a cop out to not have to share your life with anyone, and that your ma is the woman I love. Well, I learned that before I met the Lich, but I will always remember her kiss that led me back to life... It was the best kiss in the world." he said.

"You say that whenever you kiss her!" I said.

"Well, yeah. I think she needs to know that, though. That I wouldn't want to kiss anyone else, no matter... how much... I don't think I'll tell you about that, yet... We've just become accustomed to each other, after the initial interest of lovemaking subsided. We've grown to care for and love each other through our actions, even through ways besides our actions." my pops said.

"Can't you only show love through your actions?" I said.

"Kinda. But there's other ways to show love." he said and smiled. I thought this was a mystery to me, and that no matter how enlightened I felt, I will never understand love, even though I have it sort of with Gessa. Did I have it with Gessa? I asked her this.

"I don't know... I thought I did, but maybe I don't. I love you no matter what, but let's... just be friends." Gessa said.

I promised her we would, and she smiled and thanked me so ever much, that she had so many expectations for a love life, and wanted to figure it out on her own for a while. I sighed a sigh of relief. Even though... I did feel a twinge of regret. No matter, we could take our time. Then I realized what my pops said... we can show love through inaction as well. Just by being there for someone you love.

I was finally *really* content now that my family had come back to us. I decided I needed to talk to Marcos about things, as all his teachings on love and mercy seemed to ring truer than they ever did. I broke free from my ma coddling me while we were sitting down, trying to cheer me up after she noticed I was so serious. I broke free by saying, "I love you, Ma." first.

She said, "I-I love you too, little Zachary. I suppose I shouldn't call you my little anymore... You seem like a grown adult now. Talk with me whenever you are having trouble with something, anything. You'll always be my darling."

I smiled to her and told her I would, but that I needed to talk to a Blunt Knight. She patted me on the arm and said Marcos would know how to direct me, if she couldn't.

I asked Marcos if we could talk, as he was changing the oil on the bus. He wiped his hands off on a cloth and said, "Sure, Zach. Would you like to go on a short hike with me? I would like to see the wildlife around the area."

"I would love that, Marcos." I said.

We walked around the forest, the hills and plains, avoiding the rabbit barrow. Marcos picked some morning glory flowers, climbing up a ruin that was only a single wall, and nothing else. I asked him why, and he said they were for his wife, and whenever they went traveling he would always find things of nature to give to her. It was something they both enjoyed, and kept their romance blooming, like the morning glory flowers.

I told him that Gessa and I had a blooming romance, but we decided we'd prefer to be friends for now. He said, "In the right conditions, like the right soil, air, and water, love can take off in tremendous ways. I believe that you two will find love again, especially in the right conditions. My daughter... is in the midst of horrible evil. I wish to put her in the right conditions, and I do not believe that the battles that we will embark on will be the proper climate for her, but she has been through so much already... she may be like her mother in this sense, and I wish that she will continue to grow and prosper despite the suffocating grasp of hardship."

"I went through hell, maybe a literal hell, and Gessa was the person that kept me going the most. She made me stronger than words can pronounce, and I never want to hurt our relationship." I said.

He stared at me for a second and said, "I said the same thing when talking about Daisy. This... enheartens me. I am glad you cherish Gessa so, as I do." he sighed, looking up at the sky, and asked, "Well, Zachary. Is there anything more you need to know about fighting? I believe your struggles are only beginning."

"No. I wish to not fight, or even eat meat. I would like to become a Blunt Knight... but I've realized that sometimes I must kill, even though it pains me." I said.

"Spoken like a true Blunt Knight. You have all your life to think on the vows, and whenever you are ready to commit to them fully, you may come to me." Marcos said.

"Thank you, Marcos." I said.

"You seem... a little different. You have rarely smiled, and the only thing that seems to make you happy is wandering nature with me." Marcos said.

"I... don't know... I should be happy, I should be overjoyed! But I feel as if the weight of the world is on my shoulders, and no matter what, it will only get heavier and heavier, even if I become as strong as the gods." I said.

"Remember that you do not have to take on this weight alone. We will always be here for you." Marcos said.

I suddenly felt very relaxed, and said I wished to go back to the others. Marcos clasped me over the shoulder, shaking me and smiling, and I smiled back, and we walked back to camp.

But it was protecting my family that was part of the burden. I knew and remembered that each one of them could protect themselves as well as me... but I wanted to be the first to strike, the first to act against the threat of corruption and evil in the world.

I heard Barnabus singing with my pops, and they had finished when I got back.

I sat quietly by the fire, I didn't want to talk to anyone... even though I wanted them all to understand...

That the Lich was alive, was going to bring the world into hardship, and try to kill me.

That he wanted Gessa.

It made me so frustrated! I just wanted to be happy and joyful again! Why couldn't I grasp that feeling? Nature and life never seemed so distinct and acute to me, and I wasn't horribly depressed... but I knew something bad was going to happen!

My ma said, "You're always the happiest when you have hardship. When everything is nice and perfect, is when you know everything is going to go to shit. Don't think about it too hard, Zachary."

So I decided to have a drink, and drank with my entire family. Patricia was having a talk with Marcos, and I slurped on my brew, just trying to forget... and remember. I could never forget the four. I looked at the BC+Z heart on my arm. I looked at the picture of Rich again. I felt the weight of my axe on my back, and remembered Shake Spear and Athunhel. And it was impossible to forget the last one, Life. Everything was incredibly vivid, and I took pleasure in my senses. I hadn't told everyone yet, that I could see them from miles off, notice their hair growing, feel the earth rumble at the slightest footstep, hear anything that was said even though they thought it was private. I still tried to keep their privacy, as I didn't want them to get nervous around me, so distracted myself from their conversations, but still I heard Barnabus and Mary kissing some ways away, I heard the sharp sound of Edgar sharpening his knife, and I heard Gessa crying on her lonesome. I decided I'd give Gessa space though, as I didn't want to ruin our new agreement. Edgar was getting more and more nervous lately, and sharpened his knife to dull that nervousness. Barnabus and Mary sounded pretty happy though.

My pops and Floyd went beside me, and we talked about the Lich. My pops told me of every horrible thing that the Lich said, lying and trying to torture him, trying to kill him, or make him take his own life. He had heard the Lich talk to him, through the curse he was freed from.

I drank, to stifle my fears.

My pops put a light to his pipe.

"Well, Draziw, I kinda thought you had something to do with the Lich, but I never knew you *were* the Lich." my pops said.

"I was, and wasn't. I believe it to always be the organism, and at first it tempted me and gave me power, but I was consumed by it. I do not remember everything that I had done... which is a shame, as it is a relief. I do remember my life as it was good, and I hope someone remembers that story as well."

"Well, you got all the time to tell." my pops said.

"I believe we have more important matters to concern ourselves with. Another day, perhaps." Floyd said.

"So how do we kill it?" my pops said.

"It is dead, it is death." I said.

"Zach, you should know better than to raise others to their imagined pedestals. Nothing can be death, death just happens. It is just the end of life." my pops said.

"How can you be sure? What if it is the god of death? Like... really, Death? What if we are all going to meet it at the end?" I said.

"Well, Zach. Think of it like this... religion has thousands, even more than thousands, of ways to interpret death. No one knows which one is right, but if you live your life according to that death, then your life will reflect that. Some people try to do good, just not to fall into Hell, but that is not really doing good. That is doing something because of a threat. Think if your soul would go to Heaven no matter what, no matter what happens, or... something Edgar's told me before, like you go back into everything, and you are simply life looking in on itself from a different perspective." my pops said.

"Edgar told you that?? But it sounds like I would lose my identity, and just be everything! That sounds kind of terrifying!" I said.

"It's much better than being consumed by a monster... and life, no matter what, is better than being controlled by a monster who threatens you. Being everything isn't so bad, felt pretty good actually, and I've only ever felt that once, from some crazy drug fountain." my pops said.

I let my newfound strength slip, and said, "I feel everything. The biggest things, the smallest things."

"I know, Zach. You've been hiding it, but I can tell you sense everything. We're not so dumb not to notice the change in you." my pops said.

"Thank you, Pops. I have power now, I have love, kindness, peace, and life. I will use this power for good, as it can only be used for." I said.

My pops seemed surprised, and said, "Well... good. I'm sure if anyone can learn from evil... I mean, true good, it is you. You really do seem like you've matured. I'm glad for that... I didn't want to have to have a kid forever! Now I have an adult to talk to, who better understands the world."

I laughed, and said, "Yeah, Pops. I'll never understand everything, but I can try to."

"Spoken like a true scholar. I believe you've learned from Gessa, as well as the Lich." Floyd said.

"I wish... I could talk to the Lich. Like there was some way to reason with him." I said.

"You don't want to do that. I was trapped by him, and he followed me through some sort of afterlife. At least I think it was an afterlife... it could've been something else." my pops said.

"What was it like?" I asked.

"Well... sort of like blankness. Like we were all together, at least in death. I don't really know. Sort of like a blank... page. It was a strange feeling, but I felt my heart beat again, and I knew I wouldn't remain there forever." my pops said.

"Could we make the Lich realize life is fine? That it is good?" I asked.

Floyd said, "It has long ago given up that feeling... It is the most cursed soul, and we should pity it for that reason... It is hateful, decrepit, and utterly alone. It strives to be that loneliness forever... as I have done, but I always enjoyed reading fortunes with my insight."

"Yeah, you crazy kook. I didn't know what the hell you were talking about when we first met, but it all made sense in the end. I think you should do something more productive with your time..." my pops said to Floyd. Floyd laughed, and said while he was in this world, he would travel and help wherever he could, down to the mundanest things, because sometimes really all we need is a little help in mundane matters.

He said to me, "Sometimes we are seeking something besides the mundane... but the mundane can be the most pleasurable. Do not be sucked into demons and darkness... and the Lich. Be one with normality and reality."

I thanked him, and talked with my pops and Floyd about the old days... and it was nice. Like being a kid again. I decided I'd talk with Gessa as soon as she finished with the long crying session she was having... that I heard, and broke my heart more than any words can describe.

32

The Wheels on the Bus

I didn't really know what to do anymore, so I was glad that I could just follow and be with my family for a while.

Zach was waiting for me as I was walking back to the others, as I was wiping off the tears on my shirt. He was smiling, saying it'll be nice to have somewhere to go. "There's nowhere to go for me that's safe..." I said to him.

"It'll be alright Gessa! Look, I've found some rare wildflowers your dad helped me pick! And... here's a beer, if you want." Zach said.

I smiled to him and accepted his gifts, smelling the flowers, then chugging down the beer. I wondered if alcoholics and botanists were related, in a sense. I'd have to get drunk too, if I had to spend all my time on flowers...

We walked back to the others, and Zach's father said, "Alright, let's get this show on the road. We're going to the Emperor's lands. Everyone, on the bus!" So we filed into the bus, Zach's mom chatting with everyone about trips, my father laughing at something Jacob said, and my mom wrapping an arm over Mary's shoulder. I looked back at our campsite, because not everyone was getting into the bus. Zach, Patricia, Edgar and Floyd were sitting back.

"Ar-Aren't you coming with me? Zach?" I went over to him and asked.

He shook his head, and said, "We will go to the Lich. Patricia, Edgar and Floyd have decided to aid me in this matter. Floyd told me about a bastion of the dead, his previous safehouse, where the dead tree he created is. We will go there."

Zach's parents appeared over my shoulder, and his dad said, "Yeah... Good luck, and please, call with Venny's new phone, every night."

"You better call your ma! That's the least children can do for their parents, just so we know you're still breathing." his mom said.

"You're going too, Edgar?" I asked.

"I will find another way to make amends. We will be in touch through Zach. If I can save everyone, all at once... then there will be no need to make every single amend!" Edgar said, smiling.

"Sounds to me like you're cutting corners." I said.

"I suppose... but everyone I needed to make amends to is now dead or gone. I spent a long time trying to track everyone down, but most end up missing. I will try to be... a hero." Edgar said.

I grimaced, and said to him, "Thank you Edgar, for being a father." and went and hugged him. He was surprised at this, but slowly, tentatively, hugged me back. He deserved this hug.

Then I went and hugged Zachary. My best friend. My first boyfriend. We hugged, and I didn't want to let him go. "Venny and Absinthe created a cell tower a long time ago, and have just gotten it working again. I'll be in the area, and will meet you again in a few months." Zach said to me.

"And don't you forget it! Whatever happens, you're meeting us in France no matter what!" Zach's mom said to Zach. Zach smiled and said of course.

His dad shook his hand, and his mom hugged the daylights out of him. We went into the bus, and all waved goodbye to the four. The others had already said their goodbyes while I was busy crying. The bus started off, and I stared back at Zach, Patricia, Edgar, and Floyd, and blew them all kisses.

I immediately called Zach.

"Hello? Gessa?" he said through the phone.

"I want to say you were the best boyfriend a girl could have!!" I said quickly, not knowing how much time I had on the phone.

He laughed, and said, "Thanks, Gessa. You were the best girlfriend I've ever had." I sniffled, and told him to be safe again, and to keep the others safe. We talked for a little bit, just about stuff. I remarked on the cows in the field we were passing, and that my father drove smoothly, if a bit cautiously.

We kept on talking, Zach and I chatting, and he even said my black hair was actually very gorgeous. I said I hated it, but thanked him anyway. The comment did make me feel better about my hair, my body, my mind, which had all changed, and would continue to change for the rest of my life.

Even though we could talk endlessly, I didn't want to ruin the moment, so I told him goodbye.

We kept on driving, and what is there really to talk about driving? Endlessly going from one place to the next, just admiring the scenery. I was feeling sleepy, just looking out the windows, not getting a good night's rest and fearing to fall asleep again. Barnabus and Mary were drinking and making jokes with my mom and Zach's mom. Jacob was in front with my father, giving guidance on which way to go next. Zach's dad seemed the most forlorn to the group, just sitting and staring out the window with his motorcycle in the back of the bus. I went to talk to him.

"Hi, Uncle Matt." I said, sitting down beside him.

"Heya, Gessa. How's it?" he said to me, smiling.

"I'm alright. I was wondering if you were sure that it was alright leaving Zach and the others behind?" I said.

"Yeah, I have my doubts too... but our first priority is you, Gessa. We will keep you safe, no matter what happens. The others are sort of our assault team, aiming to approach the enemy, and you're sort of the important person the enemy wants to assassinate. We've had many jobs like this as guards. It's usually easier when some of our forces are sent out as an assault team, so the enemy doesn't simply bide its time, and has to make actions according to our wishes." he said.

My eyes opened wide, and I said, "Really? I just thought we were going on a family vacation, or some shit!"

He laughed, and said, "Nope! There won't be any time for vacations while our true enemy lives, the Lich. Just taking your hair is a spooky way to try to scare you... and all of us. Making it seem like he has more power than he does. But who knows how much power that monster has? I didn't even think it was real for the longest time."

"What if... we just ran away from it? Got far away, somewhere safe?" I asked.

"That's the problem... we don't even know where it is." he said seriously, "Our allies will be able to keep you safe, and finish the monsters. And another reason I didn't want to bring Zach... those rebels plaguing the Emperor's lands are led by Gar."

"Zach's... birth father?" I asked. Zach told me about him once, when he was fuming about orcs. His own monster was his genetic father, kind of like how my monster was Edgar for a while.

"Yeah... Although Zach agrees with me, saying that he would prefer not to kill him... strange, as he said that there was no doubt in his mind that he *would* kill him... And strangely, I believed him. He's grown up a lot. You both have." he said.

"You either grow up quick or go quickly to your grave, right?" I said, remembering the dream I had of him.

"What's that? That's pretty clever, Gess." he said. I smiled.

Jacob got the radio on and popped in a cassette. "This is a mixtape I made! Any comments or appreciations are most welcome!" Jacob said back to us.

I listened to the slightly sombre music, and wondered about life. I never expected Jacob to have this side of him.

I went to Zach's mom, and said, "Hi, Auntie Melusine. I want to change my hair." She obliged, and made it red like hers. I looked in the mirror and smiled back at myself. Take that, you old boogeyman.

It soon became night, and Zach's dad was working on his motorcycle in the back of the bus, my mom was sleeping next to Zach's mom, and Barnabus and Mary were drunkenly stammering at each other.

"Y-You can't throw in a joker! That's... *too* classy!" Mary said to Barnabus.

"It's the best! Fuck 'em with style, and they don't question a thing!" Barnabus said.

"You... need to learn how to play fair games..." Mary said.

We got to a town in the night, and my father fell asleep, as Jacob still listened to his music. He was jamming, listening to some hard rock of a muffin man.

I decided to cuddle up in my seat, and fall asleep.

In the morning, my hair was black again, even darker. I didn't remember the nightmares, but I knew they were terrible. I dyed my hair every day, but still, it would turn black.

We kept on driving, going from destination to destination, stopping to get food and supplies. Zach's dad would sometimes ride his motorcycle ahead or behind us, which Zach's mom would keep him company on.

We decided to camp at a campground one night, and had an uproarious night of drinking, games, laughing, and joking. The nightmares weren't that bad that night.

We finally got to France, and I had called Zach every day. Simon and

Melissa stood waiting with an entourage of armed guards, and welcomed us into their empire.

33

An End to a Beginning

I walked with Floyd, as Edgar and Patricia were chatting amiably. Gessa would call me every day, or I would call her. I missed her already.

I asked Floyd about his life, and he told me a story. It was a long story, and a time consuming one, but it enlightened me a bit about his life, and I needed to know whatever I could about the past, and the present, for the future. We trod on the footsteps of greater and lesser men and women, walking through time. We were all and everything, and I was Zach.

I didn't want to tell Gessa about wanting to kill my birth father. I would end Gar, if I couldn't reason with him first, that is. He put a stain on the orcs, on Shake Spear, on Athunhel, with his killing. With his destruction and rampages. My pops thought that my plan to find the Lich was solid, and taught me as much as he could, even though it was more of a refresher than anything new. Still, it was nice to train like we had in the old days. We would be the assault force, and I was sure with the healing skills of the knightly Patricia, the indomitable barbarism of Edgar, Floyd's magic and wisdom, and I, were the best for the job.

That's my story for you, the beginning of it, anyway. We grew up, we loved, we killed, and we found old and new friends on the way. My life, all of life's fight, was only beginning.

I let Aphrodite and Nickels, the young coyotes, go free, and I watched as they ran off into the horizon, all grown up.

www.ingramcontent.com/pod-product-compliance
Lightning Source LLC
LaVergne TN
LVHW010313070526
838199LV00065B/5545